MW00987656

Belongs to
Dianne

"Quilters have an immediate connection to the main themes of this book; family, friends, and community. Ann Hazelwood has captured this connection in an intriguing story that quilters will love. The story and place will be familiar to the reader. This is a novel a quilter can call her own."

—Chris Stergos, Patches Etc.,
Quilt and Button Shop,
St. Charles, Missouri

"Ann Hazelwood knows a few things about the human spirit, family and dreaming big. Add a mixture of the love of quilting and all the things Missouri historic and otherwise; you will experience the words and passion of this unique and gifted author. Enjoy the experience!"

—Tom Hannegan, Streetscape Magazine,
St. Charles, Missouri

The pattern for this block is available at:

**http://www.americanquilter.com/
lily_hazelwood
Pattern from EQ7**

The Potting Shed Quilt

ॐ

a novel by

Ann Hazelwood

American Quilter's Society

P. O. Box 3290 • Paducah, KY 42002-3290
www.AmericanQuilter.com

Located in Paducah, Kentucky, the American Quilter's Society (AQS) is dedicated to promoting the accomplishments of today's quilters. Through its publications and events, AQS strives to honor today's quiltmakers and their work and to inspire future creativity and innovation in quiltmaking.

EXECUTIVE BOOK EDITOR: ANDI MILAM REYNOLDS
GRAPHIC DESIGN: LYNDA SMITH
COVER DESIGN: MICHAEL BUCKINGHAM
PHOTOGRAPHY: CHARLES R. LYNCH

This book is a work of fiction. The people, places, and events described in it are either imaginary or fictitiously presented. Any resemblance they bear to reality is entirely coincidental.

American Quilter's Society
P. O. Box 3290 • Paducah, KY 42002-3290
www.AmericanQuilter.com

Additional copies of this book may be ordered from the American Quilter's Society, PO Box 3290, Paducah, KY 42002-3290, or online at www.AmericanQuilter.com.

Text © 2013, Author, Ann Hazelwood
Artwork © 2013, American Quilter's Society

Library of Congress Cataloging-in-Publication Data

Hazelwood, Ann Watkins.
  The potting shed quilt / by Ann Hazelwood.
    pages cm
    ISBN 978-1-60460-063-6
  1. Quilting--Fiction. 2. Family secrets--Fiction. 3. Missouri--Fiction. I. Title.
  PS3608.A98846P68 2013
  813'.6--dc23
                    2012051157

CHARACTERS

Anne Brown
Owner of Brown's Botanical Flower Shop
in Colebridge, Missouri

Sam William Dickson
Anne's fiancé

Sylvia Brown
Anne's widowed mother

Julia Baker
Sylvia's younger sister

Jim Baker
Julia's husband

Sarah Baker
Jim and Julia's teenage daughter

Ken and Joyce Davis
Sylvia and Julia's brother and his wife; they live in Ohio

Sue Davis
Ken and Joyce's daughter; she lives in Colebridge and is single

Mia Marie Davis
Sue's newly adopted daughter

Muffin
Sue's dog

Helen and Joe Dickson
Sam's parents; they live in the Chicago area

Pat and Elaine
Sam's sisters; Pat, a quilter, lives in Tulsa; Elaine lives in Chicago

Ted Collins
Anne's former boyfriend

Wendy Lorenz
Ted's current girlfriend

Sally
Flower shop employee; she is single

Kevin
Flower shop delivery man; he is single

Jean Martin
New flower shop employee; she is from Bath, England

Al Martin
Jean's husband

Gayle
Shop owner of Gayle's Glassworks,
located next door to the flower shop

Donna Howard
Owner of Donna's Tea Room on Main Street

Brenda
Jim's mistress

Steve Simon
333 Lincoln hired hand

Officer Wilson
Colebridge policeman

Tom Kelly
Realtor

Greg Branson
Sue's lawyer

Evelyn Brody
333 Lincoln neighbor

Walter
Mrs. Brody's nephew

Carl Hogan
Historical Society employee

Nancy Barrister
Anne's school friend; she lives in Boston

Richard Barrister
Nancy's husband

DECEASED CHARACTERS

Charles Brown
Anne's father

Martha Davis
Anne's grandmother

Marie Wilson
Sylvia, Julia, and Ken's sister

Albert and Marion Taylor
Former owners of 333 Lincoln

With Appreciation

One does not fulfill one's creativity and success without the help and support of one's family and friends. I would like to acknowledge and thank the following:

First and utmost my heartfelt thanks go to my husband Keith Hazelwood and my sons Joel and Jason Watkins, who continue to tell me how proud they are of my work. I love you!

My writer's group, The Wee Writers, especially Jan Lewien, who does early editing for me. Jan, Hallye, Lilah, Mary, Janet, and Ann are all very dear to me.

My friends Dellene, Bobbie, and especially Terry David, who's helped me out with her handiwork. Terry Gulickson and my sister-in-law Mary Hazelwood help me create outside the box with their ideas and humor.

Last, but certainly not least, is the AQS staff, especially Meredith Schroeder and Andi Reynolds, who believed in this fiction series. I feel they are on this journey with me, and I hope to make them proud.

CHAPTER 1

I was wearing my silly straw gardening hat and favorite torn jeans as I walked down the aisle. Then I noticed brown edges on my bouquet. What would people think of the owner of Brown's Botanical Flower Shop carrying such pathetic flowers at her own wedding? Perhaps brown was the color scheme, I thought, noting brown wilted flowers gracing the pews. "Not to worry," I told myself. The real purpose here was to join Sam Dickson in holy matrimony. But when I reached for his arm, the face attached to it was not Sam's, but Ted's, my former boyfriend!

"No, no!" I cried.

"Anne, Anne, wake up." Sam gently touched my shoulder.

"What? What?"

"You were in a pretty deep sleep, weren't you?" He grinned, humoring me as he fastened his seat belt.

The plane was about to land. I was exhausted from the stress of meeting Sam's parents for the first time, so I must have fallen asleep into a total nightmare. I didn't answer him at first until I got a grip on what I'd just dreamed.

Waking more thoroughly into reality, I decided not to share this nightmare with my fiancé. I concentrated instead on our recent holiday visit with his family. I thought the visit went well, despite their cautious reaction to our becoming engaged so quickly.

My family saw it coming and seemed to embrace our future plans when we told them at the Christmas Eve dinner table. On this visit to his family early in the New Year, Sam's two sisters, Pat and Elaine, and his parents, Helen and Joe, were pleasant enough, but I felt their reservations. Over all, though, they all seemed to be happy for us, as Sam had reassured me they would. He dropped me off at my home, which I shared with my widowed mother, Sylvia.

"I'll need to get some work done tonight at the flower shop," I said as I kissed him goodbye. "I can handle this luggage. I'll call you later this evening."

"I love you, Annie." He blew me another kiss. Sam was the only person to call me Annie, except my Grandfather Davis.

Mother was glad to see me and helped carry things to my room. "I can't wait to hear every detail about your trip," she said with much excitement.

"You will, Mother. But first I need to get to the shop quickly. I stayed away a bit too long. We have a couple of funerals that need my attention."

"Oh, did your staff mention who they might be?"

"No, I didn't ask. Unless I'm there taking the orders, it doesn't always register. Hey, what's been going on here? Is there anything new?"

"Well, your Aunt Julia and Uncle Jim are busy planning their little wedding to renew their vows." She shook her head in disbelief. "Your cousin Sue is waiting to hear when her plane trip is scheduled to leave for Honduras to pick up little Mia. I hope this adoption goes well and she isn't disappointed once she gets there. I have the quilt frame all set up in the basement ready to put in Mia's quilt top. I think the size is still sufficient for a two-year old," she mused. "I'll try to get that taken care of soon so we can call the others to help us quilt Mia's quilt."

"Oh, I can't wait to see this little darling in person." I was changing my clothes and yelling back down the stairs. "The photo Sue showed us on Christmas Eve looked so cute and she appeared to be pretty healthy. I wish I could be as excited about Uncle Jim and Aunt Julia's ceremony on renewing their vows!"

I met Mother at the bottom of the stairs. "It seems like such a scheme on his part to win her back, if you ask me. Do you think I should have a little talk with Aunt Julia about me discovering his affair with this Brenda person he works with?"

"I'd leave well enough alone. Remember, they said they had cleared some things up between them and decided to start fresh with this ceremony. Let's be happy for them."

"Did you work at the book store this past week?" I changed the subject.

"Just one day a week is fine with me. Working part time is working out and I really wanted some time to get all the Christmas decorations put away."

"I sure hope they were able to get some of that done at the shop. I won't be home for dinner." I grabbed my coat and a soda out of the refrigerator to take with me. "I'll fill you in on all the details of the trip later, but I think all and all it went well."

CHAPTER 2

Sally was helping Kevin load the van when I arrived at the shop. Brown's Botanical Flower Shop was my second home and Sally and Kevin were a big part of it. Kevin kept busy with deliveries, and Sue helped out on occasion, but Sally proved to be my right hand. As I began visualizing a bigger picture for my shop, I could foresee Sally becoming the flower shop manager somewhere down the line.

"Welcome back!" Sally gave me a big hug. "I should also give you my official congratulations!"

"Oh, yeah," Kevin smiled big. "It seems like just yesterday that Sam sent you flowers to get your attention. I just met him once, but he must have swept you off your feet! When's the wedding?"

"I know! It's been quick for many to realize. I'm quite sure of my decision, but it will be some time before we marry. I'd like to have time to plan our wedding and then figure out our living arrangement."

They both were relieved to hear that I didn't have immediate plans and I could see that they were much more interested in discussing what orders had to be done.

"Anne, here is a resumé that was dropped off last week by a Jean Martin," Sally said, handing me the forms. "She told me that she heard from Sue that you might hire another person before Valentine's Day. She's in her forties I would guess, quite attractive, and new to the area. Her husband was transferred here from Kentucky, where she designed arrangements at a place called the Village Flower Shop. She has a charming accent," Sally paused for a breath. "She's originally from Bath, England. I liked her."

"Great! Does she know we just want part time?" I asked while I looked through my written messages.

No one responded so I assumed they knew what we needed.

"I'll call her in for an interview because Valentine's Day is coming soon, like you said, and Sam is taking more of my time." I blushed at the mere mention of his name.

My cell phone was ringing and I saw it was Sam trying to reach me.

"Yes, Mr. Sam, what can I do for you?"

"Aren't we all business like? I guess I have to get used to your behavior during business hours. Can you take time for a quick bite to eat at Charley's around five o'clock? I miss you and it has been hours since I dropped you off at the house."

"Well, aren't you sweet!" I whispered as I moved back toward my office in case this call got personal. "We are really backlogged here so I'm not sure I should."

"You're going to have to eat. How about I pick us up a salad from there and deliver it to you about five thirty? I know how much you love their steamed vegetable and grilled chicken salad. Will that work for you?"

"I can see your mind is made up, so that's fine. Sally and Kevin hope to leave at five o'clock. See you then Mr. Dickson!"

Here I was trying to get back to my paperwork and scan my e-mail, but now my mind was sidetracked by someone I adored. He was trying to step inside my business world just to spend a few minutes with me. This was nothing I was accustomed to. I never allowed Ted or anyone else to do so.

Would I be able to handle this? Was this relationship going to impact my independence? Why wasn't I more grateful for his thinking of me? Would I get used to this, and would things settle down after a while?

This man was going to be my husband, which was still hard to believe. As so many reminded me, it wasn't going to be about me anymore. I looked down at my gorgeous pearl engagement ring set with two diamonds, and that made me smile. Then I remembered how surprised I was when Sam proposed to me, right here in the shop. He had gotten down on one knee and would not get up until I said 'Yes.'

It was a dream come true and now my heart couldn't wait to see his big smile and have his strong arms surround me.

But...how would I get any work done with this man in my life? Was Anne Brown, professional businesswoman, caving in? Hmmm.

It was five thirty on the dot when Sam tapped at the back door. His arms were holding two bags containing our salads. He put them down and it was no time before we were kissing and hugging each other.

"You're spoiling me," I told him sweetly. "I've never had this kind of personal attention. Should I assume this is a picture of the future?"

"Well, my mind has been running wild since our trip. We have our whole life to plan and I'm anxious to do it all. I then remembered I have a partner who is going to want to have a say in all this."

I laughed and told him he was indeed being silly and should slow down. I agreed that he now had a partner to consult with and told him I had one, too. As I laid out our food on the counter, Sam said he had been thinking about a timetable for us. 'Whoa, mister,' I thought, though I smiled at him instead as I brought out an unopened bottle of merlot from my little wine stash in the back closet. This stash had come in handy more than once, and now I needed a delaying tactic.

"Anne, would you ever consider moving in with me so we could be closer to each other while we plan our wedding?" He had moved in close to me. Before I could react, he continued. "I would love that so much, but I know you well enough that you'll dismiss the thought. Promise me you'll at least think about it. You don't have to give me an answer now."

I fiddled with opening the bottle while I corralled my thoughts.

Finally, I said, "Oh, Sam, you're right. I can't even think about this question. You have no idea how time consuming my job is. Living with Mother is perfect for all I have to do now. Having another move before our marriage would add to my stress." I gazed into his eyes and took a deep breath. "I promise to make sure we have time together. I need you and love you with all my heart. I would have never considered your proposal if I didn't."

I moved even closer to him as silence took over the room. Had I made a mistake, defending my independence against his wishes?

"Okay," he finally said. "I'll use my energy and thoughts in helpful ways—like actually opening this bottle of wine." He smiled at me and pulled the cork. "The sooner I can get you to commit to a wedding date, the better. I want us to have our own new place soon to begin our life together."

"I agree." I put my arms around his neck. "It will be such fun planning the wedding and deciding where we want to live. It's just all overwhelming right now. I'll start thinking of wedding details with Mother and you can take the lead in scoping out places we might want to live, how's that?"

"I love it, and I love you." He kissed me fully and I nearly swooned. Hmmm.

We poured the wine and toasted ourselves in laughter as we served ourselves dinner out of a bag. It was probably the first of many bag dinners in our future.

CHAPTER 3

Jean Martin's interview turned out to be better than I had hoped it might be. Her experience in floral designing was much better than my own. She was childless after eleven years of marriage and seemed perfectly happy with that. She spoke highly of her husband, who had been transferred to a company near Colebridge. I discovered one of her best qualities of all in the interview; she was a quilter! When she had left her quilt guild back in Kentucky, she was serving as their president, and all of her spare time now seemed to be absorbed with quilting.

I took a little time to fill her in on the "basement quilters," but did not dare tell her about Grandmother Davis, who had made her critical spirit known, and my sweet Aunt Marie, recently departed after we had just finished a quilt but "came back" to visit us. These two spirits were part of our group whether we liked (or believed) it or not. I thought this topic would be better addressed with a glass of wine at another time.

Jean started working the next week and brought her English accent as a bonus, which we thought was quite interesting and even humorous. Her response of "Jolly good!" to most everything made us smile. Sally took the lead in getting her trained. Sally's skills continued to please me, and confirmed that I did need to promote her soon.

Valentine's Day was sneaking up on us and the shop was adorned with my favorite color, red. All of the shop owners on Main Street knew this. My red geraniums out front in the summer were part of my signature look. Red roses dominated the shop orders, creating an atmosphere of love and romance.

Sue and Sarah, my cousins, were coming in to help us with the rush, but I wondered how on earth I was going to have the time or energy to accept Sam's invitation to Maverick's restaurant on Valentine's Day evening. I couldn't disappoint him, but the only one without plans was Sue. I'm sure holidays like this were dreaded by a single woman like her. It was a good thing she had Mia's adoption to look forward to. The busy day had arrived, and the faster I worked, the more stressed I became.

"Let me stay late, Anne," Sue said, as she saw me spinning my wheels. "This is an important day for lovers like you and Sam. He's been pretty patient this week!"

"That would be awesome, Sue, if you don't mind," I said thankfully. "I really need to go home and change. Oh, dear! I don't have a Valentine gift for Sam! I never gave Ted anything. Do you think Sam is going to expect something?"

"I don't know much about those things. My parents are always nice to send me a card. It may as well be a sympathy card as far as I'm concerned! Actually, I look forward to taking home a pizza and curling up with this good book I'm reading. I do, however, think you should have at least a card for Sam, which I will be happy to sell you from our card rack." She smiled and hugged me. "It sounds like Sam will want time from you more than anything."

"You're so right Sue, and your plans sound pretty good to me. I'm a romantic and think the day is pretty special, but this year is our first Valentine's Day, so I don't know how much to make of it all. I think I can be creative and…" I grinned back at her, I believe I know which card will work."

"Your mother said we're all getting together Sunday afternoon to put Mia's baby quilt in the frame."

"Yes, she said something to that effect, so I'm glad she's called everyone," I said, cleaning off the counter. "It will be good to be together and fill everyone in on meeting Sam's family. Has Aunt Julia said much about the wedding ceremony with Uncle Jim? I really want to hear about that. It's next month, right?"

"I think so. I hope it doesn't interfere with my trip to Honduras. I expect that I'll be told in the next couple of months and I don't think there will be much advance notice."

"Then we better get busy on Mia's quilt." I swept faster as I cleaned up the floor littered with stems and leaves. "I wouldn't let anything interfere with picking up that little dark-headed beauty!"

Mother was looking for my return from work, assuming I would have a romantic date with Sam for the evening. I walked in the door holding some white roses and one of our Valentine cards for her. I made it a point to never forget a tradition that my father had with her on Valentine's Day. He always brought her white roses. I knew she would be feeling melancholy today.

"Oh, Anne, this is not always necessary," she smiled through and through. "You should be saving this expensive inventory for your customers." She caressed the soft petals. "I guess in the back of my mind though, I was hoping you'd do this. I remember my mother would get white lilies all the time, because they were her favorite."

"Dad would want me to think of you, as he always did on this special day," I said, kissing her on the forehead.

She gave me a hug and got busy arranging the roses in a vase while I ran upstairs to change into something that would look like this was a special evening. Sam had certainly boosted my ego in telling me now and then how sexy he thought my shape was, so I found myself wearing more snug-fitting clothes around him. I settled on a knit blue dress that brought out my blue eyes and blonde hair. Pearls, my favorite jewelry, would be perfect for this look. I was making the final touches to my hair when I heard his voice downstairs.

"Anne, look what Sam brought for me!" Mother exclaimed. She held a heart-shaped box of candy in her hands.

"You know how to spoil everyone, don't you?" I teased him, walking down the stairs.

"It's really a bribe," Sam said as he looked me up and down. "Sylvia's going to help me get you to set a wedding date, because I don't know if I can accomplish that by myself."

"We'll see about that!" I quipped as we went out the door.

CHAPTER 4

Maverick's was just as romantic as the first time Sam had taken me there. It was forty-five minutes outside of Colebridge but well worth the drive. All the indoor plants around the restaurant in the dead of winter were refreshing, just like my shop. Each table had a white tablecloth with a small nosegay of red roses surrounding a lit white candle. My merlot and Sam's malted scotch appeared magically, as if Sam had called ahead. I was ready for some relaxation and time with my fiancé. This was sure better than the salad out-of-the-bag that we had shared the week before in the shop.

I asked if he had any more information about Uncle Jim's wedding ceremony to renew his and Aunt Julia's wedding vows. Jim and Sam worked together, and had it not been for their friendship, he would not have brought Sam to our Thanksgiving dinner. Uncle Jim had told us his friend would be alone and he knew just where he would be welcomed. I'll never forget that introduction because when I think back, it was love at first sight, for both of us.

"It's interesting that you should mention that," Sam noted. "He asked me today to say a few words at the ceremony and said Julia was going to be asking you to do the same thing."

"Really! And just what am I supposed to say?"

"You're still suspicious of Jim, aren't you?"

"I just find this whole attitude change in both of them a bit much to accept. Aunt Julia said she didn't love him anymore and was convinced there was someone else in his life. What happened to her? She seemed ready to be single again and move on. This just doesn't add up, Sam." I sipped some wine. "Now, of course, dear Mother said they probably had a meeting of the minds and perhaps set their suspicions aside to stay together for Sarah's sake."

"Wow, I don't know what to say, Anne. I told him I would be happy to say a few words about the two of them. Jim is my friend and I think they're doing the right thing here. You've got to admit that trying to work things out for whatever reason is better than divorce."

"I'll reserve my response until after I talk one on one with Aunt Julia." I folded my arms in front of me.

Sam was about to say something when the server came to take our order. Sam suggested we just think about the two of us and take advantage of the slow romantic music playing in the room. He just knew how to handle my mood and temperament. Suddenly I felt bad about expressing my suspicions on such a special occasion.

We walked onto the small dance floor, dancing closely with the slow pace until a livelier song came along. I began to swing to the beat but Sam grabbed my arm to return us to the table, where dinner was now being served. Phooey. I was just getting ready to show him my moves.

The conversation throughout our delicious meal was light and even sexy. Flirting with Sam was fun and daring, unlike Ted's predictable moves. The evening was a Kodak moment of love and romance I had not experienced before. Growing up, Mother always referred to "Kodak moments" as if the experience was a picture happening right now that you never wanted to forget. I had picked up her habit as I began to have my own Kodak moments.

"I feel like dessert, how about you?" Sam suggested, rubbing his tummy.

"I don't know how I could, Sam, I am so content right now."

"Would you share some of that sinful chocolate cake that you know I am such a sucker for?" He was asking me like a child getting permission.

"Of course." I lifted his hand to kiss. "How could I possibly refuse?"

Thinking this was the time to produce my card for him, I placed it in front of his coffee cup when he turned his head. When he noticed it, he grinned from ear to ear.

"I wasn't sure what exactly to do for Valentine's, to be very honest with you, so I had to be creative." I felt my face blush.

He opened the card, read the personal written message, and then said, "Really?"

I had told him in clever words that I would cook a romantic dinner for him that included some very seductive entertainment. Then I asked if he preferred me to wear a full apron or half apron. He leaned back as if someone else had made the offer.

"When, where, and please tell me it will be soon! Forget the apron!"

We laughed and he kissed me on the lips, right in the open view of other couples sitting around so conservatively at the other tables. It was at that moment the dessert arrived with a small beautifully wrapped box on a silver tray. The little red bow had my name on it.

"This is for me?" I could pretend to be naïve when I wanted to. He just grinned.

I unwrapped the neat, tiny package and found a wonderful pearl bracelet that had a gold clasp accented with a diamond in the center. I gasped and stared in disbelief at such an expensive gift.

"I had the same jeweler design this bracelet to match your ring!" He purely sparkled with delight.

"I can see the resemblance immediately, Sam! I absolutely love it, love it, love it! Thanks so, so much!" I rose out of my chair to meet him halfway around the table.

After a kiss on the cheek, he helped me put it on my wrist with his large, gentle hands. I felt like I had when I first saw the engagement ring. They were the most beautiful pieces of jewelry I had ever seen, not to mention the most expensive. They looked so beautiful together. My suggestive card seemed silly and totally unbalanced compared to this lavish bracelet, but then again, he had looked at me that special way when he'd read it...

The rest of the evening went as perfectly as any Valentine's Day could go. Sam was careful not to pressure me for setting a wedding date. We just enjoyed the look in each other's eyes that told us we would share this forever. Being able to dance and hold each other close, not saying a word, was enjoyed until nearly closing time. Our evening ended with what had been building up for hours, which was an intimate reunion at Sam's loft. Oh, yes!

CHAPTER 5

Despite many questions from others about wedding plan details, I stayed focused on my daily routine—running a flower shop. Sam was busy with work as well, and when he had spare time, he was scouting Colebridge's housing market and driving through neighborhoods that his realtor friends suggested. I was so pleased that Sam loved the historic beauty of Colebridge as much as I did. In his job, he might have lived anywhere, but he seemed to be especially impressed with our town's culture and willingness to grow and develop.

Meanwhile, Mother had everything planned for our first quilting of the new year. It would be good to be back in the basement where we all had learned to quilt from Aunt Marie and had gotten to know each other, better than I would have ever imagined.

Aunt Marie's death would be a sad reminder as we gathered once again. Mother and her sister had been so close. I know she missed Marie terribly, but she did not bother me with her sorrow since I was always on the go and had Sam on my mind.

As we prepared to quilt in our basement again, the question in the back of my mind was whether Grandmother Davis would again make her spirit known in our presence. As far as we could tell, she had removed the worst of our stitches, kept a thimble at Sue's place even though Sue didn't want to use it, and opened the pages of a quilt book to get my attention. Believe it or not, these things had happened and we had no other explanation.

I was helping Mother fix a vegetable tray for the afternoon when Sam called.

"I know you're about to start your quilting party, but I wanted to tell you about something I found this afternoon." His voice was alive with excitement. "I was driving around to find a house Ray at work told me about when I saw this driveway leading up a hill. The mailbox at the bottom said 333 Lincoln Street, but no name was on it. I drove up to this magnificent house, which is obviously empty. What a place! It's really grown over with weeds and tree limbs are down everywhere. You can tell the house and yard were quite a showplace at one time. There's a sign out front saying it's for sale by owner. Do you know anything about this place?"

"I think I know the driveway you're describing, but I assumed it was a private drive and never went up there. You can see part of the house at some point when you drive further north, right? I'll ask Mother what she knows about it."

"That would be great, honey. I've never seen anything so intriguing. I'm going to call the number and find out more information. I can't wait for you to see this place!"

"I know how you love those old historic places, so you'll have fun with this. I'll let you know what Mother has to say, but right now I hear the others coming in the door, so I have to go."

"Okay, but call me later when they leave, ya hear?"

"I will, sweetie, but I have to go." I hung up smiling at his enthusiasm.

The chatter swelled as Sue and her little dog Muffin were followed inside by Aunt Julia and her daughter Sarah. Everyone piled into the kitchen.

"Hey, everyone!" I smiled. "Welcome back, quilters! Leave your coats and grab one of these snacks to take downstairs."

"I made Sarah's favorite peanut butter cookies yesterday, so I brought some of those," announced Aunt Julia. "It looks like we'll have all kinds of goodies to make us fatter. I was trying to lose a few pounds before our wedding, but it isn't happening."

We all laughed coming down the stairs and I ignored the reference to Aunt Julia and Uncle Jim's wedding reenactment. When we reached the bottom of the stairs, I saw the familiar frame we had so enjoyed as we sat quilting Julia's fan quilt. It was waiting for us to attach Mia's quilt, which Mother had basted according to Aunt Marie's instructions. We had learned how on Aunt Julia's quilt.

"Let Anne and I pin this side," Mother instructed. "Julia, you and Sue pin this side."

We remembered just enough to pin closely to the attached ticking on the frame. It did not take us long because Mia's baby quilt was less than half the size of Aunt Julia's queen size quilt. The finished top was a bright, multi-colored, animal quilt with simple pieced stars that Isabella from the quilt shop called "Variable Star."

"Oh, it's beautiful!" said Sue with true admiration. "I can't believe this will be wrapped around my own daughter! Thanks so much, all of you. Where should we start? I'm going to sit here where I sat last time."

"Sure, we can all take our places and Sarah can sit where Aunt Marie sat," I suggested as a compliment for Sarah. "Is that okay with you, Sarah? It may bring you some good luck."

"Are you sure you want my stitches in this quilt?" Sarah sheepishly asked.

"You bet," said Sue, already threading her needle. "This will be such a keepsake. If I remember, Sarah, your stitches were pretty darn good for a teenager."

"Here's Aunt Marie's thimble box," said Mother removing the lid. "See if you can find a small enough thimble to fit you."

"You're really going to make me wear one, huh," teased Sarah. "Here's a gold one that's kind of cool. It fits, too! Hey, look! It has an 'S' engraved on it."

"That was not one of Marie's thimbles." Mother was clearly surprised. "Let me see that. Most of the thimbles in her box were rather large. That's why we didn't have you wear one when you first tried your hand at this. Did any of you bring this? Julia, have you seen this before?"

"No, I didn't Sylvia," Aunt Julia responded with hesitation. "Good heavens, this is beautiful and, I bet, quite valuable. Who could have once owned this with an 'S' on it?"

"I would be the only name with an 'S' initial," said Mother, giving it a closer look. "I've never seen this before."

"So, Sarah, I would say you have just been given a wonderful gift to start your quilting," I stated boldly. "I think Aunt Marie wanted this to be yours. It's in her thimble box and none of us have a claim to it, so it's all yours!"

We all fell silent as we had before when we tried to absorb an apparently supernatural happening. Without alarming Sarah, who did not have much prior knowledge about the spirits in the basement, we felt it best to move on and not comment any further.

Sarah took to it nicely and didn't fight the presence of it on her finger like Sue had done when we started Aunt Julia's quilt. We started stitching in earnest.

"Mother, Sam just called and he has a question for you," I said, changing the subject.

"What's that, Anne?" Mother still looked at the thimble on Sarah's finger.

"Do you know who lives on top of the hill at 333 Lincoln Street? It's that old house that you can barely see from the street. I don't think anyone has lived there for a long time."

"Oh, boy, let me think," she pondered. "Taylor, their last name was Taylor. Many times people referred to the Taylor House and that it was haunted. I remember reading in the paper that the Jaycee organization wanted to use it as a haunted house years ago. I heard it didn't happen because there wasn't room for parking on the street and they couldn't get permission from the owner. I always heard it was very fine in its day, especially the gardens. I've never gone up there. Why on earth does Sam want to know?"

"He's been driving around checking out neighborhoods and houses," I explained. "He says it's for sale, so he drove up to check it out. He said it's amazing and he can't wait to tell me all about it." I rethreaded my needle.

"Good heavens, why?" asked Sue. "Surely he isn't thinking of buying that big old house for the two of you? A haunted house on the hill doesn't sound too cool if you ask me!"

"Oh, Anne," said Aunt Julia. "You all should be thinking of a brand new house. They're building some beautiful homes in the western part of Colebridge and I think Sam could afford a really nice one."

"Well, no big deal," I said. "He just seems to be intrigued with it. He loves old things. He has some very interesting antiques.

21

He'll have fun with this. I'm just glad he's keeping busy. I told him he was in charge of scouting houses and neighborhoods and I would start on the wedding plans. He doesn't have a trip out of town for a week or so, which is nice. Aunt Julia, your wedding date is getting closer," I announced, changing the subject from Sam and me to a topic I had to get out of my system. "I hope all this messy winter weather is out of the way by then."

She looked up from concentrating on her quilting. "Yes, I do too, but in early April most of the days are generally mild. I haven't had time to really fill you in since you and Sam came back. You know it's going to be at Trinity Church, of course, on April 10, and I decided to go ahead and have the reception in that pretty room off their entry area. I am sticking to fifty names on my list, but Jim, of course, would like to include more. To my surprise, Bill Paxton and Pam Mayor said they could be there. They stood up for us back then. Do you remember them?"

"Oh, that'll be nice," Mother said, not looking up from her quilting. "They were going together then, right?"

"Yes, and I really thought they would get married, but it didn't happen," said Aunt Julia. "The Q Seafood and Grill is going to cater. The food will be rather light and the wedding cake will be a gift from his sister, Christy. That reminds me; Anne, will you be kind enough to say a few words at the ceremony? Sam has agreed to do so and I thought it would be a nice touch to have the two of you involved."

"Sam told me about Jim asking him," I said in the nicest tone I could. "What do you want me to say, or should I comment on any particular thing?"

"Oh, you know, just something about being pleased about the occasion."

I couldn't believe my ears! How could she ask any of us to

make a comment like that after she had complained about Jim's suspected infidelity and her plan to leave him when Sarah was older? How could I respond the way I really felt with Sarah sitting right there? Mother's look told me I had better respond quickly and with the right answer.

"Sure," I answered softly. "Let me think about it, though. We can discuss the details later. Will you be taking a little honeymoon afterwards?"

"No, I'm afraid not, the way the date worked out," she said sadly. "Jim said they are about to close a deal in Atlanta, and until that is secure, we shouldn't go away. I imagine a few weeks later we could go and the weather will be warmer, also."

"Where do you want to go, Mom?" Sarah asked with interest.

"I've been thinking about that, actually, and I think I'd like to go back to Sarasota, Florida, where we had our honeymoon," she smiled.

"That would be nice," Mother graciously responded.

"Yes, the resort is still there, so I thought it would be a nice experience."

I told myself that I must be very naïve when it came to relationships. How could Aunt Julia even think about being alone with my uncle after she confessed she no longer loved him? Who was she kidding? Was she trying to put on a show for her daughter, who seemed to be caught up in the romantic notion? I would bet Jim didn't tell Julia about there being a Brenda in his life. Harrumph.

It was time for a break from stitching. "Can everyone make next Sunday again?" Mother asked as she passed around the plate of cookies. "I think we can get this all quilted in two or three meetings. That way you will have it ready and waiting for Mia."

"Great," said Sue with a grin. "I may even take it with me for

Mia to snuggle with on the way home."

"Since I am now an 'expert' on binding quilts, I will do that for you, Sue, as soon as we have it quilted," Aunt Julia said in jest. We snickered.

"Not to change the subject, but I hired a new employee at the shop," I spoke around a delicious cookie. "Sue, you met her, and she's quite a good designer, isn't she? I also learned that she's quite a good quilter, too. She was president of her quilt guild when she left Kentucky, and she's won some local awards for some of her quilts. I saw a few of her quilt pictures. Would you mind if I asked her to join us next Sunday? We could use the help. She doesn't know very many people as yet and I'd love for her to meet you all!"

"Why sure," Mother said right away. "She could probably teach us a few things!"

"Yes, that would be great," said Aunt Julia.

"What's her name? Does she have any kids?" Sarah asked.

"Her name is Jean Martin, and no, she doesn't and she made it clear in the interview that she and her husband liked it that way," I explained. "I thought it odd that she made the comment at all, but I guess she knew I would be wondering about that."

"Oh, goodness," said Aunt Julia, rising from her chair. "We have got to get going. Sarah, you have a lot of homework and I need to get my report together for the Garden Club tomorrow morning."

"What is your report on?" asked Mother.

"Medicinal herbs. I saved some dried herbs from my garden last year, did a bit of research, and I found out all kinds of good things."

With that announcement, everyone decided to leave at the same time.

I thought it pretty remarkable that we accomplished what we

did with all the chatter. Perhaps we were getting better and quicker with our stitches. I think we also discovered we could chat, eat, and quilt at the same time. Who knew?

We had made a dent on another basement quilt and received another paranormal gift—the subtle reminder of Aunt Marie's spirit in the form of a personal thimble for Sarah. Hmmm.

CHAPTER 6

I could smell and almost picture the birth of spring at our doorstep. Now that Valentine's Day was past, Easter and pastel colors were taking over the shop. Jean was happy to arrange things for the first time and Sally seemed to be fine with it. Their relationship was working out well. They both could use a new friend, from my observation.

Sam had been pestering me to take some afternoons off to look at some of the houses he liked. I didn't want to discourage him. It was bad enough I couldn't decide on a wedding date. He first suggested June 17th, my birthday, but that was too soon. Next spring I could handle. I could only picture a garden wedding, so it would have to be next year. It was good to have this time to plan and prepare.

After all, Sam and I had only known each other since Thanksgiving of last year. I think Sam was mentally ready to meet a potential wife when I met him. I no more felt that urge for a spouse or needed a man in my life after disappointing Ted and letting him go. After meeting Sam, however, I fell in love hard and fast. If he wanted me now for his bride, I was on board, willing and able. I couldn't ask for more, and I wasn't going to look back.

But…would I be risking his patience by pushing the date until next spring? So far, I felt I could convince him. I would have Mother talk with him and tell him that planning such an event with my busy schedule would be challenging.

"Sam called while you were on the phone, Anne." Sally was sweeping up stems and leaves. "He'll be here in a half hour to pick you up."

"Will we have everything ready for Kevin by the three o'clock delivery?"

"Sure! I finished up the Morton order and Jean is working on the last piece for the Johnsons. I'll finish cleaning up and balance the drawer, so don't worry. You better get used to some of this! Most husbands want to see their wives once in a while."

"I know, I know," I replied as I was finally sitting down at my desk after trying to get there all day. "I'm going to get better at this—you wait and see! We're going to visit the houses he found and then stop at Charley's for dinner, I'm told."

I saw Jean rearranging a shelf out of the corner of my eye. "Don't forget to put Sunday afternoon down for quilting," I reminded her. "Bring your thimble. I think one o'clock would be about the right time."

"Jolly good," she said with excitement. "I plan to bring some banana bread that's my Grandmother Riley's recipe. It's a yummy delight for sure."

"That sounds great, Jean, and Mother will appreciate the effort. There's Sam parking out front, so I'd better go."

"Toddle off now, will you," she ordered, opening the door for me. "We'll do nicely."

Out the door I flew with a good feeling of everything being under control. That was not always easy for me to do. Sam's warm greeting of a hug and brief kiss on the lips were just what I needed.

"Hey, what's this?" I asked, looking at a steaming hot coffee in his hand.

"I stopped at Starbucks and bought some coffee to take with us! You like the Pike Place Blend, right? It may get chilly if we look around outside and it sounded good to me."

"Thanks, baby. How observant and sweet of you." I took it out of his hand. "I can really use this. Are you always this considerate, or are you trying to impress your fiancée?"

"Yes, especially my bride-to-be, and I intend to cash in on that," he teased. "First we'll stop at Foley house, which is pretty close to here. The realtor said that a doctor just moved out of it. It should be nice. I just looked around outside and the street is full of nice, older houses, so I thought it was worth a look."

"Oh, I think I know the house." I sipped my coffee. "Mrs. Foley has been a widow for some time and I don't know how well she's kept the house up, but I always thought the curved windows must be very old. It always appeared to be as charming on the inside as it was on the outside."

Off we went, and I could tell Sam was much more excited about our adventure than I was. We were there in no time, and my first impression of the house was as cold as I felt. I wrapped my scarf tighter around my neck as we got out of the car.

I shouldn't have been surprised, but a man was there to open the lockbox and show us inside. "Anne, this is Tom Kelly, an acquaintance as well as Realtor."

"Nice to meet you, Anne," he said, handing Sam the house key. "I'll wait in my warm car, if you don't mind." He winked at Sam and moved off.

"What was that about? Isn't he going to show us around inside?"

"I've asked him to let me be your guide, Annie." Sam grinned at me and I realized again how much into this house hunting he really was.

The door opened hard and we walked into a musty smell of tobacco and potpourri that created an unpleasantness that was hard to ignore. Going into the living room off the entryway, we walked on worn floral carpeting that belonged somewhere in the 18th century.

"Well, I think we can assume the Foleys were heavy smokers."

I told myself not to overreact to what Sam had chosen to look at. Then I told myself to keep an open mind as I entered the kitchen, because Mother would faint if she saw any kitchen in this condition. The outdated fixtures were one thing, but the buildup of grease and soil in the corners of the floor and counters was pure neglect. Perhaps Mrs. Foley didn't see well and didn't have a housecleaning service. I told myself that I didn't belong there, but I waited for Sam's response.

"Do we want to bother going upstairs?" He gave off some hesitation, thank goodness.

"I don't think this house is ready for us, honey, and besides, I really need some fresh air." I walked toward the door.

"I love this location and that staircase but I'm not sure we would ever be able to remove the smell." He, too, was moving toward the door. "Okay, so one down. Let's move on."

The fresh air and still-hot coffee were just what we needed after that cold encounter at the Foley house. He handed the key to Tom and told him the address of the next place we wanted to see. Tom said he'd meet us there.

"This other house sounded neat because of the view of the

river, which I have enjoyed so much from my loft," Sam explained. "The owners are still living there, but they won't be home. They started to rehab but then he got transferred and they stopped everything. I think this has some possibilities, but I didn't see the inside. The price is very good because they want to leave town as quickly as possible."

As soon as we pulled up, my first impression was puzzlement that Sam would like such a plain, uninviting house. Tom was waiting for us to let us in but headed back to his car once we were inside.

"I know it's not much from the front, but I think I know how to create a better look, so don't worry about that," Sam said, trying to sound convincing. "We could put quite a bit of money into it at this good price."

When we went inside, neither of us expected to see such major work going on. My eyes went to stained glass windows and a very contemporary restoration. It appeared they had knocked out a wall for openness, and a skylight focused on a casual den that opened up into the kitchen area. There we found updated appliances and a fireplace in the kitchen, which was very cool. I could tell the owners were choosing updates to suit their tastes and so far I admired their efforts. We kept our comments short as we walked up to the second floor where we knew we could get a view of the river.

"This is a good view to have for an office," Sam said, reaching the first bedroom. "It reminds me a little of what I have in the loft. Look in here, Anne. The master bedroom has the same viewing angle. That's pretty cool."

"It's all kind of unique, and the view out these windows is a big plus. I wish I saw all of this finished. They do have some neat ideas."

After another few minutes indoors, we went out to the backyard, where I was not so pleased. It had a small creek running along the yard's edge that said to me that there would be erosion of some kind through the years and that it might have already started. We both took note of not being pleased with the yard in general, said as much to Tom, and got in our car. He knew where we were headed next.

"Well, you may as well know the houses I like are all going to be older, but I'm just more comfortable with that," Sam said as we continued our drive. "They have so much more character, but if you end up not being comfortable with that, we can head to the subdivisions."

"No," I responded immediately. "I am not a subdivision person. I have to have a sense of a unique neighborhood, where each house is different. This is all really new for me, Sam. I didn't even go away to college to live, so I only know about living in the house I grew up in. I don't think I'll be too picky about a house, but having my own yard to plant in is important for me. Mother had things the way she wanted them in her yard and she wouldn't let much of that change. She got older and I got busy with my shop and we were pretty content to let things be as they were."

"I understand all that, Anne. I want you to be as excited about a house as I am. I also want it big enough in case any little Dicksons decide to join us."

Hmmm, little Dicksons! Now what? Did he expect an immediate response? I honestly had never thought much about having my own children. Ted always talked of being a father and said it was part of his dream one day. I could never respond with the same enthusiasm, but thought that was part of my lack of feeling for Ted. Sam had told me more than once he wanted a family. Him, I loved. I knew I had to say something to answer his little joke, but what should it be? Keep it simple, I told myself.

"We'll see, I guess," I responded, not looking him in the eye.

"I know nothing would make your mother happier, not to mention how pleased my family would be." He drove us along to the next stop.

"Hey, I'm not a married woman yet, so slow down." I smiled at him but I was churning inside. Things might be moving too fast for me, truly.

Up the hill we drove to 333 Lincoln Street, the place Sam said he was saving for last because it was the best. Curiosity was certainly getting the best of me as we arrived at the top of the hill. We pulled into a circle drive that took us to a large porch with double doors. White pillars stood proudly on each side. Overgrown shrubs and winter debris nearly covered the beautiful brick sidewalks leading away in various directions. Part of the drive had debris scattered about. The once-beautiful, large Victorian-style home was frozen and cold, as if someone just packed up and left it to die.

"Now, don't panic and try to keep an open mind," Sam pleaded as he opened my car door. "It's an amazing place. Tom says the own-er, a member of the Taylor family, is anxious to sell it since it's been sitting vacant for so long. With them out of town, he knows little of the house's history. But look at those columns and those large windows. I'm dying to see the inside."

I remained quiet, trying to take it all in as I tried to concentrate despite the cold air. No doubt it was a pretty wonderful home in its day, but this house would require a major restoration that would cost a fortune. Again Tom unlocked the house but let us move around on our own. Once inside the massive doors we walked into an elegant, large entry area bigger than my home's living room. Wallpaper was peeling up from the carved baseboard and cried for attention. The historic home was cold, cold, cold.

Shivering, I walked into the living room where a nice size fireplace was the focal point. How I wished there was a big fire waiting for us. Sam made many pleasing sounds as he walked from room to room on the first floor. I remained quiet and overwhelmed. You could see outlines where large paintings once hung on the wall. Who were the Taylors, I wondered?

The kitchen was surprisingly small but all the required equipment was there. I could care less for myself, but knew Sam would love a well-equipped kitchen for his cooking. To my surprise, he loved the way it was laid out, as he showed me the large pantry and the maid's back entrance to the upstairs. A nice glassed-in back porch was off the kitchen that looked liked it held many a story. It would be the perfect mudroom for children coming in from the back yard. Children!? Where did that thought come from? The slanted floor I had seen before on many historic porches and I assumed it had to do with water drainage of some kind.

"Amazing, amazing," were Sam's continuous words of praise. "Anne, look out these dining room windows."

The dining room and what looked to be a study or library had built-in shelves, as well as their own fireplaces. The view out the dining room was a lovely view of a garden; lovely at one time, anyway. "It's amazing, Sam, but a little too amazing for me."

"Let's go upstairs," he said as he quickly moved ahead of me.

The wide, curved stairway was impressive even though a few spokes of the handrail were missing and some of the varnish seemed to be wearing off. You could see where the stairs were carpeted at one time. Wow. These stairs would keep anyone in shape, I thought to myself as I arrived at the top.

There were at least five large bedrooms and a smaller room off the wide hallway. There was a door that opened to a back stairway leading down to the kitchen—the maid's back entrance. Hmmm, a maid. I made a mental note of that. Maybe Sam could sweeten this deal if it came with a maid for me!

There were large closets that must have been added a bit later and the small room could have been a nursery at one time, since it was off the biggest bedroom. Sam thought it also could have been the maid's room. I saw more hideous wallpaper that must have been quite the rage some time back. I loved red, but not the heavy red velvet brocade lining the hallway. Sam started to tease me about not having to change a thing if we moved in, because there was so much red.

"I think it's colder in here than outdoors, Sam." I was shivering madly.

"Don't you want to go up to the attic?" He found a narrow door leading up from the hallway.

"You go up," I shook my head. "It might be pretty creepy."

Sam flew up the stairs in a flash. His energy and interest showed a side of him that I hadn't seen. He was like a little boy not knowing which toy to play with first. It made me happy to see him this way. I really didn't think he cared that much about my reaction. He was in a zone of fascination so deep I might just have been a fly on the wall.

As I tried not to think of the cold, I couldn't help noticing the extra gingerbread trim in various corners and the handsome woodwork in each room. The master bedroom, which I had decided must be the one because of its generous size, had a bay window that lined up with the bay window below on the first floor. How comfy this could be, waking up to morning coffee in this grand room with a view.

I had to admit to myself that it would be interesting to know about the former owners, the Taylors. They lived a fine lifestyle here to be sure. Did I remember hearing Mother say they said the house might be haunted? I think that could easily be the case, but who would it be? Could it be someone who may have died here? I would have to ask her again about that. I wasn't feeling anything strange.

"Okay, my love," he announced coming down the stairs. "It's fascinating up there but a bit too dark without electricity. They left a few things behind, which might be interesting to go through. It's a mess, but I guess the family didn't want to move that stuff."

"Sam, I can't imagine how expensive this place must be, and besides that, you really can't be serious about us considering this for our home, can you?" We headed back down the stairs.

He got quiet for a moment. Had I come across too strong?

"I'm not worried about the price, as it's flexible, but yes, Anne, I think this would be a fascinating project and a gorgeous place to live," he said in a hard voice. "Can't you look past the dirt and disrepair and see how beautiful this was and could be again someday? What scares you most about this? You could never find such qualities like this in most homes, including a new one. It would cost a fortune to build a house like this."

"We have jobs," I started talking, trying not to panic. "At least I have a job that keeps me very busy. You travel a lot, so who would oversee any restoration and everything else that would be required, like upkeep?"

"I have given this quite a bit of thought, and I knew what your response would be and that it was going to be challenging." He stared straight into my eyes. "We may have a big battle over this before it's over, but can't you at least for now have an open mind about the idea?"

"Oh, I'm sure I could, but how many battles would follow for us with this kind of project?" Now my voice was rising.

"Okay, let's go," Sam was shaking his head as he opened the door into the cold. "I don't want to leave without seeing the backyard and garage. I also want to know where the property lines are, if you don't mind. Stay in the car if you're cold; it won't take me long."

"I want to see it, too, so don't get crazy on me," I said, knowing I had gone a bit too negative.

We closed the big front doors in silence and followed the sidewalks leading here and there. The yard was large with landscaped areas that were overgrown and sad. I spotted boxwood bushes that I was so fond of. The first time I smelled a boxwood bush, I fell in love with it. I knew they grew very slowly, so these must be very old. I also knew they could be trimmed and sculpted into most any shape. Rose bushes rambled everywhere.

Sam had disappeared into the garage, but I followed the sidewalk to what appeared to be a small potting shed. The vines nearly covered its small windowpanes, some of which were broken. The once-green shed was peeling and faded, indicating it had been here a long, long time. Oh, how precious this was and so hidden from the front of the house! I pulled and pulled to open the door and finally walked onto a brick floor that led to potting counters covered with lots of clay pots and dead plants.

There was a small raised bed of soil on one side and larger containers stacked on the other. Rusty tools lay about like someone just left and never returned one day. This was now becoming amazing to me. How could anyone leave this? The very small structure had a purpose here at one time and it was still standing, waiting for someone to rescue it.

Now I could see the bigger picture Sam was talking about. I could imagine someone growing seedlings in the soil and filling all the pots with beautiful plants that would compliment the gorgeous house. There were worn wooden shelves above the windows. How did the former owner use those shelves? I wondered.

I could see my bazaar vases and clay pot collection displayed around the room. Was there a gardener here at one time or was it a hobby of Mrs. Taylor's? There was no doubt that no one had been active here in a very, very long time. Despite the broken windows, spider webs, and nasty vines that had grasped onto anything secure, the potting shed had a charm about it that I couldn't describe. I wanted to start cleaning it up; I could see the potential. It felt warmer in here, and I was sure the morning sun would hit it in the right direction each day.

"Anne, Anne," I heard Sam calling. "Where are you? Hello!"

"Sam!" I yelled with excitement. "Come in here and look! This is awesome!"

"I can't believe you're in there," he grinned, pulling away the vines that had greeted him. "You talk about me going into the attic! This is a whole lot creepier and you're getting all dirty. It doesn't even look safe!"

"No, no," I exclaimed, picking up one of the clay pots. "Come look at all this. This was an active greenhouse or potting shed years ago. Someone spent time here growing things. A gardener most likely worked from here to tend this huge yard and flowerbeds. I could hide and get lost forever back here. If I had this behind my house growing up, my mother would have never found me. Can you imagine starting all the plants from seeds, watching them grow, and dispersing them all around this house? I can almost smell the fragrances and feel the hot, humid air. This is where plants are born before they come to a place like Brown's Botanicals."

There was silence as Sam stared and listened. I knew he would not understand a bit of what I had just said. I had even surprised myself and suddenly brought myself back to the reality of this old estate. How could I expect anyone to understand the beauty here?

"You should hear yourself, Anne. What if you could play and hide in here whenever you wanted? This whole yard, with its gardens, cries out for someone like you. The house cries for me and I can't ignore it, despite your discouragement. Now you know what I mean after seeing this potter's shed."

"This is crazy, Sam," I replied, dusting myself off. "We must come to our senses. We aren't even married yet. Taking this big old house on is not timely and would be very costly."

"You let me worry about that," he said, helping me wipe off the spider webs. I couldn't keep my hands off the place. "I've got some stock I could sell and I'll be putting my loft up for sale. I might enjoy doing some of this work myself when I'm not traveling. I could go ahead and buy this and start working on it. It might be close to being habitable by our wedding date, if you're still thinking next spring."

I couldn't think clearly. What was he saying? I didn't know the asking price, but I was starting to realize that Sam had given this a lot of thought before he saw the house with me. He was going to buy this house with or without my approval. Would this be a good thing, a burden on our relationship, or an independent way to start our marriage? I wasn't sure I liked the answers. Was our independence taking over our joint decision-making? Hmmm.

"Sam, I couldn't let you do that. This is a decision we should be making together. I want to be a part of the investment with you. I don't want you to buy this house without me."

He came over to me and put his leather-gloved hands on each side of my face. He stared into my eyes with such admiration and determination.

"Anne, I love you so much." He brought his lips to mine and kissed me deeply. "Let's go get something to eat and talk about this over a hot bowl of soup and a glass of red wine."

CHAPTER 7

Not much was said about 333 Lincoln as we drove to Charley's on Main Street. Exciting ideas and scary thoughts dominated our minds. When we arrived at Charley's, we asked for a quiet booth where we could talk, as the bar and tables were loud and very busy with happy hour customers. We placed our orders from memory, made small talk, and waited for the wine to be served before 333 Lincoln surfaced in our conversation.

"Sam, I think what I'd first like to get settled is a wedding date," I announced out of the blue. "There is no sense discussing a house till we have a sense of when we will need a house as man and wife."

"I couldn't agree more, so what about next week?" He was now being silly and bumped his shoulder into mine.

"I wish it were that simple." I touched his cheek with the back of my hand. "I feel things are going too fast now. We need to set a date we both can live with and then we can plan accordingly."

"Valentine's Day of next year sounds pretty romantic. How about then? Don't you think there would be time enough to plan a nice, small wedding like we talked about?"

"I have to have a garden wedding, Sam," I squirmed at the thought of a chilly Valentine's Day. "I can't picture it any other way. How about May, a little over a year from now?"

"Too long, way too long, Anne." Sam was very serious. "Why such a long wait? Your mother will certainly be a big help with any planning and I know my sisters would be helpful."

He was reaching out to me, so I had to reach out to him. "I'd be happy with a small group of family members and friends, wouldn't you?" I suggested. "We could just have one couple stand up for us, and I think we should have lots and lots of flowers, don't you?"

The mention of a lot of flowers made him chuckle, which gave me more time to speak.

"I think I'm seeing it more clearly now Sam. I want it to be very manageable. I want the ceremony outdoors in a beautiful setting."

I took a deep breath and said, "How would September 12 be with you? That was my parents' wedding anniversary. The weather should still be fair outdoors before fall comes in." I watched his face for a reaction. "That's just a few months from now."

"I think we have a wedding date." Sam threw his hands in the air in delight. "I like it. You must promise me to stick to that date and delegate as much as you can so you don't get stressed out about this. I want Jim to be my best man since I don't have a brother. You decide who you want as his partner."

"Pinch me, Sam." Now I was giggling. "This is becoming real and very pleasant to my ears. I'll have to give that some thought. I did think the sunken Rawlings Garden in our city park would be a beautiful place. I've delivered flowers there before and it has so much to offer."

"Great, so that's settled!" He raised his glass of wine. "Here's to Sept. 12 for the rest of our lives! Have your mother call to book the garden on that date and get some suggestions on caterers."

I lifted my glass in frightful joy. What had I just agreed to? Setting a date was more real than the commitment to get married.

"Having a smaller wedding would be less of a financial burden on my mother, although she said I could have anything I wanted because my dad would want it that way."

"She doesn't have to pay for all of that, Anne. I can help."

"No, you can't, because you and I have a house to buy at 333 Lincoln!" This announcement nearly had him falling off his chair.

"Anne, oh, Annie, are you serious?"

"Only if you let me also invest in the purchase!"

"It's a deal!" Sam raised his glass of wine again. "I'll drink to that, too!"

"You'll drink to anything," I smiled, reaching over to give him a squeeze.

I couldn't believe what we had just agreed to. In ten minutes tops, we had set a date, described the wedding, and made a decision to buy a house. I had no doubt that with Sam's love and determination, 333 Lincoln would be ours. He said he would get busy making the deal while I would be planning the wedding of my life with my one and only love!

CHAPTER 8

The next morning I slept in an hour later than usual. I stayed in my bed trying to comprehend all that had taken place the night before and wondered how and when I would tell Mother. I reached for the bedside phone and called Sally at the shop.

"Hey, I'm going to be delayed this morning," I told her in my sleepy voice. "Will you be okay? I think Jean will be in at eleven o'clock."

"Oh sure, the orders are pretty light and I'll go ahead and get started on them. Will you be in before lunch?"

"I'm pretty sure." I mulled over a long list of things to do in my mind. "Call me if something comes up in the meantime. Be sure to check in the deliveries as soon as they come in. We've been waiting on the carnations to complete some of the prom corsages. There are also a couple of boxes for UPS when he comes in."

"Not to worry. Say hi to your mom or whoever you're with!"

"Hey, what's that supposed to mean?" I joked, knowing exactly what she was referring to. "I'll have you know I am home in my own bed and Mother and I have wedding plans to discuss."

"Oh, cool! Finally! Fill me in when you get here."

"I will," I said, hanging up the phone.

Mother was putting dishes in the dishwasher when I went into the kitchen in my bathrobe. She was dressed for work, which reminded me of her trying to have a life outside of just being my mother. She squinted in wonder when she looked at me.

"Hey, sleepyhead. No walk this morning?" She poured my coffee.

"I can't believe I slept this late. I had a little too much to drink last night, I think." I ran my fingers through my messy hair. "The good news is Sam and I made some decisions and settled a few things over dinner with a few glasses of wine."

"Well, hurray!" Mother gave me her full attention. "Do we have a wedding date?"

"Yes, we do," I nodded to the positive. "We had to compromise, which I guess is a good sign of things to come. We decided on a garden wedding on September 12. Does that sound like a good date?"

"How sweet of you both, Anne." She kissed me on the forehead. "Your Dad would be pleased. The date sure worked out well for us! Hey, we're talking September 12th of this year, I hope!"

"Yes, and I'd like it to be at Rawlings Garden at eleven a.m. We want a light champagne lunch, and Mother, we want the wedding to be a lot smaller than we first talked about. We want just close friends and family. We agreed that I would have to ask for help and I promised him I would not get all stressed about it. We'll have just one couple stand up for us to keep things simple. So, what do you think?"

"Oh, my dear, it just sounds perfect!" She was beaming. "It should still be lovely weather, and you'll be all settled for the winter. Oh, Anne, I am so happy for you!"

43

Mother started to tear up as she gave me a hug. I wanted her to enjoy the moment before I broke the news about the Taylor house. She started babbling about this and that, things that had to be done, and then she fussed around the kitchen making sure I would eat something. I didn't absorb much of what she was saying, as my mind was wandering.

"I haven't decided who my maid of honor will be because I'm thinking I may have to choose one of Sam's sisters. What do you think?"

"Oh, I never thought of that," she said, sitting down with me to have more coffee. "You have only met them once, right? I think Sam would want you to have someone you are close to. I am guessing he will have Jim stand up for him, am I right?"

"Yes," I nodded. "You got that right. They are thick, I'm afraid. I just hope Jim doesn't end up being a bad influence on Sam, but that's another conversation. Hey, what time do you have to be at work?"

"Not till noon today, but I wanted to run a few errands before then. What about you? Are you taking the day off?"

"No, but I told Sally I'd be in by lunch. I have something else to share with you, Mother. Sam and I are going to make an offer on the Taylor house."

"You have got to be kidding me, Anne." She looked shocked, even horrified.

"We did look at some other places and I really thought we'd be looking for weeks and weeks, but I have to admit we both, and I'm repeating both, fell in love with the place. Sam was going nuts with enthusiasm as we went through the house. I was pretty numb taking it all in until I walked the grounds and saw the gardens and potting shed. Mother, you just won't believe how amazing it all is! I've always dreamed of my own greenhouse and boxwood garden, and there it was! We both felt we belonged there. I know it's hard to explain. Does it make sense? Say something, Mother!"

"My word, child! Have you both lost your minds? How much is that place? I hear it needs everything done to it! Who will do all that and how long will it take? Don't you want a nicer place with a minimal amount of maintenance? You're both busy people. Don't you think you both need to think this through?"

"When Sam puts his mind to something, he moves," I said, trying to stay calmer than she. "I think this is why he has been so successful. His positive manner tells him ways he can make things happen instead of why they can't. I saw it happen before my eyes. The house might be partially finished enough for us to move into after the wedding. We decided it would be something we would both work on in our spare time. I think it might even help my flower business in the future, if I can start growing some of my own things in the winter. Sam wants to work on it when he isn't traveling and I can actually see him doing that. Oh, Mother! I am more excited about our adventure together at 333 Lincoln than the wedding itself. Does that make sense?"

"Anne, Anne, this is a lot to take in." She took a deep breath. "But you're a grown woman with a good head on your shoulders. You work hard and deserve a good husband, a successful business, and a magnificent home. My darling Anne, I want nothing but happiness for you, and you have my blessing."

This was all I needed to hear to make my happiness complete, and I hugged her tight.

"I have to ask your honest opinion, Mother. I want to be a financial partner in this house. I don't want to live in Sam's house, if you know what I mean. I want this to be ours. I was thinking of using the rest of the money left from Dad's will to invest in this house, instead of it being my business cushion. The shop is holding its own, even with the extra employee, so I think I feel comfortable doing this. We won't know the final price until Sam gets done negotiating with them, but I think what I have will be sufficient."

"It's your money, Anne." Mother smiled with approval. "If that's where you want it to go, I don't see why you shouldn't. I can always help you, too. You know that."

"You need to protect yourself, Mother. I don't ever want to do that to you. I want you to have a comfortable life without any worries. I'll be fine and feel a lot better if Sam is not carrying the load in all of this. You have offered to cover the wedding and for that I am most grateful."

With all that said, we hugged in tears with excitement for the future ahead of us. I couldn't wait for her to see the house and the potting shed.

Then I started to think. What if we couldn't buy the house after all of this? Would we be able to do it all? I think I could eat on a picnic table and sleep in a sleeping bag if it meant being there with Sam. Then I reminded myself that Sam came with a whole loft full of furniture and I would have some things from my home as well, so maybe we could and would live like regular folks. I needed to go back to the Lincoln yard soon. Spring was at our doorstep and I wanted to start planning. I wanted to make sure that the flowers and shrubs that were there could begin to blossom in their own time.

Yes, I was getting the cart before the horse, no doubt!

CHAPTER 9

Sam was delighted with how happily Mother received the news about the purchase of 333 Lincoln. He was certain a deal could be struck with the owners' distant relative who was in charge of the house. We immediately decided to apply for a pre-approved loan together, in hope of a quick purchase.

I was feeling more mature than ever. Anne Brown was buying a house! A big house with a big yard and potting shed that I had only seen in my dreams. I felt confident my father would have approved of this real estate investment.

The shop girls, Sally and Jean and Sue, were thrilled about the wedding date being set. I hadn't had a chance to visit with Aunt Julia yet but knew Sam was keeping Uncle Jim informed. In no time, there was a message on my cell to call Aunt Julia and I was sure she had heard about the house purchase as well.

"Sorry I haven't called you," I told her when I returned the call. "Things have been crazy, as you may have heard."

"Anne, this is so exciting! I am so happy the wedding will be this year. I have to admit when I heard about the Taylor house, I about fainted."

"You and me both," I laughed lightly. "As soon as we finalize everything, I'm sure you and Sarah would like to go with Mother and me sometime to see it."

"I think we can do that. I don't know about Sarah; she usually has much to do after school, but just let me know when."

"Oh, that would be great." I felt relieved that she took all the news well.

The next couple of weeks were intense, but everything worked in our favor, so we moved quickly on the sale and then finally had a closing. We were homeowners! I couldn't help wonder why they accepted our first offer so quickly. Was it because of the ghost everyone kept telling us about? Sam was totally at ease with the entire transaction, as if he did this every day. I had to pinch myself at each step, knowing how this purchase would not only commit us financially for a long time, but would require much of our time and attention.

We celebrated the closing by grabbing some Starbucks coffee and driving up the hill to 333 Lincoln. It was now ours. I, still Anne Brown, owned half of a house! That was totally scary till I remembered the charming potting shed waiting for me around the corner. We got out of the car, stared up at this magnificent, lonely house, and raised our cups as we congratulated ourselves on the rescue. We kissed and hugged, knowing it would not always be this romantic and fun. What would really, really be in store for us? Hmmm.

Aunt Julia had continued to remind me about wanting to check out the new purchase, so the next day I agreed to show her around, not remembering Sam had our only set of keys at this point in time. After work, Mother and Aunt Julia promised to promptly pick me up after the shop closed at five o'clock. They were right on time and pulled up across the street. I left a few instructions for Kevin, who was also leaving, and grabbed my coat. Aunt Julia came in alone and expressed her curiosity and excitement.

"I'll drive," she offered.

I agreed, waving to Gayle who was leaving her glass shop next door at the same time, and got in the back seat of Aunt Julia's SUV. As soon as I shut the door, she fired off the dreaded question.

"Hey, Anne, have you thought about my request to be a part of our ceremony?"

"Sure, I'll think of something, but I have some questions for you." I took a deep breath as we drove away from the shop. "I couldn't be happier for you and Uncle Jim working things out, but I think you owe your family an explanation on how in the heck you went from plan A, which was leaving Uncle Jim after Sarah got out of school, to plan B, where all is wedded bliss?"

"I know, I know," she paused. "I do owe you all an explanation."

"No, you don't," said Mother sharply. "I think what you and Jim are doing is wonderful and the details are none of our business."

I was taken aback by Mother's strong tone, but Aunt Julia responded as though nothing was wrong.

"I had a 'coming to Jesus' talk with Jim some time back and a lot was said and confessed. He really broke down, feeling guilty about some things, and promised he would do anything and everything to keep our family together. I never saw him like this. Immediately he started making an effort to please me, including a romantic side of him that I had not seen in some time. He can turn on the charm, you know, which is why I fell for him in the first place. Besides; Sarah is growing up so fast, and I'm going to need help with her in these years. She needs a father's influence right now, so I've convinced myself to try to remember the Jim I fell in love with."

Feeling guilty about him and Brenda, I wondered? Was that what he confessed? I sure couldn't reveal anything about Brenda without her telling me first. Was this another cover-up from Uncle Jim? Hmmm.

"Okay," I said, not wanting to make this a bigger issue. "I think I understand how you feel and I do admire you for that, but I hope you don't wear blinders, just because you agreed to this. Was it his idea to have the vows renewed?"

"Oh, sure," she half-laughed. "He likes to put on a show. He's that way with everything. I did put my foot down about asking no one to this ceremony but family and a few friends. He would have invited every client he ever had and then write it off as a business expense." Yup, she was right about that! Just then we drove up the hill to 333 Lincoln and the subject was dropped.

"Oh, my goodness, Anne!" Mother got out of the car. "The more I see of this place, the more overwhelming it appears to be! Can you really believe it's now all yours?" No, she had no idea how surreal this all was, but I had to show confidence about our decision. Their heads were up, down, and everywhere as they sized it up.

"I'm sorry I wasn't able to get the key from Sam today, but there's a lot to look at out here." They followed me around the outside of the house. "Look at all these brick sidewalks underneath the debris. If they could talk! They all lead you somewhere, like to this once-manicured rose garden." I pointed to a circular area of rambling rose bushes.

"Oh, Anne, look," Mother called, going off in her own direction. "This is a weeping willow tree. I love them and always wanted to buy one. They say they grow well around water, like a lake or pond. This has been here a long time by the size of it. This is all overwhelming, Anne!"

"Anne, Anne, do you and Sam know what you're in for?" Aunt Julia asked without expecting an answer. "How in the world will you know where to start?"

"I know, but follow me over here to where this potting shed is," I called as I opened the door that barely opened and needed replacing badly. "This is what sold it all for me and it's what I've always wanted. I can play in the dirt and grow beautiful things everyday! Did you ever see so many clay pots? Some of these are pretty interesting."

"You and your silly pots!" Mother teased. "No one's been in this little shed for quite some time!" She and Aunt Julia pulled spider webs and vines out of the way as they cautiously walked in and looked around. It was a little creepy actually, and it probably was a mistake to bring them here before any clean up took place.

"I've never been in a potting shed," said Aunt Julia, shaking her head in disbelief. Mother seemed a bit dismayed, too.

"Wonder what this is?" I asked as I looked under one of the workbenches. "Something's wrapped up here. Oh, dear, this is big-time dirty." I pulled it out, dragging all the dirty debris with it.

"Here, hand it to me." Aunt Julia removed it from my hands. "Holy cow, whatever it is has something heavy inside. Yucky for sure! Why is this under here? I wonder how long it's been here?"

"Look at that, Anne, whatever you have there is wrapped in an old quilt!" Mother turned back a corner to see more.

I couldn't pull the quilt off fast enough, laying it on the counter. I was starting to sneeze from the dust and leaves attached to the quilt. The quilt fell to the ground as I examined a large pottery vase in front of me. This was cool, whatever it was. This was the kind of dirty treasure I had a knack for spotting at garage sales.

"What do you think of that?" Aunt Julia said with awe. "It's pretty interesting, Anne."

"There's got to be a mark on this someplace." I turned the piece over and over, looking intently. "Oh, Aunt Julia, you're getting so dirty, and we'll never find a mark until this is washed off. I love it, don't you? This should clean up nicely. We need to take this with us. What can I put this in so I can get it home safely?" I looked around the abandoned shed.

"Well, here, you're not going to leave this behind!" Mother stated as she picked the quilt off the ground. "It's a frightful thing, but you can still wrap it around that vase for now."

She took the quilt outside to shake it out. When she opened it up, we could see it was really a quilt top, not a finished quilt. The fresh air and better light, which was fading, helped us concentrate on the fabric burdened with dirt and leaves.

"This is a Crazy quilt, Anne," she said as she opened it further. "I think Grandmother had one of these. Look at all these fancy stitches. Boy, oh boy, this is a mess."

"Go ahead and wrap it back up around the vase," said Aunt Julia as she began to sniffle. "I have some plastic in the trunk, so don't worry about the car."

"Here, be careful with this Aunt Julia," I instructed as I handed her the dirty treasure. "I want to walk around the house and show Mother more of the garden. There's a back porch off the kitchen. Maybe we can get in there."

Everything was locked up and I didn't want to force anything open. I also didn't want to leave. I couldn't resist pulling a few weeds along the way as we walked our way back to the car. Mother kept making comments about the poor condition of most everything she saw. No doubt I was going to hear more about this run-down estate from everyone in the days to come.

"You're going to need so much help, Anne." Mother shook her head. "I'll have to quit my job and become a gardener. What kind of plan does Sam have to begin a project like this?"

"He assured me that we would pay to have most of this work done and then he can work on some things when he's not traveling. We have a fair amount of time to get this place cleaned up before our wedding."

Aunt Julia and Mother rolled their eyes and their body language said they were now ready to go, but I wanted to examine a few more things while I was there. As I looked more at the house, I was beginning to see what Sam saw right away—a vision of the finished product. I could just see wicker furniture with large ferns placed about the south porch of the house. The trees were shading most of the porch, which would be delightful in the summer. My cell phone went off, which took me out of my fantasy.

"Yes, Sam," I answered like I was in a cave. "Mother, Aunt Julia, and I are standing in front of our house. I'm pretending that I will be inviting them in for a tour and a cup of tea."

Sam laughed and I could tell he was pleased that we were having a good time. He was so excited as he brought me up to date with arranging for an electrician and carpenter to start giving us bids on the needed work. I knew I couldn't keep up with his planning, but that was okay with all I had on my plate. He had to hang up, so I told him I'd see him tomorrow. Things were all moving so fast. Were things moving too quickly?

"Are you all ready to leave?" I finally asked them as they stood chatting. "Don't you think this house is one of best kept secrets in Colebridge?"

"This is very exciting, Anne, but maybe it should remain a secret," teased Aunt Julia. "Seriously, I do think this place could be amazing." She turned to look at her sister. "Are you sure you heard it was haunted, Sylvia? Anne, don't you want to know a little more about the haunting rumors? What if it's like one of those TV shows or movies where you don't know how scary it is until you move in? It's everything I can do just to put up with the spirits in your basement!" We all laughed.

"Well, you know how rumors like that take on a life of their own when there's an old building," Mother was doing her best to assure me. "None of it is probably true."

"Anne, have you heard any details about the ghost?" Aunt Julia persisted in teasing me.

"Heavens no," I answered. "Just like the spirits in our basement, I think if they're here, then they're going to love Sam and me. We're going to bring this place back to life and hopefully we'll not do anything that would disturb them.

"Oh, my gosh, look at the time!" Aunt Julia broke the spell. "We need to get going."

CHAPTER 10

Mother and I were exhausted by the time we arrived home. There was too much to think about, such as when could I really start this mammoth undertaking? I heard plenty of reasons on the way home about how difficult everything would be.

Annoying as they were, raining on my parade like that, I expected these cautious reactions. Besides, for now I had a treasure to uncover, so I brushed the negatives aside.

I carefully carried the vase and quilt into the garage so as not to drag any loose soil inside the house and placed it on the workbench. I couldn't wait to look for a signature or something that would tell me more about my discovery. I shook debris off the outside of the quilt and made sure it sat securely on the bench. Then I brushed myself off and went inside to wash my hands in the kitchen. Mother suggested that she warm up some leftover soup and make some ham sandwiches. I prayed she would not continue to question the house purchase, now that she had seen it.

I went to my room to change my clothes and threw myself across the bed to digest my thoughts. My dreams were becoming larger than life. Sam had been my main focus until I saw this house. How could that be? The thought of the two of us enjoying such a place was really beyond my wildest dreams. I was not turning back!

Sunday was a good time to put all the commotion from the 333 Lincoln visit aside. Mother talked me into going to church with her. She was so devoted and such a good church member. I grew up in the Lutheran school and church. We knew most everyone. It actually was good for business to belong there as I provided most of the church's flowers with the added benefit of acquiring plenty of business from its members. It was a good time to meditate with my own personal faith. Going to a parochial school had given me a day-to-day communication with God. I knew it had given me the strength and courage to be what I am today. I also knew Mother's faith was strong, as was Father's. When he was still alive, we always held hands around the table to pray. After he was gone, Mother and I rarely bowed our heads to pray at home.

I sat quietly, looking at couples coming down the aisle together. Would I someday be one of them, bringing a child to Sunday school? Sam's determination to be a father wasn't going to go away. I'm sure Mother had thought this would be the aisle I would be walking down some day to be married, but fortunately, she embraced the garden wedding idea.

My mind continued to wonder if our yard at 333 Lincoln could be transformed in time for a wedding. That task would be nearly impossible, but choosing Rawlings Garden was certainly appropriate, even in early fall. I could picture myself in a sheer white gown with white flowers flowing from my hair. Oh, dear! What is this sermon about? I shook myself from my daydream.

Later that afternoon, Sue was the first to arrive right on time for the afternoon quilting. Aunt Julia brought Sarah again, which surprised me. Being a teenager, Sarah amazed everyone with her interest. It might've been our experiences of spirits in the basement that intrigued her. Jean arrived fifteen minutes later.

"Didn't mean to hold you up," she said with her sweet smile.

"You know Sue." I introduced them. "This is my Aunt Julia and her daughter, Sarah. And the 'hostess with the mostess' is my mother, Sylvia."

"This is a most pleasant occasion, Mrs. Brown, I mean Sylvia." Jean said using her English manners. "How jolly this will be! I do so appreciate the invitation, and I simply adore anything to do with quilts!"

Per our tradition, we moved downstairs into the "quilting basement." Jean nodded as she looked about the basement. "What a cozy assembly room, I guess I may call it. Every cottage in England has one, and I'm told this may qualify."

"Oh, it's an assembly room all right," I joked as the others chuckled.

"I have a spot right here for you, Jean." Mother pulled out a chair for her. The rest of us took our usual places. "It won't take us long to finish this quilt for Sue's little girl, who'll be arriving soon—all the way from Honduras! Do you know this Variable Star pattern, Jean? We had a little help finishing this top, but we all want to put our stitches into this little baby quilt. It will be fine for a boy or a girl."

"Yes, yes, so special," said Jean. "It is adorable and it is such a blessing. It was the first bit of news Sue shared with me the day we met in the shop. The fabrics are precious!"

"Did you bring your thimble?" I asked Jean, wanting to get started.

"Yes, indeed I did, Miss Anne," she grinned. "This was my

dear Grandmother Riley's thimble. She did a bit of sewing, though I don't know if she quilted. She was quite a knitter though, by golly!"

"It's beautiful." Aunt Julia looked it over. "You know, Jean, we're all still beginners."

"Sure," she said. "This matters not on something as personal as this."

"I suppose you've met Sam by now, am I right?" Mother asked.

"Oh, my dear, yes! What a handsome bloke, and such a gentleman."

"And did Anne tell you about purchasing 333 Lincoln?" Mother asked as she quilted along.

"I heard her speak of such, and Sally brags of its history. I am most anxious to see the place for myself someday!"

"We had a most interesting visit to the house recently, Jean," I started to explain.

"How's that, Miss Anne?" She looked up from the quilt.

"When I took Aunt Julia and Mother to see the place this week, we went into the potting shed in the backyard. Inside, we discovered something wrapped up under one of the workbenches." I paused from my stitches. "Something was big, heavy, dirty, and wrapped in an old quilt top. When I unwrapped it, we saw a wonderful vase. I knew it had to be valuable. I need to really look it over after I clean it up. This vase is not going into a floral arrangement for the shop like my other finds. This is going on one of the fireplace mantels at 333 Lincoln."

"Where is the find?" Jean asked in a serious tone.

"I had to leave it in the garage because it was so dirty."

"I would love to see the quilt more than the vase," said Jean. "I adore antique quilts."

"Oh, Jean, this one is pretty ratty and dirty."

"Let's go see," said Sue. "May we have a look right now?"

"Yes, I say we have a look." Jean started to rise from her chair.

"Oh, dear," Mother protested. "The garage is a mess. I'll spread newspapers or something on the kitchen table. You all can come up there, get some dessert, and take a look at the mysterious treasure there."

"That's a good plan." I joined Mother as she climbed the stairs. "You all keep quilting while we bring it into the kitchen." The four of them started stitching again.

I went into the garage and observed that the garage was never a mess, but figured Mother didn't want us all in there. I carefully carried the wrapped vase into the kitchen and placed it in the center of the newspaper-covered table. As I unwrapped the quilt from the vase, the backside of the fabric faced up. I noticed the quilt pieces were all attached to paper, which I thought was rather odd. I kept the vase sitting on the paper side of the quilt for all to see. We called downstairs that we were ready and were joined by the others.

"So let's have a look, shall we?" Jean asked in anticipation.

"Gee, Anne, this all looks pretty yucky if you ask me," said Sarah. "What's so cool about this thing?"

"I just love unusual containers, you all know that, but I've never seen anything like this. Have any of you?" I asked.

"I am blind when it comes to American pottery," said Jean as she looked closer. "I want to see more of this quilt. It strikes my fancy, I can tell you! May I take a look, Miss Anne?"

"Oh, sure." I removed the vase from the table to give her access to the quilt. "Jean, what's the deal here with all this paper on the back?"

"This is foundation pieced," she said. "English paper piecing is similar and Americans are intrigued with it. It helps give body to the shape of the fabric patch, which is typically pretty small. I know about this as I learned how to do it in a quilt shop in Kentucky. I understand how it got its name because I have seen some quilts like this at home. Silk and satin quilts are more common there." We were staring in awe of how much Jean seemed to know. Aunt Marie had been our quilt expert and she was gone. This was a great treat!

She continued, "Historians call this a Victorian-era Crazy quilt. Quilters mostly used newspapers or catalog pages as their foundation, because it was not expensive and it's what they had stashed in their homes. It would secure the piecing and then later be removed before a batting and back side would be attached. Crazy quilts usually didn't have a batting because the fabrics were already so heavy. The Crazy quilts that I have seen usually have a fabric foundation, not paper. Instead of quilting the layers together, they knotted them, as we say. I believe you Yanks say 'tied.' This poor lovely soul never made it to its destiny. It's a bloody fright of a thing now, for sure!"

Jean picked it up gingerly and turned most of it over. We backed up so as not to get dirty from anything. We all just observed Jean, who was taking a great deal of interest in the pile of soiled fabric. She continued to examine each detail of the quilt, making funny sounds with each discovery.

"Ooh! These cloths I see here may be as late as 1920. Most Crazy quilts were made as early as 1880 of satins, brocades, velvets, and silks. This has a bit of all that."

She made another noise, then looked up at us and said, "I was taught by Miss Ellie that you date a quilt from the newest fabric in the quilt, because many quilts are made from bits and scraps the quiltmaker would have stashed away from clothes, bed covers, curtains, and the like. They were sometimes referred to as 'parlor quilts,' for they were to thrill the eye, not warm to the body. Right now, this poor thing cannot do much of either, wouldn't you say?"

She chuckled and then turned the top over to the back side again and looked closer. Our fascination with Jean's knowledge had put my wonderful vase in the background for a few minutes, but now the others, losing interest, helped themselves to the three desserts arrayed on the kitchen counter.

"These papers are most unique, Anne." Jean tried to see what they had written on them. "From what I'm seeing, these are all letters cut up into the different shapes. You can see they are all handwritten, and even though they are on different colored paper and different colored ink, they all seem to be in the same handwriting. That is very odd. Take a closer look, Miss Anne."

"Well, someone got sick and tired of saving someone's letters and cut them up!" Aunt Julia said, all practicality.

"Why wouldn't they just use newspaper, and then we could read all about it!" I joked.

"Don't give a laugh." Jean continued her close examination. "These letters or sonnets could be most exhilarating for a variety of reasons. I heard once that after someone passes on, they would cut up paper pieces of their memories and put them into a quilt one way or another. This happened mostly after the war, someone said. Oh, I would like to create one of these dandies myself someday!"

After several sneezes from Sarah, Aunt Julia told her to go back downstairs to avoid more exposure to the dust. Mother kept picking up loose pieces of dirt and fabric as they found their way to the floor.

"This had to belong to the Taylors in some way," I thought out loud. "I just don't understand why this vase was protected like this. And why on earth was it put under the workbench like that? Someone wanted to protect it, perhaps. Or, maybe a burglar or servant came along and decided to hide it for taking later."

We started getting silly with interpretations of why the vase and quilt were there. It was the best entertainment we had had since the spirits had kept us guessing in the basement with the last quilt we quilted.

"Miss Anne," Jean hesitated. "Would you mind if I took the quilt home for a closer look? I will tidy it up the best I can and study all this a bit."

"Oh, Jean, what a great idea," said Mother. She was clearly anxious to get it out of her kitchen. "Anne will be doing some checking on this vase with one of her antique dealer buddies on Main Street, I suspect."

"Yes, Jean, I would love that if you're sure you want to fool with this old thing. It's pretty dirty!"

"I won't give it a wash, you know that, don't you?" Jean reassured us. "This kind of quilt you cannot wet clean, but I can air it out, and I also have a way of lightly vacuuming a quilt with a screen over it. It works! This is most fascinating, my ladies!"

With that decision, everyone decided to be on their way. Sarah continued sneezing as she and Aunt Julia went out the door. Sue helped Mother clean up in the kitchen after Jean wrapped up the quilt in the newspaper on the table. I could tell that she had a feel for the antique things in life that had a story to tell. All in all, I was very pleased with the afternoon, and couldn't wait to tell Sam all about it. I was sure the vase was meant for me to keep at 333 Lincoln.

CHAPTER 11

Monday morning was wet and dark. A good morning for me to get another hour or two of sleep, but with me leaving the shop earlier more frequently, duty called. Forget trying to get in a quick walk with this depressing weather.

Mother was sleeping in for a change. I decided not to wake her and grabbed a Starbucks coffee and a raspberry muffin on the way to work. I should have something to look forward to, I told myself.

I loved having the alone time in my shop of colorful blooms and smells. I guess I pretended it was all for me. Then I thought of that charming potting shed. It was likely getting rain inside from all the broken windows. I didn't mind rainy days here because the shop was always humid, warm, bright, and cheery. The drops of rain on the windows were like rain on my garden. At some point, I must write about the seasons of a flower shop, I thought.

Oh, I did love to write. I had not had a moment to write my thoughts on anything since I met Sam. Here I was experiencing some of the happiest moments of my life and I had no time to put them into words! I wasn't even sure Sam understood how much I loved and even needed to write. I had always wanted to start a writer's club to keep me focused on one of the things I loved, but now it seemed all I had time for writing were checks for bills, although I did take the time to do some occasional quilting in the basement.

Sam returned to my thoughts. Thinking of him made me smile inside and out. Our future home and my precious potting shed offered such excitement to look forward to. This amazing house must have its own story to tell. If I were to write about 333 Lincoln, I would best begin by journaling every day about the restoration and what we might learn about its history along the way.

I wanted to know everything I could about this forgotten house with its gardens. Who could possibly leave this place and why? How could they have neglected that precious potting shed? When was it built and who put it there? Why was the intriguing vase left there? How would anyone know if the place was really haunted? Had others tried to live there since the Taylors? Were they driven away? It didn't appear like that from what Sam was told.

Thinking about the vase I realized I had not had time to really clean it or ask anyone on the street about it. I was still lost in my thoughts when Sally came in at her usual time and brought me back to reality. I had lots to fill her in about the house, the vase, and the quilt discovery.

"I brought you a blueberry muffin from Starbucks, Sally. I know how you love them."

"Oh, you are the best boss ever!" She picked up the delicious muffin. "I love those things. I slept a little late this morning. It was so dark; did you notice that?"

"Yes, oh yes, I did." I stretched. "I had a big weekend I can't wait to tell you about."

"Good morning!" Gayle came in from the glass shop next door. "I met your nice little English girl last week, Anne. I love her accent! How is she working out?"

"Great! And, she's a quilter." I smiled.

"Since when is that required here?" Gayle laughed.

"She joined our little quilting group at the house after I learned that she is quite the quilter! She had a good time and even took on a project for me. She and her husband don't know many folks, being new to the area. I hope you reach out to her, Gayle."

Just then the phone rang. I went to the design room to answer and let Gayle and Sally continue chatting. It was Sam, with a voice I would never tire of hearing.

"How was the quilting?"

"Good morning to you, too!" I answered with a smile. "It was great. I'll tell you more about it tonight, I hope." I could just picture him smiling on the other end of the phone.

"Yes, a beautiful day isn't it!" He laughed. "I do have to be in the office all day, but I'll be free for dinner to catch up. I miss you, Annie dear!" He paused for me to take in the compliment. "I took some photos of the house yesterday so we'll have some record of 'before' pictures, and they turned out quite good. How about I pick you up at your house around six thirty, so you have time to change or whatever?"

"Oh, that would be great; I'm anxious to see the pictures. Did you get the potting shed, too?"

"No; I don't think the potting shed is in a photo by itself, but I'm sure you'll be the one taking many of those pictures. You're really excited about this, aren't you, Annie?"

"Yes, indeed, just like I'm excited about September twelfth!" Sam laughed.

"I'll see you at six thirty," I said, reminding myself that this horse before the cart had me thinking more about 333 Lincoln than the wedding. Hmmm.

When I hung up, Jean had arrived at the shop. She was her perky self, and then proceeded to tell me what a grand time she was having with the quilt. She was thrilled with the muffins and devoured one as she talked.

"The sun is supposed to be out tomorrow," she noted. "I will air out the quilt first thing in the morning. It has impeccable stitching on the front side, Miss Anne. The pretty flowers and designs are quite dashing and there is some silk ribbon embroidery, but no sewn dates or initials are to be found. The hand painting is quite good on some of the pieces. In paint there is one 'M,' at least I think it's supposed to be an 'M,' or maybe it's a 'W.' Don't mean to waffle, but we should be able to figure that out. By golly, I think that the most amazing thing is that all the papers seem to be letters of some kind! If I had to guess, they were love letters, because there are words that pertain to romance."

"Thanks so much, Jean." I felt her excitement. "Hand painting —wow, I didn't notice that. The initial will be helpful as we learn more. I want to find out about everything in that house, and so far that's the only thing that has any information about it. The Realtor we worked with was not helpful at all and didn't seem to care. Sam said there are a few things in the attic, but I don't know when I will have the nerve to go up there and check that out. We were lucky just to get the former owners' names—Marion and Albert Taylor."

"Did you say Marion?" Jean asked.

"Yeah, why?"

"That could be our 'M' on the quilt I just mentioned. Marion could have stitched this quilt!"

"Oh, that would be cool." Now my curiosity was up. "Your keen observations will be so helpful."

The phone rang again and it never seemed to stop ringing all day. It was going to one of those "what do I first" kind of days. Two funerals and a fund raising event at The Pillars Banquet Center were more than enough to keep us all hopping for the day. Folks in town would always say, "If it's happening at all, it's happening at The Pillars." That was one good reason The Pillars wasn't in consideration for my own wedding.

At five o'clock, Sally and Jean had to leave and the last delivery was on the truck. It felt good and I knew it had been a "good money drawer day," as we called it. I had locked the door when the shop phone rang once more. I crossed my fingers that it wasn't something that had gone wrong with any of the orders.

"Hey, Annie," Sam smiled across the wires. "I'm about to meet some of the guys from work for a drink. If it's okay with you, how about I grab a pizza before I pick you up and then we head over to my place? I thought you might want to know that you can throw on some jeans to be more comfortable."

"That sounds wonderful." I relaxed all over. "Besides, the privacy of your place will make it easier for me to attack you, my dear. I really miss you and have a jillion things to talk to you about."

"Awesome!" He sounded very sexy. "However, you may have to choose between attacking or talking. I'm not very good at doing both at the same time."

The heads-up on this plan gave me extra time to finish up at the shop and return a few phone calls. I really did love this guy.

CHAPTER 12

S am's generous kiss in the car was stiff competition with the wonderful smell of pizza from Pete's Pizza, a local favorite in Colebridge.

When we arrived at his loft, it wasn't difficult to decide which to indulge in first. Sam's grip and his urgent removal of my coat told me that the pizza could wait and then be warmed up. We initiated our passion in the kitchen and ended up on the large floor pillows, where we had often exchanged our heated attraction for one another. His beautiful words of passion and love were incredible to me. Every time he would just say my name I wanted to melt. He knew the right words and the right moves. I wondered how in the world I rated in comparison to his other lovers. For a quick second I tried to think of any other comparison to our love and I couldn't think of any; certainly not with Ted. Perhaps Wendy was enjoying sex with Ted in a way I couldn't. Would that be a good thing or a jealous thought? Why was I even thinking about that now? Hmmm.

"I'm starving," Sam announced, heading for the kitchen. "How about a cold beer and hot pepperoni pizza with lots of onions?"

For some reason the beer sounded good with the pizza in spite of my love for merlot. The food went down quickly. I watched Sam take much bigger bites than I remembered seeing. I was happy just watching him eat!

"We've been so busy I haven't had a chance to tell you what I discovered in the potting shed the other day with Aunt Julia and Mother." I took a drink of beer to wash the last piece of pizza down my throat.

He stopped in mid-bite. "Oh, and what might that be?"

I began telling him the whole story of how we were checking out the grounds and the potting shed. Then I filled him in on the beautiful vase wrapped in an interesting quilt. He could see and feel the excitement as I shared how I was going to need a lot of help to identify the vase and also from the basement quilters to solve the mystery of my find. To my surprise, Sam was quite intrigued and was especially interested in why there were letters cut up on the back of the quilt.

"Speaking of help, I may have found some much-needed labor support with the house," he inserted with matched excitement. "Tonight at Charley's I had a few offers to help with some of the initial cleaning up. Paul Becker gave me some good leads on restoration guys. Jim also said if he was free, he'd give me a hand. Brenda from our department said if we needed any decorators, she knew them all!"

"Who did you just say?" I nearly choked. "Who there tonight?"

"Paul, Brenda, and Jim," he calmly stated. "We were all in the same meeting and decided to grab a cold one at Charley's. Why?"

"This Brenda." I chose my words carefully. "She's married, right?"

"Sure, I think I met her husband once. Why do you ask that?"

"Because she, Brenda, is the one supposedly having an affair with Jim!" I blurted it out before I could think. "It didn't take me long to hear that when I was at the Christmas party. I didn't want to say anything to anyone, hoping it wasn't true. I sure didn't want to tell Aunt Julia. Then, when I heard about their wedding renewal, I was glad I didn't say anything. Now you tell me she and Jim were together. Didn't you say they were leaving to go out of town? That's incredible!" I paced back and forth in the kitchen.

"Hey, slow down." Sam looked shocked at my actions and words. "Who told you this? Jim and Brenda travel a lot to the same places, but so do others, like myself."

"I didn't get the name of the lady at Martingale's who told me. I was so shaken from what I heard. She said it'd been going on for years. I then asked another person if she worked at Martingale's. When she said yes, I asked her if she knew a girl named Brenda. She said yes. I asked her if she was at the party because we had a mutual friend and I would like to meet her. She said no, that Brenda's husband usually did not come to these things."

I paced the room. "You can see why this is bothersome. Uncle Jim has conned Aunt Julia into believing everything is hunky dory, and I would bet anything he is still involved with Brenda."

Sam got up silently and walked to the window, looking out on the river. I decided to let him think a bit. I wasn't sure if he was going to attack me for accusing his friend of something untrue or if he was trying to digest my suspicions. I walked over next to him and stared at his handsome profile.

"Talk to me, Sam. Am I off base on this or not?"

He put his hands on my shoulders and pulled me close.

"I don't know what to say." He moved me back so he looked

straight into my eyes.

"If it's true, Jim has not shared any of that with me. He does like her a lot; that has always been evident. I always assumed it was just like good friends. I could probably connect the dots on how this could be if I put my mind to it. She, just like Jim, has been married for quite some time."

He stared off for a bit. "I don't think I'm comfortable about confronting him. I think you may be all wrong on this."

"You also don't know how long Aunt Julia has suspected there was someone." My tone was still angry. "She told us one night in our basement that his infidelity was okay because she no longer loved him, but she was going to stick it out till Sarah went to college. You can imagine how shocked we all were when Jim bragged about this wedding ceremony on Christmas Eve. Sarah is sitting there all excited and we're thinking, what in the world happened here?" I was pacing again.

"You don't know how hard it was to hold back from commenting, but they were off and running about their plans. You and I left after Christmas and there was no way I could bring it up until the other day. When Aunt Julia picked me up from the shop to go see the house, I asked her how in the world she went from plan A to plan B with Jim. She said she confronted Jim and he didn't deny he had played around, but he convinced her he would stop and do what he needed to do for Sarah's sake. When he suggested they renew their vows, she thought it would help and she'd give it a try."

"I had no idea about all this and I sure didn't pick up that she felt that way about Jim." Sam was distressed. "This is very sad."

"What does your gut say, Sam?"

"I really need to process this." He sat down. "If this is still going on, we need to intervene, you realize that? We have both been asked to speak at their ceremony and I don't want any part of a deception. After all, it's not helping Jim or Julia and it's a slap in the face to a family that I now love."

Truer words were never spoken!

CHAPTER 13

Spring was emerging quickly, but thoughts of a late freeze were haunting the back of my mind. Early seasons were good for business, but not for the magnificent yard and garden that I was about to cultivate at 333 Lincoln. It was just a couple of weeks before Aunt Julia and Uncle Jim's renewal ceremony. Sam hadn't brought up the subject of their relationship since I told him about Brenda. I felt that how he wanted to handle this sticky situation was his business.

A morning conversation with him resulted in plans to drive to 333 Lincoln after I closed the shop that evening. The weather threatened rain all day, but was holding out, which met with my wishes to visit the 333 Lincoln gardens. When Sam entered the shop to pick me up, I stopped what I was doing to take in his constant smile and sparkling eyes. They filled me with such warmth and excitement; I didn't care what kind of weather we were about to experience.

"Hey, Annie," he said, walking towards me. "I have a nice bottle of chilled wine in the car with some nibbles, as you call them. I wasn't sure I'd be able to leave work, so I thought nibbles might end up being dinner."

"Nibbles as in my favorite Gouda cheese and crackers? That's such a great idea, Sam. Why didn't I think of that?"

"Because you were busy taking care of everyone else in this town, right?"

I grabbed a light jacket and decided I wasn't staying in the shop one more minute.

"By the way, I timed the ride from my shop for future reference and it was just over five minutes," I said, waiting for a reaction. Sam laughed at my having to know that.

Already I could see changes from last week's visit as we approached our future address. Early jonquils lined the hillside going up the driveway, and small lavender crocus randomly showed their blooms. The lawn peeking through was that pale lime green that one only sees in the early spring. A dogwood tree showed buds that appeared to be a pretty pink variety. By Easter this place would be waking up to spring whether someone came along to help it or not. Mother Nature had her schedule and 333 Lincoln was not going to be left behind.

"I meant to tell you, honey, that Kevin has a friend named Steve who does great yard work and landscaping. He gave me his number and I'm going to get him going on cleaning out this rubbish and start trimming all those rose bushes and hedges."

"I take it he knows what he's doing?"

"Kevin knows how particular I am. Fear not."

I got out of the car, and like always, my eyes went to the potting shed before anything else. Sam knew this was the place that made my heart throb, more than any brick or mortar.

"Oh, Sam, you had these broken panes repaired!" I called from the potting shed. "When did you do this?"

"I didn't do it, but when I had American Windows come and check all the windows in the house, I told them to take care of those first thing." Sam examined the window repairs closely, giving his approval.

"Oh, thank you." I gave him a hug. "I think you have your priorities quite in order. This will be my shelter, honey. This will be my safe place and it will be my creative cave. It'll be where I will create life. If you can't find me; I'll be in here!"

"Whoa, Annie." He backed off from my embrace. "Are you moving in here and not in the house with me?"

"This is special, Sam, just like you." I tried to flatter him. "I never thought I would have a husband the likes of you and I never thought I'd have my own place to dig in the dirt."

After kissing and hugging him once more, I walked him about the yard while describing my plans. We ended up near the south porch as it began to sprinkle lightly.

"I'll go get the basket out of the car," he said as he rushed to avoid a downpour. "We'll be cozy right here unless you want to go inside."

"No, I don't think this will turn into much of a storm," I ventured, thinking about how it made our visit a little more romantic and exciting. Sam grinned and was never surprised by anything I decided.

It was such fun spreading out Sam's blanket from his car to make a place for us to sit safe and dry from the sprinkles. We spread the nibbles of cheese, sausage, and crackers on napkins next to our wine bottle. It would do nicely as we cuddled and snacked. Sam took a photo with his phone to capture our impromptu arrangement. As we laughed, we no doubt created a Kodak moment, as Mother liked to say. I hoped as we lived our lives at 333 Lincoln, Sam would always be open to spontaneous moments like this. I had a feeling it was one of the things he enjoyed most about our relationship. Would being Mrs. Dickson change any of that?

We were so taken by watching the rain and sharing a few kisses that we jumped from one subject to another, discussing our plans. Suddenly, in just seconds, Sam's face became dark.

"I'm afraid I have some sad news to share with you before we go back." His tone was serious. "I confronted Jim about Brenda." My heart skipped a beat in suspense.

"And what did he say?" I wondered if I really wanted to know.

"He didn't deny it." Disbelief colored his voice.

"I knew it!" I was instantly animated, as I pulled back from him. "What a jerk. Did he just think we were all stupid and he could continue with this? What was he trying to prove by having this ceremony? Well, he's going to hate my guts now for telling you, but he has to know my allegiance is to Aunt Julia."

"I know, I know." Sam agreed with me but tried to calm me down. "Just take it easy for a second. I do think Jim actually loves Julia. He wants to do everything he can to keep the marriage together for Sarah. He presents the story that he and Brenda just have a sexual thing going and that it's nothing serious."

"Give me a break." I was getting angrier. "He doesn't love Aunt Julia enough to keep his pants on, not even for their daughter." I was breathing hard. "You know, I think if he hadn't done this confession thing with Aunt Julia, with the promise of a new beginning, then this wouldn't have been so horrible. What a dirty trick."

"Well, I told him he would have to share this with her or we would." Whoa! Sam's words shocked me. "He is my friend, but now he's being deceitful and abusing part of my family. I don't want to be a part of that."

My breathing slowed down. "Good," I said, feeling somewhat better. "What did he have to say to that?"

"He was pretty upset with me. He said he would tell her but we needed to stay out of it. I'm sure this will bust things wide open with them, but better now than after the ceremony. I told him he was still my friend and always would be, but that he needed to do this. Whatever he and Julia decide from here on is their business; I'm done."

"I know, and I understand, Sam." Now I was feeling sad about it all. "I feel bad you had to get involved with this. You aren't upset with me for bringing this up, are you?"

He smiled at me. "I think this is just the first of many independent actions of yours that you feel strongly about, and I admire that!" He lifted the bottle to pour. "How about a little more of this wine to heal the souls of the accused and the accusers? Hey, it's really raining hard now. Do you want to go in?"

"No, silly, I'm happy right here in your arms." I snuggled closer. "Just listen to the sounds. I wonder if water is leaking into the potting shed?" Do I leave his arms to find out? Hmmm.

"Oh, my mother called," he announced out of the blue, changing the subject. "She wants to come for Easter. I told her that would be great. Pat offered to take care of Dad and told her the trip would do her good. I think she's anxious to meet your family."

"That's wonderful news, Sam." I leaned back from his hold. "I'll write her and get more details if you like." He grinned with pleasure.

"I'll treat everyone to brunch on Easter Sunday, so you can also plant that seed if you want," he offered. "Didn't you say Donna's Tea Room does a great brunch?"

"Yes, that would be perfect." I pictured it all in my mind. "Donna always makes everyone, including strangers, feel very welcome. Her family recipes are wonderful. Everyone always wants them."

The rain had slowed down, but Sam insisted we go into the house and make sure all was well. His ideas on how he envisioned the restoration were just as exciting to him as the gardens and potting shed were to me. I could tell Sam had been doing some clean up as I looked about the first floor.

"Have you been back up in the attic?" I had forgotten about its contents.

"Not really. You didn't want to go up there, but I don't want to throw anything away or clean up there until you take a look."

"Good." I felt relieved. "I'll go up during the daylight with someone. I have a feeling there could be other interesting items like the vase and quilt I found."

"So is the vase something good?" He walked around the first floor.

"I think it might be. Mother is doing some research on it. Even if it's not valuable, I love it and it belongs in this house."

"You kept that dirty quilt?"

"Oh, sure." I could see he was surprised. "Jean was going to clean it up as best she could and bring it to the next quilting for us to examine."

"The rain has stopped, so maybe we need to get on home. I want to check the basement to see if there are any leaks from the rain and then we'll go."

"Can you tell with just a flashlight?" I asked as he disappeared down the stairs.

In no time Sam appeared back up and was pleased that all seemed dry.

When we got in the car to head home, I told him that I had hoped to journal about the restoration and anything I learned about the house and family. When leisure time would allow this was beyond me! In my dreams I could see myself writing more and more in this place that would be my future home. It began to sink in, that my journaling would now be about a whole new life. It changed completely with meeting Sam, an engagement, a wedding, and now 333 Lincoln. It was too scary to think much further. Where would I start?

CHAPTER 14

Mother was always good about calling everyone to make sure we were on for our next quilting. When she called Sue, she hinted that she may have travel plans shaping up for Honduras to pick up Mia. Jean was talking all week about coming and said she was going to bring the quilt I found in the potting shed. Mother said she left a message for Aunt Julia but had not heard back. I didn't tell Mother about what Sam and I knew about Jim. It would be best if it all just evolved without other people becoming involved and worried. Who would be blamed and who would not was something I did worry about. Aunt Julia was not a very confident and independent person like she wanted us to believe.

"What is that heavenly smell, Mother?" I came down the stairs into the kitchen.

"I started out with these chocolate chip cookies and then ended up adding banana bread when I saw the bananas getting so ripe." She sampled her bread dough. "They will both get eaten. Sarah may come and you know how she loves those cookies. I also put a couple of card tables together downstairs in the basement so we could lay out the Crazy quilt Jean is bringing."

"It's a mess Mother," I apologized for my dirty prize. "We'll make sure we have something underneath the tables in case pieces start falling everywhere. By the way, have you learned anything about the vase?"

"I'm getting close. I really washed it well and there was no mark of any kind on the bottom. I will find out more when I go to work this week. They should have some kind of book on it if it is legitimate. I agree Anne; it is quite lovely and will be perfect to have for 333 Lincoln."

Jean was the first to arrive. With her hands full we led her to the basement to carefully lay out what we nicknamed "the potting shed quilt." Her excitement at being part of our group and also the mystery of this quilt was fun to observe. Sue followed and brought a bottle of champagne with her.

"What's the champagne for at one o'clock in the afternoon?" I was curious.

"We haven't lost our talent for celebrating, have we?" Sue asked with excitement. "I will let you all in on that when everyone's here."

"Jolly good!" Jean chimed in.

We all helped with bringing down the trays of cookies and bread, plus champagne glasses for everyone. Then we examined the quilt with the backing facing up, exposing the paper letters. It looked better with Jean's touch, but it was still a dirty mess. None of us wanted to touch it because stitching on Sue's quilt was our mission for the day. We decided to see how much of Sue's quilt needed to be quilted before we got too sidetracked with the Crazy quilt or snacking and chatting. It was getting past our usual starting time and Aunt Julia and Sarah still were not here. I didn't even want to think what that might mean.

"We better get started here ladies." Sue was full of excitement. "We have some urgency here on getting this quilt done."

"What is that supposed to mean?" Mother asked.

Just as she was about to fill us in on her news, we heard the doorbell ring upstairs. I was hoping it was Aunt Julia and yet I wasn't sure I was ready to see her under the circumstances. I went ahead and started my first cookie as Mother went to the door. It was indeed Aunt Julia coming down the stairs to join us.

"Hey, it's about time!" Sue smiled. "Where's my favorite cousin, Sarah?"

"She had a sleepover at a friend's house last night and today they were going to a movie. Hello Jean, I heard you would be joining us today!"

So far she seemed to be in good humor and I kept my fingers crossed.

"Charmed to be here ladies," said perky Jean. "I brought the mystery quilt back as you can see."

"I don't know if this champagne is for something special, but I need a glass of this right now." My aunt poured herself a glass.

"Well, I brought the champagne, Aunt Julia, because we do indeed have something to celebrate," said Sue as she poured one, too.

"Well, let's hear it," I said.

"I leave next week for Honduras to get my little Mia," announced Sue proudly.

We all jumped for joy with the surprise. Mother was the first to give her a hug and then we all took turns. Sue was so happy she was crying, which caused me to follow with the same emotion. What a momentous and scary occasion for her. This was her very first signature event in her life. Even Jean rose to give her a hug of joy.

"Can you believe it is time already? All I have in her little room is a bed. I kept thinking I had more time." Sue was wringing her hands.

"Okay, ladies, we can't leave this house until this quilt is done," announced Mother. "You heard the girl say all she has is a bed. We need this on her bed when she returns."

"I really think that's possible, Sylvia," said Aunt Julia. "I will bind this off for her and by the time she gets back, this will be done. There's nothing like pressure to get us shaped up."

"You all are amazing." Sue blew her nose. "I'll be gone almost two weeks so you have more time than you think. Aunt Julia, I am sorry to say I will have to miss your little wedding. I thought of that after I settled down a bit from the news. Yesterday I went shopping to get all the things they suggest I bring. The children are sometimes handed to us just wearing a diaper. I almost go crazy thinking about it all."

"Well, Sue, I will be the first to fill you in that you will not be missing a thing while you're gone." Aunt Julia had a serious look on her face. "We are not going to be having the ceremony, but perhaps you will be back in time to celebrate our divorce!"

"What on earth are you saying?" asked Mother in complete shock. We all stopped what we were doing and waited for an explanation.

"I feel quite foolish to think we actually had a little agreement to make the best of our marriage for the time being, but I was so very wrong. Jim told me that he didn't feel good about making decisions when he was confused and didn't think he could keep his promise to work things out."

"Oh, my God," said Sue with astonishment. "What's going on with him?"

"I think he's having a relationship that he is unwilling to let go of." She paused and then said, "And by golly, that's fine with me." Her flushed face became redder. "Anne, you better be careful with Sam. They share a lot of time together and he has to know what was going on with Jim. Men, I hate them, and I swear, I will never get married again once this is all over."

"Julia!" Mother's tone was strong. "I don't think its fair for you to judge Sam on this without knowing for sure, right, Anne?"

"Oh, Aunt Julia," I said, slowly shaking my head. "This isn't the time or the place, but when it is, I will share with you what I do know. Sam and I both were so happy that you were going to renew your vows. Are you really serious about getting a divorce?"

"You bet," she said firmly with hands on her hips. "I just didn't think it would be quite this soon. Sarah is pretty upset. Kids are so smart. She knew we were still having heated conversations. It's going to be better for her not to have this tension around the house. I told Jim he had to leave. This was Sarah's home and he is almost always gone anyway, so he could just find someplace else to live."

Jean was sitting with her mouth open not saying a word. No doubt she was feeling very uncomfortable. One minute we were celebrating a new member to our family and then the next we were told we would be losing a member of our family. Mother was holding back tears about to erupt.

"Well," said Aunt Julia. "Mother was right about me again. I can never finish anything successfully, not even a marriage." We were speechless and sad.

Jean became teary-eyed and started gathering her things as if she would be leaving.

"No Jean, please don't go," begged Aunt Julia. "I am so sorry I rained on this parade. I'll get a grip here, and besides, we have a quilt to finish. Sue, I'll have another glass of that champagne."

Jean relaxed a bit and said, "As we say in England, this is none of my beeswax but I'd be going off my trolley if this happened to me." She was choked up with emotion. "This is bloody sad if you ask me; but I give you credit, Miss Julia."

We all refilled our glasses. Aunt Julia changed the subject back to Mia's arrival. She said we would have a shower for her when she returned and she wanted it to be at her house. She thought it would be good for her to plan something fun.

Sue filled us in on who we might want to invite from her workplace. She also shared that she might not be able to help fill in at the flower shop now that she was going to be a mother.

Chatter was in the background as my mind went to Sam. How dreadful his talk with Jim must have been. I could not wait to make the call to him or, better yet, crawl into his arms for reassurance.

CHAPTER 15

I was in no mood to discuss the chain of events with Mother, and by the look in Mother's face, she did not have the words to describe her disappointment in Aunt Julia's announcement. I went to my room wanting to pour my heart out to Sam and warn him of the turmoil to come. I let his cell phone ring and ring, only to leave a message. I called his landline and left a message there as well. Where did he say he was going tonight? It wasn't like him to not pick up.

I changed into my pajamas thinking I could possibly just fall into some sleep. I felt so sad. Why did Uncle Jim have to put my aunt through this? I couldn't believe Aunt Julia thought that Sam might also be like him. Was I assuming too much about Sam's innocence with other women?

Sam was also NOT a married man, I had to remind myself. We weren't a couple until Thanksgiving. I hadn't lost sight of him since. This was another reminder, however, that I may have moved too quickly with our relationship. Our wedding date was not until September, so time would reveal things, either way. I had always read that a relationship should have four seasons together before any marriage plans should be made. Well, I would almost make the cut with a ten-month relationship.

I wasn't sleepy and needed to be doing something until he called, I thought. I put on my robe and went down to the basement. This is where I felt the closeness of people who loved me. The basement is where we shared our secrets and came closer together as a family. I decided quilting would calm me down. We still had quilting to get finished on little Mia's quilt. I still had a piece of the border in front of me to finish.

I turned on the lights, sat in my spot, and felt like I was not alone. I reached for my thimble and looked where I needed to pick up my stitches. Well, this couldn't be quite right, I told myself. I know I didn't finish this part of the border. As I looked further, the last of the quilting had ALL been done.

Oh no! Not like on Aunt Julia's quilt! Having her quilt mysteriously finished had been too much for all of us to absorb and believe; but it was true. Grandmother, oh Grandmother, are you here again? The thought of her loving, if supernatural, appearance caused tears to flow.

"You wanted your stitches in this quilt, didn't you?" I said out loud. "Please help your daughter Julia who is hurting right now. She doesn't deserve this. She actually is worried about what you would say, even though you are gone, for heaven's sake. I love Aunt Julia and Sarah. Oh, I don't know how to help." I could not hold back the craziness of it all as more tears flowed down my cheeks. Why wouldn't she go away for good and leave us alone? Thank goodness no one else heard me have this one-sided, ridiculous conversation with Grandmother Davis, who had passed away years ago.

Distraught, I blew my nose and walked over to the potting shed quilt that was spread out on the table, waiting for attention. Curiosity got the best of me and I started looking at some of the writings on the back of the quilt pieces. Why would anyone cut up these letters? They must have had some hard feelings or maybe passionate feelings to save letters and then end up cutting them apart to put in a quilt. This was all weird to me.

My heart is breaking read one line. *Small, but elegant hotel* was written on another line. *Will count the days, console your tears,* and *most heartedly, Albert* was in another piece. Albert, I thought… Albert Taylor! Of course!

Yes, of course, these letters would have to be from the Taylors and this must be Albert's own signature. What were his letters doing here on the back of this forlorn quilt? How on earth did this quilt end up in the potting shed? Did they know it was there when they moved away?

Wow, this is kind of strange and intriguing. I wondered when and why these letters were written. Did Albert write every single one of these letters? The handwriting seemed to be all the same. Jean mentioned that to us when she brought the quilt back to us.

I wonder what our fancy, old-fashioned grandmother thinks of us having this ratty, old quilt laying down here in the basement. She must think we have all lost our minds. If she kept up all her activity, we would for sure! Was she trying to frighten us or was she just really trying to communicate with us? Hmmm.

Remembering Mia's finished quilt, I walked over to the quilt frame to make sure I really had seen what I saw before. Confirming the completion, now I would have to tell the others that the quilt was done. That would be good news, but how it got done would be not so good. Should I just tell them that I went ahead and finished it one night? I couldn't deal with much more drama. I suddenly felt overwhelmed and very, very tired.

Even though Sam had not returned my call, it didn't seem to matter right now. I just wanted to lay my head on my favorite pillow, as I found myself going quietly up the stairs to my room. Feeling my soft pillow reminded me what it felt like when I laid my head on my Mother's soft neck when I was very young. She always told me as she smoothed my hair that everything was going to be okay.

CHAPTER 16

After a short walk around the neighborhood the next morning, I was off to the shop. I had a full schedule to expedite and Sam's unreturned phone call had to go on the shelf.

I loved arriving at work as early as possible for many reasons. Opening my doors when only the street sweeper was working was special to me. The hustle and bustle of Main Street was good for business, but the beauty of the alignment of historic structures and the river were breathtaking to me. Every day was a new, unexpected day on the street. I told myself how lucky I was to be doing business in this piece of heaven. Sometimes it was hard to share it with others. Main Street was my personal front yard; therefore, I resented folks who did not pick up after themselves and abused our property.

Looking at our daily schedule was always the first thing on my agenda. Two wholesale orders had to be called in early or deliveries would not happen in time for the Collier's 25th wedding anniversary party on the weekend. The Chamber luncheon I had penciled in might have to go by the wayside. I then noticed that it was the 10th, Ted's birthday. I wonder what Mr. Ted was doing to celebrate? I'm sure it's with Miss Wendy, I thought sarcastically. I hope he doesn't expect to hear from me! Last year at this time Mother cooked a special birthday meal for him, which he really appreciated. I knew my family liked and missed him, but they were getting used to my new love and seemed to like Sam.

After taking a call from a vendor concerning an order, the phone rang again.

"Why did you have the phone off last night, my dear Annie?" Sam asked half angry. "Did you go to bed early? I tried several times, and then finally decided your phone was off, which is unusual for you."

"Oh, no, I didn't realize that Sam," I apologized.

"I wasn't going to call late on your home phone and disturb your mother. I had a late night with Jim. It was awful, as you can imagine. He was pretty down. You probably heard all about it from Julia by now. He is moving out this weekend and even though Julia wants a divorce, he is still hoping to talk her out of it."

"It was a quilting that went sour; that's for sure," I said sadly. "Aunt Julia is pretty angry and I don't blame her. She is concerned about Sarah more than anything. We all were shocked about her announcing she was going to file papers for a divorce. No one knew what to say. We all want to be supportive, but it's all so sad. Everyone pretty much went home after that. I couldn't sleep, of course. I know now that at some point I'm going to have to share with her what I know about Brenda."

"I have to go to New York tomorrow," Sam sounded frustrated. "Is there a way we can have dinner and talk about this tonight?"

"I think so." I let Sally in the back door. "How about we make it somewhere close by, like Charley's, because I may have to work late if the deliveries don't come before closing."

"Great, I'll check on you at closing time to see what your situation is like. I'm meeting at noon with one of the contractors at 333 for a bid on improving that driveway. I don't know how anyone managed that narrow road in the winter."

"Oh, I wish I could get over there, too." I was envious.

"Just think, Anne; someday you will go to 333 every day after work," he reminded me with affection in his voice.

"I can't wait to hear all about it. Check to see if Steve has shown up to do any trimming on the bushes. He said he would start this week. Tell him if he has any questions on anything to call me. I gave him my cell number."

"Well, I guess you'll keep your phone turned on for Steve, right?" He teased like the happier Sam I knew.

"You're darn right, mister!"

After I closed the shop that evening, Sam and I walked down to Charley's hand in hand, but we could hardly get in the door with the all the people standing in the reception area. Who would have thought on a Monday night the place would be so packed? It must be a private party. We gave our name for a table, but the wait was going to be up to twenty minutes so we thought we would wiggle our way to the bar nearby.

As we got closer, I recognized some people that Ted and I socialized with when we dated. When Sam gave our drink order to Brad, the bartender, I glanced across the bar and couldn't believe my eyes. There was Ted, surrounded by his buddies that, of course, included Wendy. Sam didn't pick up on my observation with all the commotion and loud conversation.

"Sam," I said as loud as I could. "We have to get out of here. Today is Ted's birthday and these are all his friends. This can't be happening." I wanted to turn and run!

"Cool it, Anne," Sam said, looking into my eyes. "We'll get our drinks and move into the restaurant area."

I turned around so Ted wouldn't see me, but remarks from some of his friends didn't let that happen. I nodded and tried to get away but, as luck would have it, Wendy found her way to my eye level.

"How nice of you both to come," said Wendy, walking closer to us. "I don't think I've met your friend, Anne, or is it fiancé now?"

I thought of the commercial that says "Want to get away?'" She was gloating that she had regained Ted's interest, and she was going to let me know it. I knew Ted would savor the thought of his next girlfriend after me being Wendy since he knew I disliked her. Meanwhile, there stood Sam waiting for an introduction. I tried to ignore him.

"Wendy, I'm sorry but we had no intention of crashing this party," I explained. "Sam and I just wanted to have a quick dinner." Her eyes were on Sam; not me.

"So, you're Sam, I presume." Wendy was flirting outright!

"Yes, Sam Dickson," Sam announced reaching for a formal hand introduction.

"Well, I hear congratulations are in order." She tossed her hair from her forehead. "When is the big day?"

Before I could answer, we were joined by Ted. Now it was going to get really interesting. I wasn't sure if Sam was enjoying this encounter or not. He sure wasn't doing much to get us out of a sticky situation.

"Well, nice of you guys to stop by on my birthday," Ted gave us a half smile.

"Happy birthday, Ted," I said as I tried to gather my composure. "We really just stopped by to get a quick bite to eat and wondered why the big crowd at Charley's on a Monday night, and now we know why!"

"Good to see you again, Sam." Ted spoke as if he had already had a few drinks. "It is Sam, if I remember right? Wendy; I assumed you were introduced. By the way, how is Jim doing these days?"

"Good," said Sam, wondering how much Ted knew. "We need to check on our table, but enjoy your party, Ted, and nice meeting you, Wendy."

Sam grabbed our drinks off the bar and maneuvered us between the shoulders of strangers to get near the reception desk. I followed with my head down, not wanting to meet another person. To our luck, our table was ready. We were ushered to the second floor, which couldn't have worked out any better.

"Crap, wouldn't you know!" I complained as I sat down. "I can handle running into Ted, but I really, really dislike this Wendy person he's dating."

"She's a pretty sexy babe who's probably hard for him to resist, especially after getting the boot from someone he really wanted," Sam smiled at me lovingly. "Hey, Annie, it's no big deal. This is a small town and getting smaller, if you ask me. It was nice of them to acknowledge us in a friendly way."

"You're right," I said, looking out the window into the street. "Do you think Ted knew about Uncle Jim and Aunt Julia?"

"Well, everyone will shortly," Sam noted as he read the menu. "Perhaps the separation will be good, and in time will work things out. The good news is we are off the hook for having to come up with superficial speeches for their wedding!" We smiled, although I felt somewhat ashamed for being happy to duck that responsibility.

"I hope Aunt Julia doesn't turn on you and me" I said. You know how other divorced couples end up taking sides. If you're friends, sometimes you're put in a dilemma to choose between husband and wife. Aunt Julia and I have been closer than my other aunts because she is the youngest and closest to my age."

"And you should be there for her; just as I will be there for Jim. I hope we both can keep our relationship with Julia. After all, we will be family very shortly."

"I have pretty much decided not to tell her anything I know about Brenda, unless she beats it out of me. I don't see what good can come of it."

"I think you're right, Anne," Sam agreed as he motioned to the waitress. "Let's help them keep their heads straight and try to be kind to one another. I think we should change the subject to us and what we want to eat."

We made our dinner choices, but my appetite was gone. What was Ted thinking right now? What were Ted and Wendy saying to each other? Why was I even thinking of them?

"When I was at 333 today, it was exhilarating to tell this contractor how I envisioned the driveway," Sam explained with his positive personality intact. "I think he really got it! I don't think that two-car garage has been used as a garage in years, so I asked if he could be helpful in getting that cleared out and having new doors installed."

"Was anyone working in the yard on the bushes?" I joined him in thoughts of our house.

"Yeah," he nodded. "I had to introduce myself. This guy was a bit strange looking if you ask me. Did Kevin say what nationality Steve was? I have to say he was working hard, but there seemed to be something odd about him. He kept watching me very closely."

"I will ask Kevin more about him."

The food arrived and Sam lifted his glass to make a toast.

"Here's to the future life of Mr. and Mrs. Dickson. May they live happily ever after at 333 Lincoln."

We clinked my glass of merlot and his glass of beer which ended the toast with a kiss. Mr. and Mrs. Dickson, I repeated in my mind. Had I decided for sure whether I would take his name, or did I want to reserve "Anne Brown" for my family's sake and the future success of my business? I told myself I had many nights to mull it over. One thing I had decided was that this Anne Brown's love and dedication was now going to be with Sam Dickson.

CHAPTER 17

There were good points and bad points to Sam's leaving town for three days. When he was in town, I would do anything to be with him, so not having that option helped me focus on the matters at hand.

As soon as I locked up the shop, I was going to go by 333 Lincoln to check on some things, as he had suggested. Now that some work had begun, we did not want anyone breaking in to look for valuables. I also wanted to see what this Steve person was up to. I had taken Kevin at his word to let Steve start working on the yard, but told myself that Sam or I should have checked on some other references.

Driving up the driveway, which had already improved, the prospects of how lovely a home this would be someday were more and more apparent. I got out of the car and noticed there were no other vehicles, so I assumed Steve had already gone home for the day since it was after five o'clock. I walked towards the side yard where I saw a pile of ivy on the ground that had been removed from the side of the house.

"You must be Miss Brown!" a voice bellowed from behind, scaring me to death.

"Oh, oh, my gosh!" I said in astonishment. "Where did you come from?"

"Right over here, ma'am, where I was working on the rose trellis," Steve said defensively. I stared for a moment.

This guy was dirty from his work. His Elvis-like greased hair matched his skin-tight, white t-shirt with turned-up sleeves waiting to hold a pack of cigarettes. He was so much the opposite of his supposed friend, Kevin, who was "Mr. Joe College" in his appearance. A red handkerchief was tied tight around his neck to absorb his sweat, I presumed.

"I didn't see a car and thought that I was here alone," I explained, as I looked around.

"I'm Steve, by the way," he said, looking me up and down. "I could start today so I got a ride. My car needs some repair and I don't have money to get it fixed. I'm putting in all the hours I can here and hope you'll be pleased with my work. I guess you'll be living here someday, right?"

Before I could answer he went on. "It's quite beautiful up here; just as you are, Miss Brown. You're quite the looker, just like Kevin said you were."

I was in no mood to humor him or respond to his inappropriate comments, as he continued to stare at me like I was an available piece of action for him. I wanted to move away from him and change the subject fast. I didn't like his looks and I didn't like the idea that Sam and I didn't know anything about him. Not looking back at him, I walked over to the rose trellis.

"I almost have this repaired and these bushes all cut back,"

Steve said, trying to impress me. "I'll make sure this all gets hauled away. I know what I'm doing here. I used to work for a landscaper. This place sure has been neglected, but we'll get it all in shape before you know it."

"Thanks, Steve," I managed to say. "I know this is hard work and you've certainly made some headway here. Have you ever trimmed hedges?"

"I don't own any of the right equipment for that, but I'll see what I can get my hands on."

"Well, forget that for right now, then." I was feeling odd and confused. "Just get things cleaned up best you can. After all this debris is carried away, I may have you do some other clean up." I nervously regretted just having said that.

We walked toward the potting shed and I told him I wanted to fix it up. He followed very close behind me as I pointed out the replaced windows. I then mentioned that the workbenches needed repair, but I lost my train of thought when I saw him stare straight into my eyes, like I was supposed to respond to him in some way.

"Sure, Missy. I can do anything you want." My stomach sickened.

"Fine." I walked around him to get out the door. "I need to check on some other things while I'm here and I'm keeping you from your work."

"Nice meeting you and all." He had a grin that made me cringe inside.

I walked around the house checking locked doors, porches, and windows. I lost all interest in staying any longer and went straight to the car without saying another word to him or offering him a ride home.

Mother was glad to see me as I walked in the door. She had a meatloaf baking in the oven. She loved the leftovers for sandwiches, so she made it once a week.

"Mother, how did you know I needed some comfort food tonight?" I sat down at the end of her work space. "Tonight I need a friend, a glass of wine, a good meal, a good night's sleep and most of all, my mom."

She gave me a little hug as she had done year after year in my life, making me feel everything would be okay, no matter what. I would miss that, no doubt, when I was married, but then I would have Sam to comfort me. I knew Mother would indeed miss me. She was just getting used to not having her older sister Marie around since her death. Aunt Julia, her baby sister, was just young enough to have a different world to contend with, which now included a divorce.

"Here's some merlot, Anne," Mother said as she poured herself a glass. "I think it's nice enough to sit on the front porch until dinner is ready. I just have to whip up the mashed potatoes."

"That'll be great, but let me change clothes first," I said, going up the stairs.

Lots of thoughts were going through my mind about my uneasy visit to the house. I put on my favorite jeans and a sweatshirt from a vacation years ago. The soft yellow shir mellowed me out and it seemed to be thicker than most, indicating its better quality. It helped give me the warmth and comfort I was looking for, on what might be a cool evening.

I tried calling Sam from my room to tell him about the unpleasant meeting with Steve, but had no response. I left him a quick message. I knew there was a dinner meeting so he likely had his cell phone off. He would call me later, and this time I would make sure my phone was on. I came down to join Mother on the porch, but I didn't see her there. I called for her and she answered from the basement.

"I'm down here, Anne," she responded. "Come join me here

with your wine; I want to show you something."

Walking down the stairs I said, "I guess you saw that Mia's quilt is finished."

"It is?" Mother asked not quite understanding my statement.

"Yes, it is and I don't think you finished that border anymore than I did," I said shaking my head. "I think we've had some help again, Mother."

"Oh. Anne; we're making too much out of these little things," she said, wanting to dismiss the subject. "For all I know I may have finished that area. I'm more intrigued with this silly old quilt you brought here."

"I couldn't help but peek a bit when I was down here getting the meat out of the freezer," she confessed. "This is like a puzzle if you ask me. I keep reading these little phrases, wanting to know more, and would you believe I found the name 'Martha' written here?"

"So what?"

"Here, on this piece it says, *Martha is a confused*. Confused about what, I wonder? You know your grandmother's first name was Martha. It's not a real common name but not too unusual. Do you think the Taylors knew her?"

"You're getting goofy, Mother. The Taylor family members were wealthy people who knew a lot of people. I've told you that he traveled overseas often on business, so goodness knows who all they knew. I'm not even sure these are letters from Albert Taylor, although it is a possibility since the name 'Albert' is seen here and there. To actually find this in the potting shed of all places is mysterious to me."

We sat down near the quilt and began sipping our wine. Mother, too, enjoyed a good merlot and she groaned a bit as she sat.

What's wrong, Mother?" I tried to read her.

"Oh, my knees have been acting up a bit, especially this right one. Working those six hours a day is a bit much at the book shop. I don't know if they'll let me cut to three or four. If they don't, I may have to give it up, even as much as I enjoy it."

"Well, sure, Mom." I could feel her pain. "You don't need the job for money and if it hurts your knees, you shouldn't be doing what irritates them. Have you asked the doctor about them?"

"No, heavens, no. At my age, you wake up every day with a new ache or pain. You can't go running to the doctor every time things aren't perfect. I really feel good most of the time, but when we have to carry books around the place, I notice my knee pain more often. I'm just not as young as I used to be, that's all."

"Well Mother, I think you have your answer by listening to your body. I'm going to need your help with this house, you know, so I don't think you'll be twiddling your thumbs."

"We'll see how it goes. I just have to be more careful in what I lift." She picked up part of the quilt again to read one of the pieces.

"All these pieces in the quilt are such different sizes, it's no wonder they call it a Crazy quilt. I would be crazy, too, if I had to make something like this. Surely these papers don't stay in the quilt when the back goes on."

"Jean says it is used for the piecing and that once that is done, it's removed because it's not good for the quilt to be touching an acid product like paper. For some reason, this quilt didn't get finished. My question is, why put these letters in there instead of newspaper or some other paper?"

"Look here," Mother pointed. "This corner says *about my loyalty to you*. This one says *not able to defend*. I like this one— *lemonade on the south porch*."

"The south porch? Well, we have a south porch at 333 Lincoln. Sam and I love that porch and went for cover there the other day when it started to rain. *Have put aside your fears* is here. This is so frustrating! I wish we could connect the dots. I think it could tell us a lot about the Taylors as well as the house."

"Well, Anne," mother had her hands on her hips. "When you have nothing else to do, you can take all these apart and put them back together again!"

"Don't tempt me!" I teased. "This may get the best of me. Maybe Jean can figure out an easy way to do that. I don't have the time."

The house phone rang and Mother quickly went to answer. I continued to read messages in the odd-sized pieces of paper on the back of the quilt.

"Oh, that's great news, Sue," I heard Mother say. "I guess we won't see you until you return, so be careful, and keep us posted with e-mail or just call us. Is there anything needed to be done at your apartment? Oh, I bet Sarah is thrilled. She loves Muffin. Don't worry about her; she'll be in good hands. Julia will probably have the quilt bound by then, too. Do you want to talk to Anne? She's right here. We are having a glass of wine as we admire the potting shed quilt. Here she is."

I found myself on the phone with a very happy woman who was about to be the mother of an almost two-year-old little girl. She shared that Aunt Julia and Sarah were thrilled to have the distraction of caring for her dog Muffin while she was gone. She thought it would be a couple of weeks or so before she came home and would let us know when she returned from the airport. Her lawyer had arranged for their transportation. She was scared and excited all at once.

Sue never had a lot of excitement in her life, so this had to be overwhelming. As I hung up the phone, I knew this adoption would change the dynamics of our little family in a big way, and it was a good thing!

CHAPTER 18

After a long day, I had a long soak in the tub, and then dressed in my worn, thin, gray knit pajamas that I loved. I had begun to brush my teeth when my cell phone rang. My heart jumped, knowing my Sam was on the phone.

"Annie," he whispered, "Are you asleep?"

"Not until I heard from you. I had a nice long bath tonight, wishing you might call while I was in the tub, but you missed out!"

"Oh, but honey," he sighed, "I can visualize all of that. My timing is really off. Boy, do I wish I were there to smell and feel you. I know the fragrance of your soap and shampoo and it drives me crazy."

"Good! Nice response," I said, bringing him back to reality. "How was your dinner meeting?"

"Don't change the subject on me, Annie," he toyed with me. "I'm still in the bathtub with you! Oh, I miss you!"

"Well, someone has to run the estate of 333 Lincoln while the master is away. I went by there after work and it wasn't a very pleasant visit."

"What're you saying?" Sam was all business now. "Was everything okay? Did someone break in?"

"No, no. All is well, but I went to check on this Steve person to see how he was coming along with the clean up. I didn't see a car, so I thought no one was there till he slipped up behind me to announce his presence. He's pretty creepy, Sam. He's an Elvis look-alike with a sleazy personality, if you ask me. He made me cringe. He looked me up and down and said that Kevin told him I was a looker. I'm going to have a talk with Kevin about this guy. I think they met in the Corner Tavern one night."

Sam had a few choice words for the guy. "You get rid of him right now, Annie. This is trouble in many ways. We don't know him and the place has no security. How dare the jerk talk to you that way! Call that nursery over by the park where we bought some herbs. They have people do things like this, I'm sure. Do you want me to call him?" Sam was livid.

"No, Sam, I'll take care of it." I tried to calm him down. "You're right. I can't have a guy like that hanging around. He certainly has no manners, that's for sure."

We talked another forty minutes about everything. He reported that Jim was with him on this trip and had admitted that he was in love with Brenda, but since she was married he was going to be out of luck with her as well as his wife.

"Good, serves him right." I remembered my anger with Jim. "He asked for this trouble. I don't feel sorry for him."

Trying to keep things nice, I changed gears. "Oh, I almost forgot to tell you that Sue is leaving tomorrow afternoon to get little Mia. Aunt Julia and Sarah are taking care of Muffin. We're going to have this little girl in the family very soon! I'm so excited,

Sam. It will be so wonderful to cuddle her and give her presents."

"Someday that'll be us, baby," he reminded me. "In the meantime, we'll have to cuddle each other. You're right; this will be fun for all of us, especially Sue."

After talking to Sam, all my concerns about Steve faded away in my strong future husband's voice of comfort and love.

Next day, Sally and Jean were both working, so I could run errands in the morning. Kevin would be coming in at noon to load up for deliveries, so I would have to tell him then about my decision to let Steve go as a handyman. When I arrived back at the shop, the place was active and chatty.

"Jean, I have to tell you that Mother is quite taken with the potting shed quilt." I watched her create a baby arrangement. "We were reading some more of the pieces and nothing connects, of course. There are so many word groups that need answers and explanations. She's right, it's like a puzzle that you try to put together."

"I know! It's really a jolly good piece," she said. "If you took a shine to remove the paper, it would brighten it up directly. It doesn't have much value, but it did after all, come from your future home, by golly. If you want to learn more about the house and its owners, you might want to undo the papers a bit. It's time consuming, but once they are removed, you could match them up and be able to read the letters. They are bound to be a good read, don't you suppose?"

"Goodness, Jean. That really would be time consuming. Mother has some spare time, especially if she quits her job, but what tedious work that would be!"

"Okay, Miss Brown," Jean said with an attitude. "Mia's quilt is about done and you don't have another one quite ready to put in the frame, so why can't we all meet and work on this poor little quilt from the potting shed? I think it would be quite fun, and you never know what you might learn about the Taylors. They're probably love letters of some kind, and how splendid it would be to have those assembled. You may want to frame them up and put them in that fancy big house of yours."

"Jean, you are something," I smiled at her. "You may have something there. I really like the idea. Do you think the others will think the same? I'm sure we can convince Mother, but Aunt Julia will probably pooh-pooh the thought of it. Sue will be too busy, but maybe she would come over once in a while."

"Okay, I've heard enough," interrupted Sally. "I refused to become a quilter, but I sure can put a puzzle together. I love puzzles, so I'll help!"

"I love you guys!" I raised my hands in joy.

"What's going on here?" asked Kevin, arriving on time.

"We're just going a little crazy thinking about a project we're going to try, that's all," I explained with laughter. "Can I have a word with you outside, Kevin?"

"Oh, no, this is never a good sign." He followed me out the door.

"You are just perfect." I patted him on the shoulder. "How do you know that I might be telling you about a big raise coming your way?"

"I'm all ears, Miss Anne."

I filled him in on every detail of Steve's behavior and how upset I was. Kevin was repulsed, all to his credit.

I told him Sam and I had discussed it, and we decided that Steve would have to go. I asked Kevin for Steve's phone number, but he insisted that he would take care of it since he had arranged the situation. He felt bad about Steve's behavior and admitted he had only met him a short time ago but knew he was looking for work, so passed on the opportunity.

"He bragged about doing landscaping, so I thought he might be pretty good," explained Kevin. "I'm sorry now I even mentioned anything to him."

Knowing Kevin, he was going to take this news personally and I didn't want to make him feel bad. I tried to lighten up the conversation. "I think he might be better at singing Elvis songs." Kevin didn't smile. "I hope he doesn't give you a rough time over this. Do you think he'll take it okay?"

"Anne, I don't know him that well," he said in disgust. "We'll see, I guess."

CHAPTER 19

I had been doing a fairly good job writing in my new journal when Sam and I decided to buy 333 Lincoln. I thought the occasion deserved its own beginning. I had hopes and dreams for our first home as well as our happiness together as man and wife.

The challenge of preparing this place added another level of excitement to our relationship. I was also not kidding myself that this could lend itself to some stressful situations as well. It did not deter me from my passion and love for the place. The gardens and potting shed were the symbols to me that I belonged there. After I finished writing a paragraph about my encounter with Steve, I felt like closing the journal and writing about something totally different and way more pleasant.

I had written poetry though the years and it came pretty easy for me. Flowers and plants were most of my inspiration. I kept those writings in another book in a drawer beside my bed. I was just reaching for it when the bedside table phone rang. Mother and I picked up at the same time to answer the call, and I was so happy we did!

"Hello, you all," bellowed Sue. "I can't believe I'm here, but my lawyer and I made the trip fine."

"Oh, my goodness Sue! It's so good to hear from you!" said Mother.

"Tell us what's happening!" I practically talked all over my mother.

"I got to see and hold Mia for a bit this afternoon, but we have to come back tomorrow to make sure all our papers are in order. She cried the whole time and appeared very confused."

"Well, I can imagine," said Mother.

"I was surprised to find her quite thin. I didn't pick up on that in the photo I had of her. Of course, it was mostly her face. I think she is malnourished. Just as I was warned, she was only wearing a diaper, so I'll have to use the clothing I brought for her to take her home. This place is so pathetic. It will be sad to see all the other children left behind."

"Are you going to be okay?" I asked after hearing her worried voice. "Is the lawyer helpful and do you feel safe?"

"Oh, yes, yes," she said reassuringly. "I couldn't have done all this without Greg Branson. He has done this a few times and he knows what to expect. I just want to get her in my arms, get on the plane, and get back home where I can start taking care of her. I have my pediatrician standing by to examine her when we get home. Will you call Aunt Julia for me? I just talked to Mom and Dad and they are worried, as you can imagine."

"Be careful, Sue, and take all precautions," warned Mother. "Call us when you get home and if there is anything we can do, let us know."

"We love you," I reminded her. "We love that little Mia, too. I can't wait to give her a hug!"

With that, she hung up from so, so far away. My mood had changed and the desire to write had passed. Now I wanted to call Aunt Julia as well as the shop to check on things. I went to join Mother downstairs and found her staring out the kitchen window.

"Let's call Aunt Julia now, Mother!"

"Sure, you call her, and also remind her we are getting together Sunday afternoon," Mother said.

I did just that, worried about what kind of response I would get from her. When she answered, I went right into the good news of Sue arriving in Honduras and that she would be taking charge of Mia tomorrow. Her answers were cheerful enough, so then I brought up our gathering on Sunday.

"Some of us were talking, Aunt Julia, and since we have finished Mia's quilt and don't have the next one ready, we thought it would be interesting to remove the pieces of letters in the potting shed quilt, piece them together, and see what they say. Even Sally from work wants to help. It could be fun, especially for Sarah. So, what do you think?"

"Anne, I know this is cool for you and Sam—a discovery from your future home—but right now, that's the last thing on my mind," she muttered.

"I know, Aunt Julia," I tried to understand her mood. "But I do think it would get your mind off of things to be with us. We are here for you. We know how painful this all must be right now, but you will always have us. Please remember that! Hey, and you know what else, you have to be thinking about a little party for Sue and Mia. We'll all be glad to help with everything."

"I'll think about it," she said quickly. "Right now I need to run."

I felt uneasy. I heard the hurtful—or hurting—sentiment in her voice. I could see that my relationship with Sam was going to impact her trust with me. Oh, how I hated that! I filled Mother in with Aunt Julia's response and then called the shop.

"Good morning, Brown's Botanical; Sally speaking," said the voice on the other end.

"Good morning, Sally," I answered as cheerfully as I could. "How's everything there and did Jean make it in?"

"She sure did," Sally replied. "Orders are coming in nicely but nothing big. Gayle stopped by to give you the Merchants Meeting notice and I put the mail on your desk."

"Okay, that sounds good," I said, feeling all was under control.

"Ahh…Anne, there is something about the mail that I need to tell you right away, I think." The hesitancy in her manner had me on instant alert.

"In with the regular mail lying on the floor from the mail slot was a big note," Sally said slowly.

"Oh, who from?"

"I don't know. It has 'YOU WILL REGRET WHAT YOU DID' in large printed letters. It's kind of weird if you ask me. Do you know what this means?"

"You're right, it is weird. Are you sure it was with the mail?" I questioned.

"Well, it was on the floor with the mail. I don't know which came in the slot first or last, but it was there when I came in the back door this morning," Sally explained.

Just leave it with my mail, and I'll look at it later if I get in or check it out tonight."

How strange this sounded. Who would orchestrate a little prank like that? Hmmm.

I hung up the phone and sat down by the kitchen table where we were having our coffee and told Mother what Sally had said.

"It's probably a little joke from some kid who walked by and saw your mail slot." Mother was unconcerned. "When you have a mail slot, people can put in anything they want. Haven't you had stuff like that appear unsolicited?"

"Just political flyers and meeting notices. Sally didn't say it had my name on it, so maybe it wasn't meant for me. I wasn't going to go in today, Mother, but after we get our haircuts, I think I need to stop by there and see it for myself."

We were always pleased to have our hair appointments at the same time so we could go on down the street to Donna's Tea Room afterwards for lunch. Every three weeks, Donna knew when to expect us and always greeted us like she had not seen us in ages. I put the mystery note aside in my mind and we went about our errands and haircuts.

"Oh, I am so glad to see you girls." Donna always greeted us when we walked in. "How is that wonderful house coming along, Anne? I have so admired that place. Most of us don't know much about its current condition since little is seen from the road, even in the winter time. The Taylors were quite fine, so I'm sure it is a gem."

"Yes, I feel the same way. The mystery of the family, the house and gardens is the beauty of it all, I guess," I sighed. "It's so marvelous—and some time you'll have to check it out, Donna. We're not spending much time there just yet, but feel free to drive up and have a look around. We have carpenters doing a few things, and I'm trying to clean up the gardens. As the season goes on, though, we will be there more."

After we ordered our usual favorite, the turkey melt sandwich with Donna's house salad, Mother brought up the strange note again.

"So, do you think it could have been meant for someone else at the shop?" She was looking concerned.

"I can't imagine who." I shook my head. "I don't know Jean very well, but I think in their conversation before telling me, they would have figured that out."

Mrs. Black then approached our table and asked how we were. She had been a good friend of my Aunt Marie and had helped us celebrate her birthday. She looked about my aunt's age and was dressed in fine attire, just like my Aunt Marie would have been.

"Anne, I heard through a friend that you and your future husband just purchased that lovely home up the hill on Lincoln!" She was alive with interest. "I remember my mother talking about the Taylors and how beautiful their home was. Mother lived with us before she died five years ago. I guess one of the things that I still remember her saying was that Mr. Taylor was so handsome and quite popular with the ladies, if you know what I mean! I don't know if she had a crush on him or what, but she would indicate there were always questions of his infidelity. You know how folks gossiped back then."

"Well, that's still true today, Mrs. Black," I commented as I turned around in my chair to give her my undivided attention. "What was your mother's name? I'm trying to learn as much as I can about the history of the house."

"Her name was Esther Richardson. I was a Richardson before I married Alfred."

"I never caught your first name, Mrs. Black," I asked as though I really cared.

"Oh, I guess you didn't, forgive me," she politely said. "My first name is Vera.

"I must be going but I just wanted to say hello, Sylvia. I miss Marie so much. We had so many things we shared. One of her proudest moments however, was when she taught her family to quilt and you all got together in your basement. She would tell me all about it."

"Well, you were sweet to stop by," Mother said.

As Vera Black walked away, I made a mental note of the information she had just given me about the Taylors. I then wondered if my aunt had told her everything about our basement quilting. Had she told Vera about the spirits that joined us occasionally?

When we finished our lunch, we walked the two blocks down to my shop and found two customers being helped, which was always a nice feeling. After saying hello to both of them, I went back to my office, followed by Mother. Sally came in and showed me the torn half-piece of notebook paper that had the message in big, black, hand-printed letters: "YOU WILL REGRET WHAT YOU DID."

"I think it could just be a kid from the way this is written, Anne." Mother tried to smooth over my silent concern.

"Anne, would you mind coming outside to check something?" Kevin stood at my office door.

"Oh, hi, Kevin." His presence surprised me. "I didn't know you were here."

I followed him out to the delivery truck, wondering what might be the problem. He turned to me with such a concerned look, I wondered if it were a personal problem.

"Anne, when the girls showed me that note today, we all joked around at first about who might be the unhappy customer. Then I thought about it some more as I loaded the truck. You have to know that when I told Steve that you would not need him anymore, he really, really got mad and called you some names."

"What do you mean?" I wasn't exactly surprised but this wasn't good news.

"Excuse me for saying." Kevin continued in a whisper. "He

said, 'That rich bitch thinks she's too good for hard-working people like me. She's got an attitude and she's screwing around with the wrong person.'" I gasped.

"I told him not to take it personally, but he knew different of course. I asked him if he did anything wrong or said anything offensive to you, and he just laughed. He then said he should have been a little more direct because he thought you would have fallen for some 'quick action in the grass,' is the way he put it." Kevin was mortified and I was mad.

"Oh, Kevin, who is this guy?" I leaned against the truck in shock. "This is pretty bizarre and creepy!"

"I'm so sorry I let this happen, Anne. I should have checked him out before I mentioned him to you."

"Do you think he would really be so stupid as to write this note?" I looked at it again in my hand.

"I don't know, but he was angry, that's for sure. He isn't the sharpest knife in the drawer, if you know what I mean."

"Thanks, Kevin," I said putting my hand on his shoulder. "I'll have to think about how to handle this." I paused. "Or if I have to handle this at all. I take it you do have a phone number for him?"

"No, I don't think I do, because I just see him at the Corner Tavern. I don't think I ever called him."

"Well, thanks for telling me this, because it seems to be the only lead we have," I said as we walked back into the shop.

I was glad Mother had not heard the conversation. I sure didn't want her worrying about such a creep. My decision to tell Sam would be the next one to make.

Why would this guy think for a second that someone like me would give him the time of day? Was he really dangerous and stupid? Or was I really foolish and dumb?

CHAPTER 20

I dropped Mother off at the house, telling her I still had some errands to do. I needed to think, and for the first time, something told me to go home. In my mind, my home was now 333 Lincoln. There were times I could envision Sam carrying me over the threshold in my wedding dress and sharing every holiday with him here forever and ever, and times when that vision seemed unreal.

But I did feel close to Sam there, plus, I could be alone with my thoughts—one of my favorite states of being. As I pulled up to the house, two men were packing up their gear in their pick-up truck. It was late afternoon, cool, and for most folks, the time to go home. They were the two men Sam had introduced me to that were working on the garage. I nodded to them and went straight into the house.

The house was cleaned out, which made it a lot easier to imagine its future. I went straight up to the master bedroom, hoping Sam might appear with open arms. As I looked around the spacious room, I envisioned it all in white and cream. I loved the color of its innocence and starting anew. It made me think of weddings, love, snow, and white pages waiting to be covered in words. I sat down on the floor by the bay window area that I knew would be a favorite spot in the future. I wanted cushioned seats right here with white pillows. I could then sit here and write while looking out the window.

With my head leaning on the window sill, I had to think about what, if anything, this strange note meant. Why did my happiness at this time have to be shadowed with this guy named Steve? Would he hurt my shop, my family, or my new home here on the hill?

Would he just try to scare me and then maybe just go away?

I felt sleepy and comforted somehow. Why did I have such a draw to this place? Yes, I loved seeing Sam excited about the project, but it was more than that. I was supposed to be here. Would Albert and Marion Taylor speak to me or haunt me like the rumors we had heard about?

"Marion and Albert," I said aloud. "I love your house so much, and I promise to make it beautiful and alive again. Please guide me and know that I will respect your wishes."

Okay, I said to myself. Here I was, talking to their spirits just as I had done with Grandmother Davis and Aunt Marie. I knew they heard me, and when I confronted spirits upfront, it made me feel relaxed and confident. This made me think of merlot.

Why didn't I keep some wine around here for when I wanted it? Sam said he thought there was evidence of a wine cellar in the basement. I wasn't brave enough to check out the basement and I was not about to look down there without Sam. It wasn't a remodeled basement like the one in our house on Maple Street. It was old, dark, and musty. That part of the house could be Sam's adventure and not mine!

The hours were passing, and before I knew it, I suddenly realized that I needed to get home. Then my phone rang.

"Hi, Sam. So good to hear from you. I sure wish you were here in our bedroom at 333. I came home, hoping to find you here, but there was nothing but an empty bedroom."

"Honey, what are you doing there at this hour?" He was concerned.

"Sam, it was kind of weird, I guess, but after Mother and I had our day out together today, I said to myself, 'I need to go home.' So I came here. I am sitting here on the floor in our bedroom planning how I want it to look for us."

"Ah." I could hear him smile. "You know, I am feeling the same way, Annie. When I get to the loft, it's like I can't wait to get over to 333. I think 'home' has set in for me as well, and that's what we want to happen. If only I could be there with you right now, I would take advantage of you in our bedroom."

"Before you get carried away with your imagination, I'm fully dressed and perfectly sober. I would love to have had a glass of wine, but 333 is still a dry county. Unless you left some wine from last week?"

"No, sorry, but we'll fix that from now on. I think the one kitchen cabinet will suffice for a liquor cabinet from now on. That may have been a little bar area at one time, since that section has a marble counter."

We continued saying sweet nothings until Sam had to go meet up with Jim.

I chose to wait to tell Sam about Steve when he would return in the next couple of days. We both had better things to think about, and I didn't want to cloud his thoughts with worry while he was away.

As I headed downstairs, my next thoughts were how to learn more about the Taylors, but as I went down the beautiful wooden staircase, its prior carpet ripped away, I began thinking about what might be appropriate to replace it. Probably it should match a large area rug in the foyer.

I could see Sam's large grandfather clock in the one corner. He loved it, and it was one of the first things I had noticed at his loft on my first visit. I continued walking in and out of each room, letting the stillness and spaciousness speak to me. It was getting dark and we still did not have electricity, so I needed to think about leaving.

My last visit was going to be a peek into the potting shed. I locked the front door and faced a good wind that was picking up, bringing the possibility of an any-minute rainstorm.

I walked into the potting shed and saw a complete mess! Everything I had worked so hard to clean up and organize was a disaster. Clay pots were broken on the brick floor, dirt was dumped out of containers—and this included all the herbs I had purchased to put in the ground this weekend.

What on earth happened here? The large elephant ear plant that I brought from home was lying sideways on the floor. There could not have been enough wind to let that happen. I quickly sat it upright and thanked the good fortune that it still had its pot intact.

I looked for broken windows, but there weren't any. One drawer from the workbench had been pulled out. Its contents, which were mostly gloves and tools, now lay beside it on the brick floor. This was maddening. Now I felt there must have been a great deal of anger demonstrated here. I felt my own anger surge with and outcry against whoever was trying to upset me.

Steve's name was all over this mess. Common sense told me I needed to leave right now. I quickly shut the door behind me without trying to save any poor roots abandoned outside their soil. I needed to get in my car and assess tomorrow the added damage to this situation. I drove away as rain started to pour heavily. Such a lovely visit to my future home had become awful and unsettling.

CHAPTER 21

Sam called from the airport as I was finishing up with the last customer of the day. I asked him if we could go to his place to talk and order dinner in. He had no problem with the idea and said he would take some frozen lasagna out of the freezer. I appreciated the way he thought and I liked the way he picked up on the concern in my voice.

I quickly locked the door and Sally helped me balance the drawer. For conversation's sake, she asked if I had any further news about the mysterious note. I dismissed the topic quickly so none of them would think I was concerned. I changed the subject to what we had to do tomorrow.

I was sure Sam would be home by now and proceeded up the elevator to his floor. Sure enough, he answered with open arms. I smiled and put on a happy face so he would not be alarmed by my purpose.

"Relax, sweetie," he said as he poured my merlot. He could

sense I had something on my mind. "I'm already sipping my wine without you. The lasagna needs to defrost a bit more before I heat it up. I don't have anything for a salad, but I always have some good bread in the freezer, so we'll be fine, I think." He looked so darn cute fussing around his kitchen.

"I'm really not hungry right now, Sam. I'm sure a little something later will be fine."

He took me by the arm and pulled me over to the couch, bringing my wine.

"Let's hear what's going on, Annie," he said seriously. "You don't seem yourself."

I didn't know where to start. I told him to hear me out before he jumped to any conclusions. He knew I had a bad impression of Steve on our first meeting, but he did not know about the note that read, "YOU WILL REGRET WHAT YOU DID." As I explained the chain of events, his eyes went to fury and puzzlement at the same time. I tried to interject that the girls thought it might be a prank from an unsatisfied customer, but he wasn't laughing. So then I told him what Kevin said although I left out some of the bad language. I couldn't hold him back any longer.

"Geez, Annie!" He started to pace the floor. "Did you call the police or anything?"

"Now you said you'd hear me out before jumping to conclusions, so calm down." I got up and joined him walking around the room. "I didn't want to do anything until I talked to you. I wasn't sure it was anything more than an unhappy person who was fired. I put it aside…until something happened last night after I talked to you."

"There's more!? What in the heck happened?" His eyes were flashing as he gripped me by the shoulders. "Were you still at our house?"

I began by telling him what a wonderful evening I was having until it started getting dark and how I then left the house to go check on the potting shed. His eyes were like dark arrows as he squinted, visualizing what had happened. I told him in detail all that had been damaged, and that I only picked up my elephant ear plant before I closed the door and left. When I finished, he simply stared and shook his head.

"You are darn lucky he wasn't lurking around somewhere waiting for you, Annie," he warned. "This jerk needs to be stopped before he hurts more than a few plants. You and I both will stop by the police station tomorrow morning and make a report. I want to talk to Kevin. Are you sure Kevin doesn't know more about him?"

"No, poor Kevin feels bad enough for suggesting he help me out. Please don't be upset with him. I'm the one who should have questioned this guy."

Sam was frustrated the rest of the evening and neither of us felt like eating a bite of food. He held me close as the room got dark. He lectured me about not being alone until this was resolved. He said I needed to alert the girls at the shop in case anything odd went on there. He agreed that at this time we would hold off telling my mother about Steve.

After hearing a bit about his trip and an uneventful dinner he'd had with Uncle Jim, we called it a night. We were exhausted and Sam walked me down to my car.

"Call me when you get home," he demanded as he gave me one last kiss.

I did just that, and I felt better already that Sam was finally updated on my unsettling problem. I wanted to handle this myself as my independence commanded me, but I had to learn that Sam would be my partner now. I had to consider his opinion on matters.

After a quick walk through the neighborhood the next

morning, I met Sam at the local police station. They didn't make too big a deal out of it, which eased my mind. At least we were on record for the intrusion and damage at the potting shed. They said they were going to run a check on this Steve guy, which they would start by making a stop at the Corner Tavern where he could likely be found. They also said they would pay Kevin a visit. I hated that part. Kevin was a great and honest employee.

Sunday afternoon was something on which to focus that was fun and positive in my life. I tried to be normal in my thoughts and actions by concentrating on our next quilt project.

Mother was more excited than I was about taking the potting shed quilt apart. She prepared her delicious peanut butter coffee cake. She had a nice display downstairs using her blue and white china with a tea set to match. The smell of tea and coffee was just as inviting as the cake as I joined her downstairs.

"Mother, you really outdid yourself again." I gave her a little hug. "This is lovely. I've always loved this china and you hardly ever use it."

"Well, I haven't heard from Julia, but Jean and Sally are coming, so that's at least four of us to get started." She arranged the refreshments.

The doorbell rang and I went up to answer. As I expected, Sally and Jean came together. It was pleasing to see them getting along so well, especially with Jean new in town.

"Welcome to the basement," I said to Sally as we all came down the stairs. "Who knows, Sally, some of this quilting stuff may rub off on you!"

"I just hope those spirits stay away while I'm here," she joked as she took off her jacket.

We had just started to listen to Jean's instructions on how to remove the paper pieces from the Crazy quilt top when the doorbell rang again. Again, I left them to answer the door. I was surprised to see Aunt Julia and Sarah with Sue's little dog Muffin.

"Yay!" I yelled so all could hear. "So glad to see you guys!"

"You can thank Sarah." Aunt Julia half-smiled at me. "When she got wind of what you all were going to do, she got very excited and thought it would be really cool to do and here we are! I hope you don't mind us bringing Muffin. She's been here before, and we don't dare mistreat her by leaving her alone while her mommy's away."

Seeing who it was coming down the stairs, the rest of the gang gave them a great reception. They all had to give Muffin a hug and a pat on the head. Once she made the rounds and got her usual treat from Mother, she usually was happy taking a snooze behind one of the chairs. I wondered to myself if Sue had thought about what it would be like for Mia to have a new pet and a new mom.

I got everyone's attention and told them to watch Jean remove one of the papers so we wouldn't harm the actual quilt itself. Jean had, in fact, used her careful vacuuming-through-a-screen technique on the delicate quilt, so it was as clean as it could be in its fragile state.

"I am going to show you how to carefully remove the paper without disrupting the stitches on the quilt. Once we do that, we will make different piles of the pieces according to the color of stationery. We can later match them up together like a puzzle."

Jean did a demonstration with one piece that easily came away from the seam line with just her fingers, but she had a few seam rippers handy if we needed assistance. By teasing any stubborn bits of paper away from the stitches, we wouldn't use the rippers for cutting—just precision "fiddling." Everyone nodded as they understood what she was saying.

"But they're all mixed up," said Sarah. "Where do we start? Oh my, this line says *my dear precious tomato*." We laughed and all fell in line with quotes that got our attention. I helped Sarah take out that particular triangular piece of paper so she would not tear it.

Aunt Julia said, "Listen to this: *story of bearing my child*. What do you think that's all about?"

"Maybe when it's matched up it will make sense," I said confidently. "The Taylors had one or two children, I think, but this comment about 'bearing my child' sounds like they're talking about someone else, doesn't it?"

"*London has been dark*," Sally read. "Albert must have written this from London."

"I have the best line," bragged Jean. "This little piece says *of any affair that*. Now we know that perhaps someone had an affair."

"Oh, dear," I said as I stopped to verify the message. "Vera Black told us the other day that her mother talked about what a womanizer Albert was, remember Mother?"

"Well, she said he was known as quite a ladies' man, is the way she put it," she clarified. "She also said there were always rumors of his infidelity. We may have a clue here."

We all started chatting at once. Many pieces were carefully removed successfully once we learned the tricks of easing papers away from the very threads that had held the quilt together. Jean was definitely in charge of this very lengthy project and I couldn't have been more pleased. I didn't know about antique quilts, and I was scared to ruin one of the few remnants that the Taylor family left behind.

Mother insisted we take a break and enjoy the refreshments, although Sarah had starting eating coffee cake the minute she arrived. Someday she would be worried about all those calories. Everyone washed their hands in the powder room. Jean and Sally both wanted Mother's recipe for the peanut butter coffee cake, which made her happy.

In the thick of the conversation, the phone rang. Mother picked it up and shouted that it was Sue, calling from an airport in the states! We all tried to say hello and peppered the air with many questions, but Aunt Julia took the receiver.

"How is Mia? Did she do okay with the airplane ride so far?" She listened to Sue's reply. "Are you sure you don't need us to meet you at the airport?" She paused for awhile. "We'll wait to hear from you tomorrow, then. We'll not crowd in on you until you tell us its okay, you hear?"

After Aunt Julia hung up, we were all anxious to hear the answers to all our questions.

"They gave Mia something to help her sleep during most of the trip," Aunt Julia reported. "Sue is anxious to fatten her up as she's very thin. Sue said she was a wreck until the plane took off in the air for the United States. She was warned that even at the last second, things could go wrong."

Aunt Julia took a breath. "She said her next hurdle will be to have Mia checked by her pediatrician. I will tentatively plan on a party one evening next week if Sue agrees. I already have a couple of gift certificates for her. She has the nursery all set up, so she will just need some things to help her financially for awhile."

"I'll have them send over flowers from the shop as a welcome home gesture, and Aunt Julia, I can bring them for the party as well!" I offered. This was exciting.

After we talked about the details, Jean had us get back to work on the paper picking. Sarah was the first to lose interest; she got sidetracked talking on the phone with one of her friends. One by one, everyone parted from the basement to head home, Mother seeing them to the door.

We had agreed that it would be more rewarding when we

could actually match up the pieces to each other, so I stayed in the basement, still reading pieces of Albert's letters. I wondered how long Albert and Marion had been deceased, and if they were buried at Walnut Grove Cemetery, the oldest cemetery in Colebridge. I would ask Mother when she returned downstairs.

"I'm so pleased with today, weren't you, Anne?" Mother said with a big grin on her face. "Sue's call! How exciting! The desserts were a big hit, and we got a lot done. Jean has all the pieces so organized over there on the library table that I dare not touch a thing. She seems to know what she's doing."

"I really am driven to know more about the Taylors. Do you think they're buried at the Walnut Grove Cemetery, where so many of the really old families in Colebridge are? If you have any time, Mother, would you ask around about this family? Do you have any interest in going to the cemetery with me?"

"Not today, I hope," Mother quipped. "A good lead would be to find out what church they went to. If they were Catholic or Lutheran, then they would likely be in their own church's cemetery, don't you think?"

"Good point. I'll look into that. Well, let me help you clean up. I can't eat a bite of dinner tonight after all that coffee cake. There are so many wonderful recipes you have. I'll miss this good food when I move from here! Even though I don't cook to speak of, I want to have copies of my favorite recipes. Sam loves to cook and you never know what my future in the kitchen will hold."

"Of course, Anne," Mother leaned her head against mine. "You'll have the originals of many things I have. You will have a large beautiful home to accommodate such possessions. You are very lucky. Your father and I had a very tiny apartment starting out and things were pretty tough. When we inherited this house, we mostly filled it up with family pieces."

I loved talking to Mother about my father and their married life together. Everyone, including Sam, knew how much I missed him and had wanted him to walk me down the aisle. I knew Mother was also melancholy when she thought about having to plan my wedding without my father by her side. We both wondered if he would have liked Sam and what kind of advice he would be giving me right now.

So much for me thinking about asking my Uncle Jim to walk me down the aisle, as he was turning out to be an unpopular fellow right now, I thought. I was glad Aunt Julia didn't want to talk about her divorce today. I'm sure if Sarah had not been there, she would have.

As soon as the basement was back in order, I needed to call Sam. I wouldn't be seeing him, but I knew he would want any update concerning Steve, and, to my relief, there wasn't one.

CHAPTER 22

Enjoying more of Mother's peanut butter coffee cake the next morning, I sat at the breakfast table to discuss with her what we might purchase for little Mia. My cell phone rang. It was Sam telling me that he had arranged for Parkhill Nursery to help me with the yard and gardens. They would be arriving at one o'clock, so he wanted to know if I could meet with them for instructions. I had planned to take off the afternoon to try to clean up the mess in the potting shed in hopes I could salvage some of the newly purchased herbs.

"This will be a great help, Sam. Can you join me, or are you playing office today? I'm taking some things to store in the wine cupboard today. That's what I am going to call it. I'll be glad when all the rewiring will be done. Electricity will be most welcomed."

"I hear you! I'll join you around two or three o'clock when I finish meeting with a client from Boston. I'll need to change clothes after that."

"Great, honey. Mother just said she has a pork roast in the crock pot and that we should come here for dinner tonight. How does that sound?"

"You mean home-cooked food? I would love nothing more!"

"I'd better get moving, then. I'll see you this afternoon. I love you!"

"I love you, too, my sweet."

I arrived at work to find Sally planting annuals in the stone flower pots in front of the shop. They truly meant spring was here and summer was ahead. The whole street would be blooming again in no time. Shops were starting to leave their front doors open with the pleasant weather that spring had to offer.

Christmas was still my favorite time on the street, but having greenery and flower boxes here and there was special as well. Now that we had a watering service on a daily basis on the street, we were able to do more planting in boxes along the brick sidewalks. Jean, Sally, and I were chatting at the doorstep when I heard Kevin come in the back of the shop.

"Good morning, Mr. Kevin." I sounded as cheery as I felt.

He looked at me and said, "Are we alone?"

"Sure, right now. The girls are finishing up the planting out front. I'm glad you're a little early because Mrs. Armstrong would like her delivery before noon today, so I told her I would try to make that happen."

"Anne, I got a ride to work today because two of my tires were slashed last night." I was astounded, and his tone was angry. "I'm pretty sure this is our buddy Steve letting me know that he blames me as well for losing his job. Who else would it be? Were your tires okay?"

"Oh, Kevin!" I was shocked. "I am so, so sorry! I take it you found out this morning?"

"Actually, it was late last night. I came home around ten thirty, did some laundry, watched part of movie, then remembered I had left my dry cleaning in the car. I went to the car to bring it in. That was around twelve thirty. That's when I noticed it. I can't believe I didn't hear anything, but I may have dozed off during the movie. I called the report into that Wilson guy, the police officer, who took your report. He said he'd come by today, so I left my car and got a ride with my neighbor, who usually leaves around the same time I do. He said he didn't hear or see anything either."

"This is maddening, Kevin." I shook my head in disbelief. "It makes me wonder what he's going to do next."

"I thought he would just go away, especially since he isn't coming into the Corner Tavern anymore. It's weird that no one knew where he lived. I guess maybe he was staying with someone, which is what I figured. I don't want you to worry, Anne, but just be careful!"

"Oh, don't worry!" I was feeling very violated. "I'll be careful, but we need to keep moving forward. I'm not going to let a creep like him rule my daily life."

I got through my morning list of things I had to do, changed my clothes, grabbed a sandwich at the deli, and headed to 333 Lincoln to meet the guys from Parkhill Nursery. This house on the hill was indeed becoming my escape.

When I pulled up the drive, I could see two workers walking about the property and checking it out. I got out of my car and introduced myself. After hearing their wonderful compliments about the property, I put them to task removing some half-dead bushes and told them what I'd like to have in their places. These were young, bright, and professional workers who made me feel a lot safer than dealing with an unknown like Steve. I dreaded telling Sam about Kevin's tires being slashed. I didn't want to think about it.

I got busy cleaning up the potting shed. Thank goodness Steve had not broken any windows. The Parkhill employees advised me to get the herbs in water as soon as possible, which was my first mission. It was obvious that the shed roof was leaking in a couple of places. Perhaps it would only need a patch or two. I was not going to suggest a repair right now with all the major work that was needed on the house.

I became happier as I cleared and straightened. I was in my element and made mental notes about the plants I could still get going this spring. I admired how the brick floor had held up through the years, and how it had cleaned up nicely. I could visualize lining up unusual clay pots and vases on the upper shelf, to give the shed some sense of décor. I was making progress quickly and took a break to admire my handiwork as well as the amazing progress from the nursery workers.

Sam arrived around three thirty and I introduced him to the gardeners, who were about to leave for the day. He was impressed with how quickly I had restored the shed into a presentable condition. When the workers drove away, Sam took me into his arms to capture my full attention.

"I love when you work in the dirt," he teased as he wiped a smudge off my cheeks.

"I love when you get dirty." I gently patted some soil on his face, jeans, and shirt.

"You are asking for trouble! Do you want to play dirty?" He chased me into the potting shed and I held the door shut.

"Okay, I've got to check some things inside for the architect, so do you have enough to stay busy out here for awhile?"

"Sure, but before we leave to have dinner with my mother, I want to share something that happened today," I said, opening the shed door.

Sam looked at me with his piercing dark eyes, squinting with a questionable look. I went into detail about what Kevin had told me about the tire slashing last night. Before I gave Sam a chance to respond, I told him he had reported it to the police.

"Anne, this is not good," he finally said. "This could have been done to us as well. Until we know this guy is really gone or arrested; you need to be very, very careful. I'm sure he knows where you live and, as the owner of this place, he probably has my address at the loft as well. I bet this is a real hardship for Kevin. Tires aren't cheap."

"Yes, it makes me sick." I shook my head. "He really meant well to help me, so I feel it's my fault, too."

Sam went into the house in frustration. I continued my cleanup and then decided where I wanted to plant the herbs. My helpers had loosened up the soil for me where we found some old herbs still trying to do their thing. I planned where I would arrange them going around a sundial with rows of bricks in between. They would be attractive and healthy in the full sun, and the brick pathway would allow me to have access to cutting them as needed. It was getting dark, and I alerted Mother by phone that we were on our way soon.

"This is such a treat for me," Sam told Mother as we walked in the door for dinner. "I apologize for my soiled appearance, but it isn't entirely my fault." We grinned at the secret joke.

"My mother makes an amazing pork roast and I haven't tasted it in quite awhile. I have her recipe for a good spicy rub, but haven't made it in a long time. Thanks so much. What a treat!"

Now, you're making me nervous, Sam," Mother said, with her half apron still tied around her waist. "This is nothing special, but it's easy to throw in the carrots and potatoes and have it fill the house with good smells. Sometimes I add sauerkraut, but I wasn't sure if you liked it. Not knowing what time you kids would be done for the evening, the crock pot works really well. I have a salad and hot rolls to go with it. Go wash up and make yourself at home, Sam."

I got him a cold beer out of the refrigerator since he had hinted at wanting something to quench his thirst. I had a glass of merlot along with Mother. We made small talk with her and answered her many questions about the development of 333 Lincoln.

"Anne and I may check out the Walnut Grove Cemetery this weekend to see if we can find the Taylors' graves," Mother announced. "I did check with their registry and the two of them are there. I don't know about anyone else in the family."

"Oh, that would be great," Sam said as we moved to take our seats for dinner. "Anne and I both want to know more about them. We both appreciate any help you can be. I don't know if Anne told you, but my mother is coming next week for Easter, and I want to take everyone to Donna's Tea Room for brunch. Can we count on you, Sylvia?"

"Anne, I don't think you mentioned that." Mother removed her apron. "I can't wait to meet her! I bet she is most curious about 333 Lincoln, don't you think?"

"Yes, she is curious about a lot of things. My sister was going to come with her, but had to change her plans. She doesn't mind traveling alone, so my sister will look after my Dad."

"I will certainly be looking forward to that, Sam, and make sure she and I will have a chance to visit." We joined hands in a table prayer.

We began our meal, and it didn't take long before Mother was getting kudos from Sam on her great roast. He and I discovered our appetites and the comfort food was a hit.

"Okay, next topic," I said, taking my last bite. "Sam, I want you to come downstairs to see how the potting shed quilt is coming along. This is turning into a pretty big project. We should be able to learn quite a bit from Albert Taylor's letters. Mother, leave the dishes, and come down with us to show off our handiwork."

We made our way down the stairs. I couldn't believe my eyes when I saw the scattered paper quilt pieces strewn about the room! It looked like a mini tornado had come through. The quilt was no longer lying flat, but was heaped in a pile on the floor.

"What's this?" cried Mother. "Have you seen this, Anne? Good Lord, what could have happened?"

"This is horrible!" I ran over to pick up the quilt. "Sam, this quilt was laid out neatly on this table and Jean had sorted and matched the paper pieces very nicely on the sideboard here. What a mess! It will take us forever to straighten these all out again. Who came down here? Was Muffin running around? Was anyone down here at all, Mother?"

"Heavens, no." She gathered paper snippets.

"Well, then it had to be Grandmother or Aunt Marie!" I spoke as though they were still alive. "Why would they do anything like this? They knew surely how hard we worked at this. Wait till I tell Jean."

Sam leaned on the stairwell, watching us fly all over the room, not knowing how to react or what to pick up. He was listening to our comments and I somehow felt he was finding it all amusing. But he knew better than to say much at this point. The look on his face told me he was seeing a bit of humor in not only the mess, but in my reference to Aunt Marie and Grandmother.

"What can I do to help?" He finally asked courteously.

"Well, let's make sure we get them all off the floor before we lose some of these," I said. "Put them here in this basket so they don't scatter. We'll have to separate them later. I really can't believe this! I'm telling you, Sam, the spirits are alive and well in this basement."

CHAPTER 23

When I arrived at the shop the next morning, I dreaded telling Jean and Sally the news about the potting shed quilt. As I started to check my e-mails, Sue called me from her house.

"Welcome home, Mommy!" I happily greeted her.

"I really feel like a mommy, and I'm working on trying to get her to call me that, but right now Mia is very confused. We are pretty settled, though. A friend who is a hairdresser was here yesterday and has been a big help. She trimmed Mia's hair, went to get us groceries, and helped me get unpacked. Mia slept most of the night, thank goodness. It has all been pretty exhausting for her as well as me. I may drop by with her today if I can manage that newfangled car seat. Man, I hate to think about getting her in and out of it in an emergency!"

"That would be great, Sue. We are all dying to see her. You know she'll have to come to quilting day in the basement, so let me know what we need to accommodate her."

"I think I have enough equipment for her till she's sixteen," she laughed. "My mom made sure of that. She and Dad will be arriving this week, so we'll all have to get together."

"I'll have Mother call them and we'll have our little party for you while they are here." I was getting excited about it all. "Don't you think that would be nice?"

"No one needs to go to any trouble," she said gratefully. "I think I have most everything I need, but I must admit I cannot wait to show her off."

After I hung up the phone, I needed to unlock the door, since neither Jean nor Sally had arrived. I went to pick up the mail piled on the floor by the slot and headed to my office. Just as I did, the girls came in the back door at the same time.

"Anne, what's that?" Sally pointed at something I was holding.

"What?"

"This piece of paper with your mail." She pointed to a torn piece of notebook paper. It looked familiar.

"Oh, I didn't see this." I picked it up.

"WATCH OUT!!" was printed in black magic marker, just like the other message I received.

I sat down by my desk in utter disbelief that this young man would waste time on such a simple decision I had made. I had to react carefully, because I didn't want the girls to be afraid of anything that might affect them.

"Well, he's still getting his jollies, I guess." I laughed lightly. "The last thing he's going to do is frighten me." Jean and Sally were puzzled by my answer but nodded uncertainly and moved off to get to work.

He'll have to move on at some point, I told myself. I must have affected him more than just letting him go on the job. I think he must have felt threatened as a man. When I didn't respond to his sex-driven comment, he might have taken it as a blow to his ego and felt that I had portrayed myself as too good for him. I thought, "This guy has more problems than any of us know about."

"Anne, this makes my hackles rise." Jean sounded so prim with her distinct English dialect. "This gent is off his trolley, and you best keep Sam abreast of all this."

"Yes, but I don't want him babysitting me either." I felt defensive. "This will run its course and I will be careful. I promise."

"Sue is coming by with Mia today!" I changed the subject. "I also have a bit of bad news to tell you. I think the spirits of the basement have been active again. Sam came for dinner last night, and when I took him to the basement to show him the quilt, we found utter chaos! The quilt was on the floor and our letter pieces were everywhere, like a wind storm had flown through in the basement. It was a sight to behold!"

"You have got to be kidding," said Sally with disbelief.

"Are you talking about a bloody ghost?" asked Jean. "What kind of ghosts would do that?"

"Knowing Grandmother and Aunt Marie, there is likely a reason," I explained. "They do everything for a reason. We just don't know yet why. It took us quite awhile to collect every piece. We put them in a basket. We'll have to separate them the next time we're together. I am so sorry about that, Jean. I know you really had us all organized."

"Well, this is more fascinating as it goes along, wouldn't you say?" Jean shook her head in disbelief. "Everyone has a secret sorrow they say, or they are just full of beans and want to jerk your chain." Jerk our chain made sense for some reason. Why did they want to jerk our chain with this quilt? Hmmm.

At three o'clock that afternoon, in walked a new Sue with her new little girl. Even though I had been envisioning what the two might look like together, it didn't prepare me for what I saw. Sue was carrying this thin, tiny, dark-headed beauty that looked much younger than seventeen months. But how would I know that? She was resting her head on Sue's shoulder and had a precious little headband with a white flower that matched her little white sweater outfit. We all dropped what we were doing, which included leaving Mrs. Malden to browse the shop on her own.

"Welcome home!" I said as I ran up to give them a hug. "Look Sue, she is already clinging to you when I talk to her; just like a shy child does with her mom. How adorable is that? Oh, I would love to take her, but that wouldn't be a good idea, right?"

"What a gorgeous baby doll," admired Jean.

"Oh, Sue, being a mom becomes you!" Sally wanted to get her hands on Mia, as did we all.

Sue went into the work area where she could put down her extra bag and purse.

"It's surreal, I must say." She had a big grin on her face. "Isn't she something?"

"She's really been pretty good under the circumstances. She's way behind in her development, but the doctor reassured me that she would catch up rather quickly. She just needs a lot of love and the right nourishment, which she has not been getting." I'd never heard Sue go on like this!

"I don't have to go back to work for a couple more weeks," she continued, "so we should be settled by then. I've arranged for Alice Cromwell to take care of her after that. She said that if I wanted her to come to my place, she would, so we'll see. I think you may have met her once, Anne. She used to work with me and she decided to take an early retirement. I think she might be quite good; sort of like a grandmother type."

"Boy, you are lucky there," chimed in Sally. "That is the most difficult part of being a parent who has to work."

"I had that serious talk with myself before I applied for the adoption because I knew there would be no one else but me to support us," Sue shared.

"I can't wait for Sam to see her! He loves kids, which is scary, scary."

Everyone laughed and we couldn't make over little Mia enough. She wasn't letting go of her new mom, however. Even Mrs. Malden got in on all the fuss over her. She still managed to walk out with a beautiful arrangement for her dinner table and had a good time, too.

"Can you stop by Mother's later?" I asked Sue. "She's going to feel really left out not seeing Mia. I'm pretty sure she's home."

"I think we can if she doesn't get too cranky." Sue grabbed her belongings.

"I happen to know there are chocolate chip cookies in the kitchen, which will make Mia pretty happy," I teased.

"Well, it would make me happy, that's for sure." Sue smiled.

CHAPTER 24

It was the day before Easter, which always proved to be a very busy day at the shop with last minute orders and pick-ups. Sam's mother had arrived yesterday, but I was too busy to join them. I thought some mother-and-son time was a good thing.

Sam was taking Helen Dickson to see 333 Lincoln today and then they were coming by to show her my shop. I was looking forward to a day off tomorrow to be with the family and enjoy the new addition of Mia Marie. I knew Sam would adore her. The mystery of the day would be whether Uncle Jim and Aunt Julia would both attend the brunch.

At two o'clock the shop door opened when Sam and my future mother-in-law arrived. I had dressed a bit nicer than my normal work clothes as I knew Mrs. Dickson to be fairly proper in her dress.

"Welcome to Brown's Botanical Flower Shop," I greeted them cheerfully. "Come on in and have a look around. How was your trip?"

"Thank you, Anne," she answered as her eyes grazed the shop.

"Sam and the airplane were right on time and the hassles not too great. This is perfectly charming! Sam has told me so much about the place. These lovely girls must be Jean and Sally."

I was impressed with what she had absorbed from their conversation and I felt pleased Sam had bragged about my shop. She did seem sincere!

"Yes, indeed. I couldn't run the place without them. We've all been kept hopping today. There are always last minute flowers for everyone's plans. Here is our design room back here with a little office nook for myself. We are very crowded, but we love this building here on the street and manage to make do."

The girls began chatting with Mrs. Dickson, and Sam kept grinning at me like he was very proud and loved me very much. I melted, of course. I knew his each and every expression by now. The customers kept coming, which took my attention away from her, but I was also pleased that she could see that I had a successful business.

"We need to let these girls get to work here, Mother," Sam suggested. "Will you join us for a little supper at my place around seven o'clock? It will be simple unless Mother decides to explore in my kitchen."

"Oh, not a chance, Sam," Helen teased. "I'm your guest and I'm looking forward to being waited on. Anne, your shop is beautiful and I look forward to driving down this charming Main Street that Sam has told me so much about. I also look forward to meeting the rest of your family tomorrow."

I felt I needed to accept the invitation to Sam's, but I barely got out of the shop by six forty-five. I really wished we had the evening alone together. I still had not told him about the second threatening note I had received, but at least I had called it in to Officer Wilson so it would be on record. I didn't want to ruin his weekend, nor did I want to discuss any of this with his mother. I sure hoped he hadn't shared all the drama with her.

When I arrived at Sam's door, I could hear opera music playing in the background. Sam opened the door with a nice little peck on the cheek instead of the full kisses I was accustomed to.

"Glad you got away, Annie," he said sweetly. "We were just having a drink and listening to an opera selection that my folks enjoy. You feel like a merlot? Have a seat and I'll pour you some."

Sam was behaving so formally, I felt like I was interrupting something and they would have to accommodate a third party. Mrs. Dickson was in a reclining chair, looking very relaxed.

"Please join me, Anne," she politely suggested. "Do you enjoy any form of opera?"

"I can't say I don't enjoy it; I just haven't been exposed to much of it, you might say. What do we have here?"

Sam approached us with a lovely assortment of cheeses, fruit, and shrimp. He was quite the host. Would he continue to be that sort of gent after we were married?

"We had a sizable lunch, so I thought a variety of munchies and fruit would be sufficient," he said as he placed it on the coffee table. "I made some crab dip I also thought you might enjoy. I hope you aren't starving."

"Actually, this is perfect because we had a late sandwich for lunch and Jean brought in some brownies that we nibbled on all day." I helped myself to some grapes.

"Isn't it great Sam loves to cook?" Mrs. Dickson asked. "His father was not at all interested in cooking. Sam says you haven't had much cooking experience, as your mother has always been helpful with that."

"I have to confess, Mrs. Dickson, that I have been spoiled in that regard. I'm looking forward to learning some things from watching

Sam. He's planning quite a nice updated kitchen at 333 Lincoln."

"Please call me Helen, Anne," she said between her sips of wine. "Sam tells me you put in long hours and are quite dedicated to your historic area, which I find very commendable. Your mother must be very proud of you!"

Wow, this was a much more positive conversation than we had had on my holiday visit. Maybe she now realized that I would not be going away anytime soon.

"I think we have been good for each other. Mother has been pretty lonely since Dad died, and she looks forward to my coming home each day and keeping her involved in my activities. Some of us in the family have now taken up quilting, which is a great excuse to get together. Did Sam tell you about the quilt and vase I found in the potting shed at our house?"

"Honey, when I took Mother to see 333, she was already pretty overwhelmed, so no, you'll have to tell her all about the quilt and vase."

"Oh, that's right; you got to tour the house today. What did you think, Helen?"

"I couldn't believe it all," she said in disbelief. "It is a huge project and I don't know how in the world you two will be able to have it livable by your wedding, and the upkeep will be more than you can imagine. You are both so busy! It is true that Sam has always loved history and actually has been pretty handy with repairing some things. And, I'm sure this is a good distraction from his job. I just hope he doesn't put so many hours in the house that he ruins his chances for becoming president of Martingale. He has worked hard for that and I hope he doesn't become distracted from that goal."

Helen talked about Sam as though he wasn't in the room. I watched him react.

He stared at the floor as though he had heard these comments over and over during her visit. Oh my…I had forgotten that Sam's objective with his job was to be president of the company. He never ever mentioned it. It was always Uncle Jim who bragged about Sam becoming president someday. She's probably thinking I am also a distraction to his goal, I thought, looking at Helen.

"Helen, I've discovered that Sam is a very capable, multitasking person," I smiled with a wink his way. "He can do most anything he puts his mind to and can do it all at the same time. I'm kind of like him. I've been warned all my life not to take on too much, but somehow, busy people get things done. He has a lot of energy like me, and like me, he loves many things. We have both fallen in love with the Taylor house and are trying to learn as much about the family as possible, which brings me to the potting shed quilt." Sam smiled at me with love in his eyes. We truly were on the same wavelength.

"The potting shed quilt?"

I took full advantage of her question and proceeded to tell her every detail of finding the quilt wrapped around the unidentified vase. Then I told her how we were enthralled with reading the bits and pieces of letters that were cut up to make the quilt, and felt it could tell us a lot about the Taylor family.

What I didn't tell her about was what our basement spirits had been up to. I didn't give her much time to respond to most anything; too much information and a long day of activity had worn her out.

Easter morning arrived and Mother and I attended church. I had not asked Sam and Helen to come with us, which brought up a conversation as we drove home from church.

"Now, do you think Sam will go to church with you once in awhile?" Mother asked as we drove towards Main Street. "Do you think Sue will make sure that Mia has some religion in her life? I don't think Sue goes to church much, do you?"

"Those are all things we'll find out," I said, not to further the conversation. "I hope Aunt Julia and Uncle Jim both show up at Donna's for brunch today. I can't wait for Sam to see Mia."

We entered the lovely Victorian Tea Room, and Donna, as always, treated us like family. She had a nice long table reserved. Helen and Sam were already there, but no one else. We were a little early.

Introductions were made between Mother and Helen. It went smoothly and I thought they might, indeed, have lots to share.

"Thank you so much for my corsage, Anne," said Helen. "I love orchids. I can't remember when I last had a corsage."

"I am spoiled, Helen." Mother put her arm around me. "I must give a special thank you to her as well. Isn't it a nice touch? Anne is always very thoughtful and I think it comes from the nature of her business. It's people always thinking of other people."

"That's a nice way to put it." I felt happy all over. "I'm pleased to do it. You are both very special people."

In the door walked Sue with Mia, who was all dressed up in a pink dress and matching bonnet. She was more alert than she had been a few days ago, and wriggled her way out of Sue's arms to the floor where she could toddle around. She was so cute and precious pulling at her bonnet until it was completely off.

Sam immediately went up to her and got down at her eye level to say hello. She smiled at him but then went toddling back to Sue. Sue picked her up and when she did, Mia looked back at Sam as if to tease him. Sam held out his arms in case she might reconsider. She put her head down with a sheepish smile and leaned into to him for approval. I could not believe my eyes, but there he was holding her in his arms! How had he managed what we all had tried to do?

He playfully touched her chin and she giggled. He walked over to his mother, and when Helen tried to talk to her, she hid her face in Sam's neck, which turned into a delightful snuggle of sorts. I was so envious of his feat and could see him being the best dad ever! He took a cracker from the table and offered it to her. She gladly responded. Sue was shocked at their instant relationship as well.

"This settles it, Sue," I said looking her way. "We are going to have to get you a man in your life. Did you know she would respond like this to men?"

"Yes, I could have guessed, because she was quite at ease with Greg, I mean Mr. Branson, on the trip," she admitted.

Just then we were all in for a Kodak moment, which Mother typically called moments that you will never see again. I had picked up her habit. Aunt Julia, Uncle Jim, and Sarah all walked in together as if they were one family without a care in the world.

Mother took the lead and did all the introducing, which I appreciated. I was pretty sure Sam had filled in his mother about the upcoming Baker divorce. Instead of dealing with it just now, I just wanted to take it all in.

We all took our seats, but Sam continued standing to toast everyone a Happy Easter. To my surprise, he deferred to my mother, who said a short prayer of thanks. Now, this was an interesting gesture, and I wondered if this would become a common practice. Hmmm.

I was so happy and very thankful that at this moment we could all be family, no matter what problems might be ahead.

CHAPTER 25

Monday was the perfect day to visit Walnut Grove Cemetery. Mother had invited Helen. Sam was thrilled, because he had to attend to business.

To my surprise, she seemed interested in the idea of the cemetery visit, so we picked her up at ten thirty with a thought to perhaps have lunch when we finished. Helen was older than Mother, but looked fit and always presented herself nicely.

She brought her camera and commented how she had taken photos at 333 on Saturday. Mother knew her way around the cemetery better than I, plus, she had gotten a description of where we might find the Taylors' gravestones.

"This is Colebridge's oldest cemetery," Mother announced like a tour guide. "Turn here, Anne, I think we are close. We may want to park on this road and walk from here."

The grass was still wet, which I hadn't thought about, and it could have used a cutting; we left our tracks along the way. Mother had been told that the Taylors' tombstones would not be together, which was a common practice in years past. We walked a good five rows before we got lucky.

"All right, then," I said with some satisfaction. "Take a look at this. Albert Lewis Taylor, born 1890, died 1970. So he was eighty, right? Look how impressive this is! His wife spent some big bucks on this!"

The tall, red granite stone had a curved edge on top with darkly outlined leaf motifs and lilies before his name, which was carved in a dramatic black print. After the dates of birth and death were printed, "His love for God and man enriched each life he touched."

"He has fresh flowers here," Helen observed. She moved closer to the arrangement. "Someone misses him still."

"These are beautiful! They are fresh lilies. And look! He has them imprinted on his stone." I said. "Did you notice that? He must have been an important man and knew a lot of people, I suppose. We really don't know too much yet."

I looked around the area. "I wonder who could have put them here? Maybe a church or charity just laid them here. Keep looking for any Taylor name as you walk, because we think they had one child, but maybe there were more." Since we were in the older part of the cemetery, there were no floral decorations laid by the other stones. Why did Mr. Taylor have them? They seemed to make some kind of statement, but I wasn't sure what. Who was this man, so important that he still deserved fresh flowers? Hmmm.

Helen took the time to get a good picture of Albert's stone with her camera before we strolled further, reading some of the wonderful captions. There were some with embedded photos that I thought were pretty inventive for such early dates.

It wasn't long before Mother called out that she had found Marion Taylor's tombstone. I quickly walked along with very wet feet to catch up.

"Well, this is pretty modest compared to Mr. Taylor's stone," I said as I joined her. "It looks like she died five years later."

"Maybe whoever ordered this decided to be more frugal, or maybe there wasn't much money left," Mother said. "I wonder if she had a middle name."

"She died in 1987 and was born in 1895, so she lived to be ninety-two. This is quite a lovely saying," said Helen. "'Unlike the fragrance of flowers that bloom, and then fade away, a beloved memory enriches our lives from day to day.'" We all smiled.

"I wonder who picked out this stone and if she stayed in the house until she died? I wish I had more time to find out these things. I feel strange observing these stones, not having known them. Do you think I should introduce myself?"

"Very funny, Anne," Mother responded. "I can help you research the family. I have more time than you do, and it is pretty interesting, I have to say. I will go to the Historical Society's office soon. I hear they are most helpful with genealogy." She paused. "The Taylors didn't die that long ago, when you think about it."

"I don't see any other Taylor stones, do you?" We walked from row to row. "Oh, I forgot to tell you that this cemetery has a special section for children," Mother remembered. "I don't know where it is. I didn't think about asking where that might be, but we should be able to find it."

"Oh, that should be interesting," Helen said.

After she took her pictures, we got back in the car to scope out what might be the children's area. We drove back and forth on a few roads and then noticed some smaller stones up on a hill. Mother seemed to be certain that this would be the location we were looking for.

We parked as close as we could and then got out of the car.

It was a good little hike, especially for Helen and Mother, but they didn't complain. It was so strange, I thought, to have the little ones separated from their families. The tombstones were so tiny and precious. Many were very old; the engravings were hard to read. Only a few were fancy in any way until we found one that read "Miranda Sue Taylor." A small carved angel stood atop the stone that read, "Our Little Angel, Miranda Sue Taylor." Underneath the name was "1917 to 1923." I could almost feel the sorrow related to this six-year-old laid to rest.

"She must have gotten a disease or something to die at the age of six," Helen said sadly.

"I guess we don't know for sure it's their daughter, do we?" I said.

"No, we don't, but that should not be hard to find out," said Mother with great interest.

"Now I am really anxious to see your potting shed quilt," said Helen. "There could be some reference to her in his letters."

"Wouldn't that be great!" I thought out loud. "Let's make sure there are no other Taylors here, and then we'll go to lunch."

We spent another fifteen minutes walking around before we decided to leave. I had a good feeling knowing where the Taylors were laid to rest. Getting wet feet and a little exercise was well worth our effort. Plus, it was a rewarding experience to have shared the discovery with Mother and Helen.

We stopped at The Water Wheel on Main Street and sat outdoors to enjoy their delicious chicken salad sandwiches. I almost felt like a third wheel as Helen and Mother made most of the conversation, so I turned my attention to the beautiful setting. I loved all the pretty flowers planted along the creek that flowed into the Missouri River. The impatiens were blooming everywhere and had been maintained beautifully. There were also some wild lilies among the ivy, which reminded me of the live lilies we saw on Albert's grave. How odd seeing the fresh flowers on such an old grave. Was it just a coincidence that lilies just happened to be engraved on the tombstone as well?

"Did Sam tell you we want to have an outdoor wedding?" I came back to reality and jumped into the conversation.

"No, he didn't!" Helen was surprised. "He hasn't said much about the details so please fill me in. Are you sure you want to take the risk of the weather?"

"Yes, I think we can come up with a plan B for the weather," I said reassuringly. "I'll tell Sam to drive you over to see the beautiful Rawlings Sunken Garden at the City Park. They have many weddings there and it's perfect, if you don't have too many people." I felt this would be a nice hint for her not to invite everyone she knew.

"I knew Anne would have to have something with a lot of flowers," chimed Mother.

"Well, I'm sure whatever you kids decide, it will be beautiful," Helen said to my surprised pleasure. "I guess I'm miles ahead of you because I'm already thinking of those grandchildren! You know my Pat said she doesn't want children." She smiled sadly, but then she brightened. "Sam will make a wonderful father. Did you see him with that little Mia on Sunday?"

Mother and I both agreed how cute that scene had been, but I wasn't about to discuss any plans about children. We finished our lunch and decided to go back to Mother's house to show Helen the potting shed quilt. They continued talking together as if I were nowhere around.

Helen admired the house and neighborhood as we arrived back at my current home. I told her I had many fond memories there and would miss living with my mother and the many conveniences it brought my way.

Mother showed Helen around the house and put on a pot of coffee before anyone arrived for our regular afternoon get together. I didn't want to cancel just because Helen was in town. Jean was the first to arrive. Helen had met Jean at the shop, so after our hellos, we made our way downstairs.

Mother explained how we began spending so much time in the basement with our quilting projects. I showed Jean our basket of paper pieces from the quilt, all unorganized and even more crumpled than before.

"Not to worry, Miss Anne," said Jean. "I'll have these assembled in a flash." She began her mission. Meanwhile, we opened the potting shed quilt and showed Helen how we were removing the papers that all seemed to be letters from Albert Taylor. She was full of questions we had no explanation for.

"We assume they all are written to Marion," I explained. "We're just reading snippets at this point."

"I see," said Helen, shaking her head in wonder. "This is like a puzzle, as you said. Here is one that says *my mission will be longer than*. Where was he writing these from, Anne?"

"We are pretty sure that he was in London. Did you notice the different kinds of stationery, Helen? This will indeed help us to put the pieces together."

"*Sorry she was so blunt,*" read Jean from a piece she had in her hand. "Who was so blunt?" She looked at us. "As I said before, Miss Anne, there is a conflict going on here. I don't think we should assume these are love letters as we first thought."

We chatted about different theories as we poured coffee and munched on the small pieces of dark chocolate and mixed nuts that Mother had brought downstairs for us.

"This treat is scrummy," said Jean. "Did you make it yourself,

Mrs. Brown?"

"Yes, thank you, I guess." Mother laughed. "Please call me Sylvia. No one has ever told me my cooking was 'scrummy.'"

"Oh, I forget sometimes that I'm in America now and these habits slip in," Jean apologized.

"Please don't apologize, Jean." I had stopped sorting pieces to snack and chat. "We all love the way you talk and find it very refreshing. If we have a chuckle, as you say, please don't think we're making fun of you!"

Suddenly the quilt's paper pieces blew around as if someone had opened a window to let in a brisk breeze. We were so taken aback we didn't speak until Mother shouted.

"Oh no, not again," she cried. "Grab those! Oh, dear!" We had our hands full of drinks and treats and scrambled to put cups and plates down.

"Is there a window open or air-conditioning air going, Sylvia?" asked Helen, trying to catch some of the flying pieces.

"I'll get it! I'll catch it all," shouted Jean as she stooped to pick up pieces whirling about until they settled on the carpet. "There sure was a wind of sorts, Miss Anne. I've never seen the like!"

"I have the solution here," said Helen as she gathered more pieces. "I purchased some sticky board the other day for my drapery samples and it's pretty clever. You can secure your pieces, but also be able to move them about without hurting them. This would be perfect for each letter you are trying to assemble. You can get them at any art supply place."

"That's a dandy idea, Miss Helen." Jean knelt on the floor to retrieve every last piece. "I will get some today, because this plan A is not working."

I was so pleased Mother didn't mention Grandmother, who, I was sure, was up to this mysterious wind. The looks Mother and I exchanged confirmed she was thinking the same thing.

The doorbell rang as Sam arrived to pick up his mother. We all went up the stairs and began saying our goodbyes.

"I bet you're thinking that your visit to the Browns' and Colebridge was anything but dull, right, Helen?" I smiled.

"I've had a marvelous time," she said with all sincerity. "I can't wait to return. Please keep me informed about your wedding plans and this potting shed quilt. How adventurous it will be for you all to learn about the Taylors! And I certainly have seen a different side of my son. He has started many new adventures! Sylvia, keep an eye on these kids so they don't work too hard." They hugged like old friends.

Sam gave me a kiss with the promise to call later. Helen gave me a nice hug, too. I wasn't sure how much she meant the things she said, but for now, I thought she was glad she was getting on the plane to go home.

CHAPTER 26

When Mother and I walked into Aunt Julia's house, we were amazed by the effort and creativity she put into making this event for Sue and Mia so special. The theme was pink and brown polka dots. Guests were milling around helping themselves to pink punch and fussing over little Mia.

Seeing Aunt Joyce, Sue's Mother, was an added joy. She was such a sweet person, and how ironic that her adopted daughter would be adopting a daughter herself. You could tell she was the proud grandmother of her only grandchild from her only daughter.

Joyce explained that Uncle Ken could not get away, but nothing could keep her away from this joyous occasion and how nice it was of Aunt Julia to invite her to stay in her home. I thought it odd that Uncle Ken would not be curious and anxious to see his new grandchild, but then men sometimes reacted differently to things.

On the dining room table was a round, scrumptious-looking cake that read "Welcome Mia" in pink writing on the chocolate icing. Pink dots were scattered on the cake; it looked too pretty to cut.

Mia was toddling about and eating up all the attention. I wished Sam were by my side so I could see him hug and kiss her again, but no doubt there would be more times ahead. He was out of town on business for another day. We hated when we had to catch up on the phone at night instead of meeting face to face. There were things I did not share with him on the phone, like the last note I received from Steve that said, "WATCH OUT!!" Enough time had passed that I thought I might not have to tell him at all.

As the afternoon progressed, I was entertained by all the gifts generously given by so many folks. The girls from Sue's workplace outdid themselves. The clothing for Mia was precious, with many sizes to grow into for sure. Our gift certificates were not as exciting, but we knew Sue would enjoy using them. We felt family should be a little more practical, given Sue's financial challenge. We even included a certificate to Donna's Tea Room for the mommy of Mia to enjoy. She was thrilled.

Jean was holding down the shop by herself so Sally could attend the shower, too. Having just met Sue and not knowing her as well, she had volunteered to take the duty. Kevin was also around for help if she needed it. It was a Saturday, which could be awfully busy, even though the hours were shorter, so I called in to check on how things were going as I enjoyed the pink punch. Jean asked if I could stop by the shop before I went home. She would not tell me why, but I told her I would. My first thought was that there was probably a cash register problem or a charge sales question.

We ate our cake and decided we would be most helpful in cleaning up Aunt Julia's mess by leaving. Mother agreed to meet up with Aunt Joyce the next day. Joyce said she'd like to visit Aunt

Marie's gravesite now that the stone was up. I told Mother if they had time, she should also take her by 333 Lincoln and show off the house.

I arrived at the shop just in time to help Mrs. Bixby pick out a bouquet for a friend of hers in the hospital while Jean finished up another sale.

"There's a last minute delivery for Kevin," Jean called out. "Don't let him toddle off until I finish the cards on those bouquets."

I let her finish as I saw the last customer out the door. I had begun to balance our drawer when Jean came to me with a solemn look.

"I hope the party was special," she said without any expression. "I hate to ruin your good hours of the day, but I must share what I found."

She handed me another note from my "friend" Steve that looked just like the others. It read, "DO NOT RELAX!"

"Oh, for heaven's sake," I said in disgust. "This is getting ridiculous. This idiot is acting like a child. I guess I'm supposed to be really, really scared."

"You'd best heed the warning Miss Anne. I would give this to that detective gent you chatted with."

"I will." I started checking my e-mail. "I still have the other note I haven't told Sam about. Meanwhile, he gets home tomorrow and I'll see what he thinks."

I withdrew from talking, got off the computer, and then became busy with the drawer receipts.

"By the way, Miss Anne, I went to the market and found the sticky-wicky boards Miss Helen talked about." Jean was good at cheering me up.

I chuckled at her language—sticky-wicky!—and told her we

would start using them right away. I was going to take them home and have Mother start the process.

"How much do I owe you, Jean?" I asked, wanting to compensate her for time and trouble.

"Not a penny! Cheers!" she said as she went out the door.

It wasn't long until I left the shop myself. Sam and the note were both on my mind. When I wanted to feel close to Sam, I found myself going to 333 Lincoln. I did just that, stopping to pick up a cold drink at the convenience store.

As I started to drive up the hill, I came upon a large tree limb blocking the drive. I wasn't sure if it was a limb or a small tree that had fallen over. I tried to remember any kind of wind storm recently, but could not recall one. Pleased that it was still light outdoors, I stopped the car and got out to see what had happened.

I recognized the redbud tree from our yard, but how did it get here and why was it down? It was about four inches in diameter, so I couldn't do much to move it out of the drive. It was still loaded with buds and flowers, now wilting. Then I discovered it had been sawed off. I walked up the hill to see where it had been alive, and, sure enough, someone had cut it down out of the yard and placed it in the drive.

I nearly became ill trying to digest it all. Then my next reaction was to check the house and other trees and bushes for damage. After a quick assessment, I decided this was all I could find.

Feeling so angry, I called Officer Wilson's number stored in my phone. The lady who answered said she would reach him and have him come right out. I tried again to pull the tree away off the drive but it was too awkward. Was this awful little squirrel of a man going to hack away at our place little by little in revenge?

I was admiring the new herbs by the potting shed; they were coming up nicely, when I heard Officer Wilson call out to me.

When I walked down to meet him, he was taking a photo.

"I think I can pull this to the side to clear the drive. Do you think it's the handiwork of your disgruntled helper? It's a shame this poor tree didn't make it to its full growth. Do you know where it came from?" He was as disgusted as I was.

I explained where it came from and showed him when we walked back up the hill. I then brought him up to speed on the two recent notes I had not reported.

"Well, I wish you had called us right away on this. He thinks he can get by with enough to scare you a bit without doing anything seriously wrong, but I can tell you right now that we'll pick him up and get some real answers before he can do something really dangerous."

"Do you know where to find him?" I was obviously curious.

"Yeah, I think some of the other guys have seen him in the neighborhood where he has a relative that I think he's staying with," he answered confidently. "We'll get him. I think what you and Mr. Dickson need to do is put yourself some kind of privacy gate up here so folks just can't come up here so easy. For now you may want it to be locked up somehow until things settle a bit."

"I'll feel better when he's in jail or out of town," I said with conviction.

Officer Wilson nodded and I thanked him as he drove off from the now-cleared driveway. Now I had to go home and decide whether to call Sam tonight or wait till tomorrow's arrival.

CHAPTER 27

The next Sunday morning, thankful for not getting a late phone call from Sam, I planned instead how I would share the news with him later in the day. I had brought home paperwork for the weekend that had been accumulating and made a mental note of e-mails that needed attention.

Mother told me that Aunt Julia would be coming over later to help on the quilt after she dropped Sarah at the mall. She went on to church while I leisurely enjoyed a cup of coffee with my work, as I lounged in my comfy pajamas.

I walked around the safe haven I grew up in and realized I didn't have a picture of Sam anywhere around. There I was, posed with different relatives in different photos. I had made the effort to put away the one of Ted and me. I was beginning to realize that the short length of our relationship had left many unanswered questions. Did I know what his favorite color was? Did he ever have a dog or cat? Was he ever in the hospital? Did it make him jealous when I mentioned Ted? What made him really, really angry? Why were my answers to any questions about Sam always so positive and loving? Was I naïve? My thoughts were broken by a call on my cell that said "Sam." Could he read my mind and was calling to answer all my questions!?

"Awake are you, Annie?" he cheerfully asked. "I'm at the airport on my way home. Will you have time for some lunch? I know Sunday afternoons are sometimes busy for you."

"I'll pack a picnic lunch for us to eat outdoors at our house," I suggested. "Come as early as you can before the quilters come!"

"You know what I like, don't you? Do you want to meet there or would you like me to pick you up?"

"I'll be there by eleven thirty. I need to shower and dress before I raid Mother's kitchen."

"That's my sweet Annie!" he said before ending the call with his usual "love you" message.

Two hours later, the basket was packed and I was on my way to play a part in a storybook fairytale of a girl in love. I was wearing a red-and-white checked shirt and my favorite jeans. Picture perfect, I thought to myself. The temperature was starting to warm up these days and I needed to start getting more color on my body.

When I arrived at 333, Sam was already there. I did manage to get a hug and kiss before he asked if I had been there lately. I said yes, I had, as I took the basket, bottles of water, and a blanket over to the shady maple tree.

I remained calm as I slowly eased into the story of finding the sawed-off tree. He had already figured out that the fallen tree obviously dragged to the side of the driveway was no accident. Before he started scolding me, I leaped into releasing the news about the two notes from Steve.

After Sam paced and cursed to let off steam, I scored a few

good points by telling him Officer Wilson had been called. I told him how he moved the limb and that he was sure they could now go after Steve. Sam had already thought of the privacy and security fence idea and was going to implement the task on Monday morning.

It took a bit of time, but I finally convinced Sam to relax and have half of a chicken salad sandwich, a dill pickle, and some potato chips. So much for my picture-perfect afternoon! Trying to improve the situation, I laid back on the blanket to describe to Sam how beautiful the sky and clouds were. He joined me with his kind lips and ever-so-strong body that I needed to hug. I had already heard all his warning remarks about Steve from our visit before, so when we separated our bodies, I put my fingers across his lips to indicate my awareness and that he was repeating himself.

I made it back to the house before our usual quilters arrived. Aunt Joyce was already there. They were discussing their visit to Aunt Marie's gravesite, which also happened to be in Walnut Grove Cemetery. Mother was bringing her up to date on our visit there. She had driven Joyce by Albert Taylor's gravesite and noted that the lilies in front of the tombstone were just as fresh as the day we saw them. Weird and impossible, I thought to myself, but then Aunt Julia arrived and the subject was changed. We were huddled around the kitchen table, which was usually our practice until everyone arrived each afternoon.

"Did Joyce tell you that I filed divorce papers and they should go to Jim this week?" Aunt Julia asked.

"No, she didn't." I was surprised. "Wow, I didn't think it would come to this, I guess. I feel so bad for all of you! Does Sarah know it's a done deal?"

"Yes, I told her." She returned my consoling hug with a sad smile. "I knew it wouldn't work for us to tell her together. Who knows what Jim will tell her? I didn't mention that there was someone else in her father's life. I'll let him deal with that."

Julia looked at the three of us. "I just know I am finished. Please know how awkward and sad I am about all this. I know you are all fond of Jim." She paused again. Clearly, this was not easy for her. "Sarah wasn't shocked, of course. She is old enough to figure some things out and who knows what she's heard when we've argued. Jim is a good dad. He will continue to be so I'm sure, unless a wicked stepmother appears!"

"If someone mentioned that there was another person in the picture, I missed that," Aunt Joyce said angrily. "This changes the dynamics of all this considerably."

Mother was quiet as Aunt Joyce vented her anger at Uncle Jim. We then briefly mentioned Aunt Marie, who had so wanted them to work things out. We all agreed we would be extra attentive to Sarah in these hard days ahead.

It was a good change of mood when Sally and Jean arrived together chirping away like schoolgirls. After Sue, Muffin, and Mia arrived, we all went down the stairs as if we were reporting to work. Jean began telling about the second whirlwind we had actually witnessed that twirled the paper pieces onto the floor. Looks of uncertainty regarding unexplained mysteries were nothing new to our group, and there were plenty today.

Mother showed everyone how we would now have a sticky board for each letter portion we were piecing together and that the pieces would stay in place once we removed them from the quilt. We all nodded and gave our approval. Although Aunt Joyce was just visiting our group, she was quite impressed. Sue tried to keep her posted through long distance phone calls. Aunt Joyce was also busy playing Grandma as Mia wanted to get into all sorts of trouble, so we only had part of her attention. Mia was getting more and more comfortable with all of us and, therefore, she was becoming braver in her activities.

"You all continue with your puzzle and I'll watch this precious grandchild," Aunt Joyce smiled lovingly at Mia.

"*Give up her baby girl for adoption,*" Sally said suddenly. We were startled until we realized she was reading from a piece from the quilt. The announcement brought everyone to silence, as we looked at her.

"*You must not worry,* I think this says," said Jean. She sighed. "As I told Miss Anne, this quilt has a secret sorrow. I feel it and it wants to come out."

"I think this line is most curious," said Sue. "*She has always been fond of me.* Who is fond of whom here? If it's Albert writing Marion, he's telling her that someone else has always been fond of him. Can you find another piece to fit to that, Jean, on the same stationery?" With the pieces being stuck in place, it was easier to match them.

"I might, by golly," Jean answered, turning the quilt. "Here is a shape that might work. Okay, this would match the stationery and I think the shape, so this may be our first complete sentence! *And expressed so a time or two* is on this one. Putting it altogether it reads, *She has always been fond of me and expressed so a time or two.*"

Cheers of loud joy rang throughout the room, which scared Mia and had her running to her new mom. We finally had our first very small piece to our many puzzles.

"Boy, now I wonder how the *give up her baby girl for adoption* fits in?" Sally asked with excitement. "It's the same stationery, but too many pieces are missing right now."

"Here is *loving husband Albert,* so Jean, maybe you're wrong and these are love letters after all?" Mother said sweetly. "We found a piece that had the name Martha on it, Joyce. I think it said something about Martha being confused. Mother was a Martha but I'm sure there were others with that name at that time."

"I loved the line we found that said something about having lemonade on the porch," I said with a smile. "I can just see the two of them sitting there and sipping away. I think Sam and I will enjoy the south porch at 333 Lincoln just as much. I'm not sure it will be lemonade however!" This got a big laugh from everyone.

"Sylvia said she would take me by your house tomorrow before she and Sue take me to the airport," said Aunt Joyce. "I've heard wonderful things, but it sounds like the two of you will have lots and lots of work to do."

"Even so, you know, Aunt Joyce, if I had to move in it right now, just the way it is, I think I'd be so very happy. Did Mother tell you about the potting shed in the back yard?"

"I think Anne'll end up moving in the potting shed the way she loves it so much, and let Sam live in the big house," joked Sally.

I described the potting shed and how I had always wanted one. I felt it was a place where I could create life, so to speak. I also told her that it had had this treasure hidden underneath one of the counters.

"If this quilt could talk," I said wishfully to everyone.

"What do you mean, Miss Anne?" Jean said. "It is talking to us!"

CHAPTER 28

Brown's Botanical's was starting to show my absence. Only the owner of a business notices the details of what's not been attended to. If no supervision is around, things can easily be overlooked because of the employees' other responsibilities. The chatter goes on more frequently and everyone is more at ease while the time is ticking before they leave for the day. They are then entitled to go home. Their job description states their hours, but an owner's hours are ongoing.

The girls were very good with their duties, but my inattention was showing on the bottom line. The extra payroll was no longer an occasional occurrence; it was becoming normal. I'd have to soon be thinking smarter by cutting back on something else or getting back to me working longer hours. That would mean Sam and 333 Lincoln would suffer. As I was looking at the scheduling on the calendar, Officer Wilson walked in the shop.

"Come on back, officer, I greeted him. "Is there anything new to report on Steve?"

"Maybe," he said, joining me in the design room. "Is Kevin here now? I'd like to ask him a few more questions."

"I think I heard the van a little while ago, so he's probably outside. Please feel free to go find him."

He went out the back door of the shop. Sally was working out front and she leaned her head around into the back room, hoping to learn something. I shrugged my shoulders and went on crunching numbers.

"I think you are working way too hard there, Anne," said Uncle Jim as he came into my work space.

"Oh, what a surprise!" I was startled to see him. "How are you doing? I'm so sorry to hear about everything."

"Hey, I'm getting what's coming to me, so just be helpful to Julia and Sarah," he said sadly. "They're really going to need you."

"Here, sit down a minute," I said, pointing to the stool nearby. "We're family, and none of us like taking sides. You are such a great friend to Sam and will be a part of our lives no matter what—just so you know. It's really hard for Sam, too, because he really likes Aunt Julia." We looked at each other for a moment. "Where are you living?"

"I'd love to live in the lofts where Sam is, but until we get things arranged financially, I just took a monthly rental on Clark Street," he explained. "It'll do. My fear is that Sarah will turn on me and side with her mother. I hate doing this to her."

"I don't think you have to worry," I said, consoling him. "Aunt Julia was just saying what a good father you are. She thinks you will continue to be so."

"Well, that's good to hear," he eased a little. "I still think the world of Julia. I don't know how much Sam has shared with you about my friend Brenda. We've known each other forever. She is married and, as of this time, she has not left her husband, so our relationship may or may not continue."

"I hate to say this to you, Uncle Jim, but you need to encourage her to save her marriage," I advised him. "Who knows what might happen between you and Aunt Julia? You say you still love her. At some point you may court her again and start over. But it won't happen as long as there is a Brenda; I can tell you that!"

"I haven't heard the word 'courting' in a long time, Anne," he laughed. "Sometimes you are just a sweet little old-fashioned girl. Sam is damned lucky to have you."

"So what do you think of 333 Lincoln?" I changed the subject.

"I'm jealous as all heck," he sighed. "I look forward to helping Ssm with things. You, too. It will be an awesome place to bring back to life. He says you were all crazy about the potting shed, which sealed the deal."

"Yes!" I perked up at the thought. "It was a deal breaker. The family is telling me that I would just as soon move into there as the house. Hey, did you or anyone you know know the Taylors or anything about them?"

"I just knew that no one ever went up the hill since it was private property. And then, of course, there were the ghost stories that would circulate around."

"Like what kind of ghost stories?" I perked up. "What did the ghost do? What did people say would happen? I haven't picked up on a thing like that up there."

"The ghost supposedly was a mistress to Albert Taylor, but hey; this is all hearsay," he revealed. "The mistress was probably unhappy when he ditched her and she never let him forget it." He laughed.

"Are you kidding me, Uncle Jim?" I wasn't laughing. "Is that the story? He ditched her? She was the one causing the stir?"

"Supposedly," he said, trying to kid around. "Hey, don't go by me. You'll have to ask others. You know there is one neighbor up there on the east side of the house. I think that's where old lady Brody lives. She's letting the place run down, but I think she's still alive and lives there. Maybe she can tell you something. Haven't you gone over there?"

"No, but I need to." This information really fed my curiosity. "Now I really wonder if he did have a mistress. I am piecing together some of his letters that I found in the potting shed that were in an old quilt. Perhaps they will indicate something."

"Hey, I have to run." Uncle Jim gave me a goodbye hug. "Thanks for understanding and not writing me off. I love you, gal." He gave me a kiss on the forehead and off he went.

As he left, Kevin came in to tell me that Officer Wilson had left and they thought they knew where to find Steve. He had been hanging out at a biker bar across the river and it jived with what others were telling Officer Wilson.

"Anne, don't worry," he said, shaking his head in disgust. "This guy's going to be toast. There are times, as you know, I felt sorry for him. He is lost, broke, and has a low self esteem, which is why when you rejected him, he went crazy. To be honest with you, I think he just wants to scare you. I don't think he would really hurt you."

Kevin was a good guy, trying to console me and be kind to his friend, and I was sorry he had to get involved. I told him I wasn't afraid, but that Sam was having some problems with it all.

Sally interrupted our conversation by asking me to consult with a customer out front. I sent Kevin on his way with a delivery and greeted a darling young woman with a handful of Queen Anne's Lace wildflowers.

"What do we have here?" I used my most pleasant voice.

"Hi, Miss Brown," she said shyly. "I knew your Aunt Marie. My parents live next door to where she lived. I always heard you do very special things with flowers and I have a special request for a small wedding that I'm planning. I have access to a lot of these wildflowers and I had this idea that they might be able to be tinted with color in some way. My wedding is this weekend and I had a last minute thought that these would be pretty centerpieces. We can't afford anything expensive, so I wondered if this was a stupid idea or not?"

"I love this flower, and besides, it's named after me," I teased. "I always have loved it and no, it's not a silly idea. We experimented with this idea for a school play at Colebridge High last year and it worked. What are the colors you want?"

"Well, some pink and some blue would be pretty," she brightened. "My one bridesmaid is wearing pink."

"How many centerpieces would you need?"

"Oh, maybe six."

"Well, if you can bring me all the flowers on Friday morning, I'll have all six centerpieces in glass containers ready for you."

"Ummm…" she hesitated. "Well, I need to find out a price first," she said with some embarrassment. "I just wanted to see if you thought it would work or if it was a stupid idea."

"I love it and I'll do it for nothing," I smiled, feeling generous. "You can bring the containers back some time later. It won't take us long to make your centerpieces."

"I can't ask you to do that!"

"Let's just say your neighbor Marie would want me to do it for you."

"That would be so cool, Miss Brown," she beamed. "I can't believe this. Mother won't believe it either. Thank you so much!"

"Fill out this information for Sally, and don't forget to have them here Friday morning. Then you can pick them up first thing Saturday, okay?"

She was nearly in tears and gave me a quick hug. I told Sally to put the order into the computer, turned around, and Sally gave me an unexpected hug.

"This is why you are the best! This is why I love working at Brown's Botanical! 'We bring out the love,'" she started to sing.

"Stop, stop," I yelled. "Let me get back to running my sweatshop!"

CHAPTER 29

The next morning I found Mother sitting out on the front porch having her coffee. It was a beautiful day with a cool, light breeze, and the neighbor children were already at play outdoors. Years ago, I was one of them. Mother and I had many vivid memories of living on this street. The trees had gotten bigger and new sidewalks had been put in, but somehow it never changed. She looked deep in thought, and I only hoped that what she was thinking so hard about was good and not full of worry.

"Good morning," I said as I gave her a little hug. "It's lovely out here, isn't it?"

"Yes," she said stretching her arms. "I've been up since five o'clock. I just didn't sleep well last night. I think I have made a decision to tell Pointer's today that I am going to quit. I think it's time. I don't feel I am doing my fair share when I am there. All those young folks can work circles around me. Do you think I'm imagining things?"

I sat beside her on the swing. "Well, I doubt that, but I told you before that I don't like it when I hear about how you have some aches and pains from a long day. You don't have to work, Mother. I know how you like to be active and around people, but you don't need the money and you certainly don't want to hurt your health. I can give you lots to do at the house if you feel up to it. Hey, by the way—I found out something yesterday that might be helpful in our quilt puzzle."

"Oh, what's that?"

"Well, Uncle Jim stopped by to chat yesterday. We got to talking about 333 Lincoln and he mentioned the rumors about a ghost being there. When I asked him more about it, he said that he always heard that it was Albert Taylor's mistress causing trouble. How about that? Wouldn't that be something if we found something in the letters to that effect?"

"Well, I don't know about that, Anne. I think rumors can be all over the place. Besides, I don't want you to expect that there is any kind of ghost in the house. In fact, if there were such a ghost, I think you and Sam would have discovered it by now. By the way, how is Jim?"

"He's sad. He indicated that he thought a lot of this Brenda, but she was married and would not likely leave her husband. So, in other words, he was out of luck with his wife and friend."

"Serves him right," Mother said sternly. "I don't know if I can look him straight in the eye anymore. I think now that Julia might be better off without him. It's so sad for Sarah, however."

"Well, I need to shower and get to the shop." I stood up. "I think you're doing the right thing about the bookstore. You're moving on to something else. If you spend some time today on the quilt, keep an eye open for any indication of another woman. Sam has a meeting tonight, so how about I bring home a pizza and we'll work on the potting shed puzzle together? We have plenty of merlot, right?" She broke into an open smile.

"That would be great, sweetie. I'll need some cheering up after giving my notice. May I suggest that we firm up some of your wedding plans tonight, Anne? If you are still looking at September 12, there isn't much time. I know you want a small affair, but some things still have to be done. I can offer to do it all myself now, since I'll have the time."

"Yes, you're right," I agreed as I sat back down on the swing. "Sam keeps hinting that he doesn't know what to tell people when they ask about the wedding. We do have the 12th booked at the park, our pastor has the date saved and the shop will take care of the flowers, so I guess it's just the details of the reception."

"I should say so! Have you decided who is going to stand up with you?"

"Actually, I think I have, but I haven't run it by Sam or you," I carefully stated. "Aunt Julia and Uncle Jim would have been in it for sure since they are both close to us, but now I think it's a bad idea. Since Sam will want Uncle Jim as a best man, I thought I would ask Sue to be my maid of honor."

"Oh, that sounds wonderful. That's a good idea. Julia will understand. So it will be just the two of them?"

"Well, I've also been thinking of Nancy Barrister. She and I still e-mail each other and we've been friends since kindergarten. She said she was coming, invited or not! I don't know Sam's sisters at all, so I don't feel comfortable asking either one of them. What do you think?"

"I'm sure Sam would want you to have whomever you want. Do you think Nancy and her husband will always live in Boston?"

"That's a good question, because Nancy has mentioned that Mr. Barrister would love for them to come back and take over the funeral home here. I think they like it in Boston, though, and her husband enjoys working for a huge funeral business there. Sam hasn't met them. I introduced them to Ted the last time they were here. It may be too complicated to have her in the wedding, so perhaps we should just keep it the two—Uncle Jim and Sue. I'll see what Sam thinks."

"Sounds like a plan." We both left the swing and went into the house. "We haven't had pizza since we were all quilting one evening. You better get going, Anne. We'll finish our conversation this evening."

I still made it in to the shop before the others, and as I came in the back door, I saw Officer Wilson's car drive up in front. I wondered why he was here, and also what the other shop owners thought when they saw him come and go so frequently. So far, no one had asked, but I was sure Gayle next door would soon be asking. I unlocked the front door to let him in.

"Good morning, Anne," he said cheerfully.

Oh boy, I wondered to myself as I let him in. Cheery was not what I expected from an officer of the law.

"Well, I just wanted you to know that we have Steve Simon under arrest right now." Oh, my! My relief was instant.

"We picked him up last night, almost by accident," he started to explain. "He was causing a fight in a bar and the police were called in. When he was booked across the river, I went over to question him. Under the influence, I think he rather incriminated himself by responding rather violently when I mentioned you. I asked to see his vehicle. He agreed, and there happened to be a notebook inside—a notebook that had pages like the paper notes you have been receiving."

"Wow, I guess it really was him." I tried to absorb it all. "Now what?"

"We have several things to charge him with and may need your testimony at some point if it goes to court. I hope you still want to press charges. I don't think you'll be having any more trouble. If you do, then there's something else going on here."

"Thanks so much." My gratitude was genuine. "I know you have much more serious crimes to attend to, so thanks for everything you've done."

"No problem, Anne," he said, putting a small notebook in his pocket. "It's my job. Sometimes these small cases turn into big ones, and I'm glad his behavior caught up with him. Let me know if there's anything else I can do."

As Officer Wilson walked out the door, for what I hoped was the last time, Jean and Sally drifted in. Their faces were serious and curious at the same time. I filled them in with the great news, and finally we got back to work.

I didn't want to elaborate on the subject, or the conversation would continue throughout the day, but I didn't waste any time before I called Sam. He picked up his cell and was so relieved when I gave him the news. Knowing Sam, he was going to have his own conversation with Officer Wilson in case I left anything out. I told him I had made plans with Mother for the evening since he had a meeting.

"I may stop by and see you if it's not too late."

"Well, I'm not sure you should, as she was pretty pleased that I was spending time with her and she's anxious to pin me down on some wedding details. Why don't you just call me when you get home?" Here I was again, calling the shots with Sam, I thought to myself.

"I tell you what!" He teased me with an exaggerated tone. "I hope I get used to this independent woman I'm about to marry. I'm going to have to learn there's going to be limits to my

ANN HAZELWOOD

suggestions, correct?"

"Correct, and I should have to say the same for you, right?" He laughed. "So we're really perfect for each other, correct?"

"Correct, my love as always!" He answered dutifully.

As I hung up, I wondered again how I would be willing to give up the independence that I had enjoyed my whole life. Maybe I wouldn't have to give it up too much. Indeed, how much would indeed be the question.

So far Sam was respectful of my opinion, but I also knew there would be some limitations. Aunt Julia and Mother both warned me about that. My independence was something that came between Ted and me, and I think their fears were warranted. Would I recognize my limitations before I married him? Hmmm.

CHAPTER 30

A slow day at the shop allowed me to leave right at closing time, so I picked up our favorite pizza of pepperoni, onion, and extra cheese at Pete's Pizza. Located right up the hill from Main Street, it was a convenient stop and a wonderful Italian family business in Colebridge. Pete and I had served together on various committees; he and his family continually gave back to the community. His father knew my father, so we shared many stories growing up.

On the drive home the aroma of the pizza filled my car. A solo night with Mother was becoming more and more important to her. I knew she was dreading my move out of the house; giving up her job would make her even lonelier. I could identify with her struggle to have some independence but be with others, too.

"How about a little glass of wine, Anne?"

"Oh, that really sounds good. And I'm starved. The smell was really getting to me on the drive home. Hey, I'm anxious to hear how it went at the book store. Did you really do it?" I took the glass of merlot she handed me and we immediately started picking up pieces of the still-warm pizza.

"I did, and it felt like a weight had just been lifted off of me." She took a sip of wine. "Harry understood completely. He asked if I could be on call for special things. He also asked me something else, Anne, which I am thrilled about. He asked if I would write a book review for their newsletter each month. How about that? I'm now a columnist in my late new career!"

"Oh, my word, Mother, this is really cool. You love to read and this will keep you in the know at the shop, and, I might add, you'll become famous! Do you get paid for this?"

"Yes, can you believe it?" She was becoming more excited. "It's not much, but get this—I still get my discount, and the books that I review will be free!"

"This is great!" I gave her a squeeze. "Let's have a toast to your whole new career! Here's to my famous mama!"

We clinked our glasses and laughed about the fact that one never knows what's around the corner for them in life. I teased her about the fact that she may not have time to help with the wedding and house now that she had a new career, but she assured me that it all energized her. I loved seeing her like this and knew it was a Kodak moment to file in my head for the future, when I may not have her around. She was really happy; happy for herself for a change. After we finished our pizza and cleaned off the kitchen counter, I reminded her we had a puzzle to solve downstairs.

"This is really bugging me, Mother," I said as we walked down the stairs. "I want to know what I am getting into with the Taylors. I feel like I know them already, but I sense there is a secret here, or as Jean so eloquently says, 'There is a secret sorrow going on here.'"

"Didn't we find a piece in the quilt some weeks ago that said something with the word 'affair' in it?"

"Yes, let's try to find that." We picked up the quilt top. I said, "Here is one I can remove easily. It says *please dismiss her*. It's on this light blue paper, so I'll put it with those pieces."

She nodded and said, "I did do quite a bit one afternoon last week. I didn't try to match any of them up. I can leave most of that to you all. I'm getting pretty good about taking them out very carefully. I think we have only torn a few so far. Anne, look here. Am I reading this right? I think it says *visit of Miss Abbott*. You know," she paused thoughtfully, "Abbott was my mother's maiden name."

"Yeah, sure, I know." I was intent on my pieces and not paying her much attention. "But there were probably several Abbott families in Colebridge; don't you think?"

"I really don't recall that." She shook her head. "It seemed that when we did meet an Abbott, they were not related to us. But what is a little peculiar here is that we earlier found the name Martha, remember?"

"Yes, we did," I recalled. "I remember it said something about Martha being confused, right? Let's see if we can find that."

"Maybe they knew our mother," Mother said, thinking as she spoke. "What color stationery is that on, Anne?"

"Blue," I answered, pointing with my finger. "I don't remember what color the piece 'Martha' was on. We'll have to look through them all, and if it ends up on the same line, we'll have a sentence. Oh! And maybe a clue whether or not it is our Martha Abbott!" Mother gave no reaction to my suggestion.

I worked on the quilt top some more. "Here's a nice line that says *be there again with you soon*. Ohhh, he did miss her, I suppose, and this is on blue paper, also." I pried another piece of paper loose. "Oh, I spoke too soon. Here's one on cream paper that says *story is most disturbing*. What's so disturbing? This will take forever to match all of these!" Mother just worked along quietly.

After a good hour or so, my cell phone rang. It was Sam. It seemed the time had gotten away from us in our puzzle search and I hadn't remembered that he was going to call. I went upstairs for privacy, leaving Mother to the search.

"Hi there, beautiful," he whispered in his usual charming voice.

"Hey, handsome," I answered with pleasure. "Mother and I have been in the basement working on this quilt and I can't believe it's so late. We are making some headway, though! The most unusual thing we've discovered is that we found a piece that has the name 'Abbott' on it, which is my Grandmother Davis's maiden name. Last week we found the name 'Martha,' which happens to be her first name. Weird that we found both in Mr. Taylor's letters, but it likely isn't her he's talking about."

"Too much for me to digest, my dear." He sounded uninterested. "What I want to know is if you have actually firmed up any wedding plans."

"Oh, the wedding," I laughed, knowing I had forgotten to focus on that topic. "Well, not really, but earlier this morning I told Mother that I was going to ask Sue to be my maid of honor, instead of Aunt Julia. How does that sound to you? I thought about Mia being a flower girl, but she's so young, and Sue may not want to expose her to all that."

"Sure, whatever you want. Will you be having a bridesmaid? If so; I need to think of a partner for her."

"You know, I told Mother I was thinking of my good friend Nancy Barrister who lives in Boston. You remember me talking about her and I think you've met Mr. Barrister, her father-in-law, at the funeral home, haven't you?"

"Sure," he remembered. "I have met him on different occasions. So, do you think you'll ask her?"

"I think I'm happy with just Sue, to be honest," I confessed. "I think the hassle of Nancy's being from out of town will be more time spent than what I have. Are you okay with just Jim and Sue? Do you feel we need to have either of your sisters in the wedding?"

"Not really. I'm fine with keeping it small. Like you said, dealing with folks out of town can complicate things. Don't you think we need to pick out invitations soon?"

"Yes, Mother reminded me about that," I said, feeling like a small child, neglectful of chores. "Maybe we can do that this week. What is your travel schedule?"

"I leave for Minneapolis on Thursday and come back Saturday morning. How about on Saturday afternoon to order the invitations?"

"It's a date!"

"Speaking of a date, how about we take in a movie tomorrow night?" Now Sam was sounding like my boyfriend.

"I have a merchants' meeting at five thirty, but we could go after that."

There was silence, and I knew that silence. I heard this kind of silence with Ted when I put him off with my busy schedule. I was making things be on my terms again. Before he could respond, I interrupted.

"Forget the meeting. I don't think there is anything urgent going on along the street right now. Why don't you pick me up from work? We can grab a drink at Charley's and hit the movies."

"Why don't I pick you up at work and you leave the rest of the evening up to me?"

"I like it, boss man." I kissed the phone. "I need to hang up now, is that okay?"

"See you tomorrow, sweet Annie," he said, as I heard him give me a kiss back.

I walked back down the basement stairs feeling rather good that I had given Sam the upper hand for a change.

"Guess what, Anne?" Mother said with excitement. "I think I matched something here. The *visit of Miss Abbott* lines up with this fragment that says *Martha is a confused*. They both are on blue stationary, so they have to connect somehow."

"This is getting a little bizarre," I said, observing our scattered pieces everywhere. "How will we know those parts were in the same letter? We need some help here or this will take the rest of our lives. Maybe some of the girls can come over Thursday night when Sam's out of town. Tomorrow I promised to go on a real date with him, like maybe going to the movies."

"Well, how did he manage that?" she joked.

CHAPTER 31

Getting a good night's sleep got me up early enough for a brisk walk. I loved walking in my neighborhood as much as I did along Main Street and the walking trail. I could tell stories about each and every house. I did it so frequently that at night, when I had trouble sleeping, I could envision every block, tree, and building along my route.

While I was walking, I decided I would stop by Sue's house on the way to work. I was feeling on top of the world now that I didn't have to worry about Steve appearing in my life. I was making Sam happy and Mother was delighted about her new purpose in life.

I really felt I had it all. Why me, Lord? Why was I so blessed? Especially when I was out walking, this was my time to recall my many blessings and thank him ever so bountifully. This morning I had a lot to be thankful for. I wondered if Sam prayed. We had never talked much about religion. I told myself to bring up the topic the next time we were together. I knew he believed in God, but to what extent did he practice his faith? Hmmm.

I called Sue before I left the house and she said Mia was still asleep. I brought her a Starbucks coffee and one of their low-fat blueberry muffins. She had such a cute little first-floor apartment on one of the quaint streets in mid-town Colebridge. I was pretty sure Uncle Ken and Aunt Joyce had been financially helpful to her when she decided to live here in Colebridge. It had a nice little backyard that was perfect for Muffin and now little Mia.

"Well, look here!" Sue said in surprise when she saw the Starbucks coffee. "I've been missing my regular stop there since I'm on leave from work. This is awesome. Thank you, Anne! Come, sit. I did put on some coffee when you called. Is everything okay? Mia is still asleep, so I'm sorry she won't be jumping around you like she always does! How are things going?"

"Great, Sue, things couldn't be better." I took a seat on her couch with my coffee. "I was thinking this morning how lucky I was. My day will be even better if you agree to be my maid of honor at my wedding."

"What?" she said, loud enough to wake Mia. "You can't be serious! Are you serious?"

"Of course I am!" I laughed. "You and I are cousins and friends. The offer gets better, however. Would you think about Mia being a flower girl?"

"Oh, my, we'll have to see!" She was now beaming from ear to ear. "She would be adorable, but she may not cooperate; she's very young, Anne. You know how active she is already, and she'll probably be worse by then, but so nice of you to ask."

"I'm not sure of too many more details myself as yet, but you will be partnered with Uncle Jim. I hope that's okay?"

"Of course." She calmed down and looked at me. "Did you really want Aunt Julia instead, Anne?"

"No. I like this arrangement. I want everything pretty simple. You know we're having the wedding outdoors at the park. Then, under a tent, we'll have a simple lunch. The wedding will be at eleven o'clock. Of course you know me; I am counting on a wonderful sunny day!" We laughed. "We'll have scads of flowers, of course. I may need your help at the shop to make sure we can get it all done."

"Oh, I miss helping out there. I don't know when I'll be able to free up any time, though, now having Mia and all. I bet Jean is a big help to you, isn't she?"

"Yes, and we all are growing quite fond of her and the English!"

"I am just so honored, Anne," she said. "Thank you for asking me."

"I heard there is a great Asian dressmaker that works out of Miss Michelle's," I said. "We can go there to see what might be a good style for you and maybe Mia. I just want a real simple, no-frills white dress with a few white roses. I'm not sure whether I want my dress to be long or short, but I guess I better look like the bride, right? So I'd like your dress to go with red roses. I'll be the one with white flowers standing with the tall, dark handsome man."

We both giggled with excitement, and I felt so good that I had made the right decision in asking Sue. She was indeed honored.

We spent another half hour discussing details. She was going to start a diet that very afternoon, now that she had a strong incentive. I think I may have left her happier than I was by the time I left for work. She said she and Mia would be happy to join us on Thursday in the basement if we wanted more help. We could hear Mia's tiny chatter coming from her bedroom. I took it as a sign to get on my way. My mission was accomplished.

The day was a busy one. In between the orders, I brought Jean and Sally up to date on what few wedding plans I had scraped together. Sally had some good ideas on how to use roses throughout. They were going to be the main focus since they were my favorite.

I really got them worked up when I told them how much progress Mother had achieved with the potting shed quilt. Jean felt it was no accident that she had found the name Martha in the same letter as Abbott. She made it clear she would be there Thursday evening, but Sally thought she would have to study for a test. Jean felt the quilt was somewhat her project, and if she had her druthers, she would have the quilt at her house till it was all taken apart.

"Anne, you said to remind you that John from the Colebridge Dispatch newspaper was coming," Sally whispered. "He just walked in. Should I send him back here?"

"Yes, tell him to come on back, and I'll try to finish this piece up while I talk to him about an ad."

I talked and arranged a spray of gladiolas at the same time. John knew what I wanted and, of course, tried to sell me on another promotion the paper was doing for the July 4th celebration on the street. I was doing much better with results from social networking than paper print, but I liked John and felt I could do the basic ads to keep him happy.

A last minute order of long-stemmed roses for someone's lover was a good way to end the full day. Sally and Jean had left and I knew I would have to tidy up a bit, not only in the shop but myself as well. I hadn't put on lipstick since morning. Sam was on time, as always. There were parts of his perfection that were almost aggravating at times. My day never had a routine to speak of, and my hours were never defined the way a nine-to-five office job was.

"Come on in, Mr. Dickson," I said as he walked in the front door. "I'm sorry I'm not prepared for this date night right now. Make yourself at home while I do a few things."

"Of course." He smiled and looked around for any late customers. "What can I do to help?"

"Well, you can sweep this up off the floor and put it in this can," I joked. "I had a last minute order and I made a mess. I can't have all this on the floor overnight. How was your day?"

"Busy," he said, as he moved the broom to my surprise. "I have lots to do before I leave town. I want to meet the electrician at 333 early in the morning. It appears everything is going to have to be rewired. It's just all too old and now's the time to do it."

"That all sounds very expensive." I frowned.

"Not to worry, baby," he assured me when he saw my worried look. "We have a good line of credit and it will be a good investment for us. I'm having a blast having something to work on and be proud of, if you know what I mean?" He grinned ear to ear as he cleaned up the mess.

"Yes, I think I do, Sam." I paused. "For me, it's called Brown's Botanicals. This is my baby. I created it with a seed from Father's estate and I want to make him proud. It's not all about making it financially, which is important of course, but it's the reputation I have established. I love Colebridge and Main Street. It all has to work together. I also know that I have to have a balance in my life in order to do the best job here. I want to be a player in the community and yet I want someone to love and pay attention to me; just me!"

Sam walked over to me, put his arms around my waist, and kissed me on the forehead.

"This is why I love you so much, Annie." He looked straight into my eyes. "I know how devoted you are. But you can't do it all, remember. Neither one of us can, but if we support each other, we'll have a happy life. Now can we get out of this place so I don't ruin a nice little dinner at my place?"

"Your place?" I was surprised. "What about our little movie?"

"Oh, I have a movie all planned after we have a little wine, a little salad, a little pasta, a little garlic bread, and a whole lot of loving for dessert!" Hmmm!

CHAPTER 32

Mother's mood was more than great since she had given her notice at Pointer's Book Store. I wasn't hearing about her aches and pains because she had her mind on reading material for their newsletter. Plus, she was totally engrossed in the potting shed quilt. She couldn't wait till we met tonight. She prepared a shrimp dip and tasty ham roll-ups that were my favorites.

Jean said she would bring something yummy for dessert. Mother and I skipped dinner and asked everyone to come early so it wouldn't be a late work-day night for everyone. How I was going to look nice and thin for my wedding was a challenge with all the delicious food that seemed to flourish from our kitchen on most any day of the week.

I was pleased when Mother told me that Aunt Julia was coming because I wanted to ask her about how she and Sarah could play a role in our wedding, so I was glad when they arrived first. Mother joined me as I began to fill them in on what little planning we had done for the wedding.

"Aunt Julia," I said with some hesitation, "Are you sure you're okay with me having Sue and Jim stand up with us? Mia is a question mark right now. I want you and Sarah to participate, too. I'll need someone to hand out things; like you, Sarah, and you, Aunt Julia, could make sure folks sign the guestbook and are seated in the right place. It shouldn't be hard; I'm telling you, this will be a small wedding. You'll be wearing corsages of red roses, if that's okay. I really want the two of you to be a part of the wedding party, if you know what I mean."

Their eyes were glistening and I could feel the excitement building now with such wedding chatter. This was becoming a reality, not just a passing thought for the future. How could I be this lucky? When I was little, I was afraid that if a good thing would happen, something bad might happen next. Oh, dear, they were taking a while to answer. Had I hurt their feelings?

"Actually Anne, I'm relieved you didn't pair me up with Jim," Aunt Julia confessed. "I think I would have had to tell you no. Remember, not too long ago I was planning a small wedding, too!" She wasn't smiling.

"Now, Mom," said Sarah in disgust. "Don't act like that. Anne, it's very cool that Mom and I can have a part at all. I love red roses! We'll have to start looking for new outfits! Right, Mom?" There was no question that Sarah had already pictured the whole event and loved it. Aunt Julia smiled at Sarah with approval and then at me.

"Great, it's settled," I said as I heard Jean coming in the door.

"I saw Sue parking her car, so leave the door ajar," she suggested.

We all had gathered in the kitchen to say hello and give our loaded kisses and hugs to Mia; then we went to the basement. Approaching the quilt of letters, they all marveled at how much

Mother had accomplished since the last get-together.

"After what you shared about this Martha and Miss Abbott, I suggest we have a look at just those pieces that are the same blue stationery," said Jean, looking at the quilt.

We all agreed and gave Jean the task of trying to put the blue pieces together as we looked and removed those that matched.

"Sally said to give her a ring if we find out something special," Jean said enthusiastically. "She is as jolly about this as I. She is such a good shop mate, that girl."

"That's great, and how lucky for Anne," said Aunt Julia. "Have you had any strange activity from Grandma lately?"

"Grandma?" questioned Jean.

"Thanks a lot, Aunt Julia! I haven't told Jean about her spirit and the occasional visits."

"Well, you better, if she's going to occupy this basement!" Aunt Julia suggested with a laugh.

"Is that what the stir of quilt pieces was all about, Miss Anne? If you don't want to tell me, I'll put a stick in it. Remember, in England we have spirits everywhere we go. I would really fancy hearing about the ghost or spirit as you call them. There's one at 333 Lincoln, too, from what I hear."

"Who told you there was a ghost at 333 Lincoln?" I asked her in astonishment.

"You cannot speak of 333 Lincoln to anyone without someone waffling about the place being haunted," said Jean with a laugh. "Am I right, Miss Anne?"

"That's what they say." I was quiet for a moment. "Uncle Jim said he heard the ghost was an unhappy mistress of Mr. Taylor's."

"That's right, Anne," agreed Aunt Julia.

"She may have just been a slopper," teased Jean.

"A what?" I wasn't sure I heard her correctly.

"Oh, you would maybe say a tramp or no-gooder over here."

"Albert Taylor involved with a slopper!" I announced in jest.

We all laughed as Mother began passing around the little goodies she had prepared. She was bragging about Sue's brownies to Jean and thanked Sue for making a contribution with her busy schedule.

"I'm sorry. It seems like all I ever bring is brownies," she said. "I guess a lot of moms do that. Mia likes them for sure!"

"Where is Muffin today?" I picked away at a paper on the quilt.

"We left her in her cage," Sue sighed. "I had my hands full with Mia and her toys, plus the brownies."

"Before I forget," Mother started to say. "Anne has a birthday on the 17th, so I'm inviting you all for lunch on the patio at Donna's Tea Room. The weather should be wonderful if it continues like it has been."

"It's all her idea, and that's cool, but no gifts, you all." I was somewhat embarrassed. "I have been getting enough attention, but you know how mothers are!"

"Oh, my word, this is the big three-o, right?" Sue teased.

They all chimed in with the answer, kidding me unmercifully. I would be getting married at thirty, I said in my mind, trying to ease all the joking.

"Sam's birthday is the day after the 4th of July, so I thought we'd have a little picnic supper at 333." I changed the subject. "I'm cooking up a great little surprise for him when he arrives there. Kevin is helping me with it. I'm not telling any of you guys because I really, really want it to be a surprise. Just bring a potluck dish to share. I'll let you know more details later."

"How are you coming on those pieces, Jean?" Sue asked.

"Well, these two say *of course none can compare with your muffins and strawberry jam.*"

We all laughed and decided we could have fun completing some of these silly comments. This mysterious puzzle was indeed going to have surprises.

"I wish you could find the piece that connects to *sorry she was so blunt*," begged Mother. "It's on cream paper. I wonder who was 'so blunt.'"

"I think this might work here," Jean was holding a triangular shaped piece. "Have a look at this, Sylvia. It says *regarding my being the father of her child*. It now reads *Sorry she was so blunt regarding my being the father of her child*. Is this our first complete sentence?"

"Oh, my word," said Mother. "What a bizarre and intriguing statement that is!"

"Someone told Marion that Albert was the father of her child," I repeated. "Am I hearing this right?"

"Yes." Aunt Julia walked over to see the lined-up papers.

"Can you find the next sentence, Jean?" Sue asked with increased interest. "It's on cream paper again. We'll help look for this. We found this one earlier that read *she has always been fond of me*, so we must be talking about the woman who's having his child. We need another name besides Marion."

"Oh, my gosh!" Mother paled. "We do have other names, remember?"

"What names?" asked a bewildered Sue.

"Several have been mentioned," reminded Mother. "We have a *Martha* and a *Miss Abbott*."

"You mean like our mother, Martha née Abbott?" Aunt Julia faced Mother.

"I think it's weird, too, but look at this, Julia." Mother pointed out her references on paper.

We all stopped picking pieces out of the quilt so that we could concentrate on the one letter. We were all thinking it through. "*Seeking financial help*," read Aunt Julia as she turned the pieces different directions. "This is hard."

"Here's a piece that says *we have our own little girl*," read Sarah. "Where does this one go?"

"The Taylors did have a little girl, so that makes sense," I said. "Let's get back to the other women in this letter. Are there any other women's names beside Martha and Miss Abbott?"

"This could not be our mother that he's referring to," pleaded Mother. "She didn't live around here, so he must mean someone else." We all remained open to the idea, however.

"Don't forget we found F. Scott Fitzgerald's name over here," reminded Jean. "Oh, but here we go. This piece lines up with *a couple of novels by.*"

"Well, at least that seems to go together." Sue said as she nibbled on another brownie.

"This is better than *a night on the highlands*, chimed Jean in her English dialect.

We all became hysterical with laughter. The success that we were having was primarily due to concentrating on this one cream-colored letter, bringing us closer to completing the messages. There was the added mystery of having a name similar to my grandmother's name in the letter, which made it more fun for most of us except Mother. Somehow she got very serious when her mother's name was mentioned.

Sarah was getting bored and wanted to go home. Jean said that Al would be expecting her soon. The two changes in focus began to break up the gathering.

"I don't want to leave but must," explained Jean. "Your treats were just scrummy, Miss Sylvia. Thank you ever so much. My curiosity is all awake. I will be over in my spare time to help you with this, if you don't mind."

"Stop by anytime, Jean," said Mother as we all walked up the stairs. "Thanks for the brownies, Sue, they were delicious, as always. We'll have this about ready to read the next time you all come."

With everyone gone, Mother continued to carry dishes from the basement and I cleared the kitchen counters and filled the dishwasher.

I sensed something was on her mind. I went down to see what was taking her so long with more of the dishes, and there she was, picking at the potting shed quilt.

"How would the Taylors know my mother?" she asked with concern.

"Well, that is a very good question," I gave her a hug, wanting to console her. "I have a feeling it's not our Martha Abbott that Albert is talking about."

I know I didn't convince her, but I eased her mind by making light of the subject. We both went quietly upstairs to our bedrooms. We each had lots to think about.

I hadn't heard from Sam, but he knew about my plans with everyone tonight. I always wondered what he might be doing with his spare time when he was out of town. I wondered if Uncle Jim was with him. Why did that thought make me uncomfortable? I guess Aunt Julia had had a lot of these nights wondering where her husband was. I would be glad when Sam wouldn't have to travel as much. If he got the promotion that Uncle Jim told me about, he wouldn't be leaving me as much.

My bed felt unusually good as I snuggled with my favorite pillow. Sam, Martha, Miss Abbott, and my wedding party were all names swimming in my thoughts at once. Who was who? Where would all this end and when? Hmmm.

CHAPTER 33

The best part of having my birthday on June 17th was that weather in Missouri was just about perfect. The flowers were fresh and had had plenty of rain. Roses were popping up all over. The Knock Out roses, as they were known commercially, were perfect for Main Street. Wooden floral barrels were placed on each block corner and lush hanging baskets of mixed flowers hung from the gaslights. They were so beautiful. We still might have a few cool nights, but not yet the heat of a grueling Missouri summer. It would be a lovely day, no doubt.

Sam was back in town, and everyone seemed to look forward to having lunch on the patio at Donna's Tea Room. The month also held memories of my father; his birthday had been the 28th of June. When I was very young, he would give me a dollar on my birthday as a fun gift. I cherished it until I chose to give it back to him as a gift on his birthday. He would tease me that he got to spend the dollar nearly all year and I had just eleven days. I knew how special

I was to him. Mother loved to remind me of this story. I don't think he ever had a cross word to say to me; however, a certain look on his face warned me of any concerns he might have had.

It was a Sunday morning, which worked out great for everyone to be available for lunch. I got up and decided I'd take my morning walk along the river instead of through the neighborhood. When I came down the stairs to tell Mother I was leaving, she greeted me as though I was ten years old.

"Good morning, birthday girl," she said as she gave me a kiss. "I can't believe my baby is thirty years old! Look at all you have accomplished in those thirty years! I am so proud of you. I want to give you my card and gift this morning—otherwise, I would tear up in front of the others like mothers do. So here, take a minute before you leave."

I was still plenty sleepy and not ready for any excitement. I sure wasn't ready for any birthday activity. I sat down with some reluctance at the counter where she had a cup of coffee poured for me. Just watching her enjoy the moment was giving me much more pleasure than what was happening.

I was taught to open the card first before the present, so I did. It was touching and made me tear up a bit. Then I looked at the small package wrapped in white with a red bow, as she had wrapped so many of my gifts over the years. When I carefully unwrapped it, I saw a lovely diamond ring.

"What is this about, Mother?" I asked in astonishment.

"Don't be alarmed, but I wanted you to have the ring that Grandmother Davis left me from her mother," she explained with pride. "You probably don't recognize it, but I had it resized and cleaned for you. The jeweler had to replace a small diamond that had come out on the side, but it is the same ring." She paused to hug me. "I never felt comfortable wearing it for fear I would lose it. After your father died, I never got dressed up enough to even think of wearing it. It is worth quite a bit more today than back then! I know you love pearls, Anne, but this is very special, and I would feel so much better if you had it."

"Oh, Mother." I shook my head in disbelief. "I don't know what to say. It's so beautiful! I don't know if I even knew you had this. Look at how it sparkles! I don't think I'll be able to wear this. What if something should happen to it?"

"Yes, you will wear it well, my dear," she said reassuringly. "You and Sam are going to have a nice lifestyle and will go to wonderful places where you can put this on and feel like a million dollars! I'm so glad you like it. I can rest easier, knowing you have it."

I hugged her with all my strength and tears flowed freely in gratitude. I was so touched by how much thought she had put into this generous gift. I thought I had been overwhelmed by my engagement ring, but this was different—so full of tradition and responsibility. It fit perfectly and I would cherish it forever.

"I guess I can't dig in the dirt or cut flowers with this on my finger, can I?" I joked. "Wait until Sam sees this."

"Anne, can I ask you not to wear it to the luncheon today?" Mother had a mysterious look on her face. "I don't know how your Aunt Julia will react. You never know how she might take such a thing. She always claims she is the black sheep of the family, and frankly, she may not know I had this ring from Mother. I think we all got some of Mother's jewelry when she died, but I don't remember what everyone received. I know when Mother gave me this she made it very clear to tell me who it was from and that it was worth a lot of money. I always thought I would keep it in a safe place, and if times ever got hard, I would have the ring to turn to. I think that was her way of telling me that I had some security."

"Thanks, Mother, I understand. I will take great care of this and I'll never forget this birthday, for sure! I'm going to put it back in this box, put it in a safe place in my room, and get on with my walk. It may be my security as well, Mother—you never know! You have really made my day!" We hugged again.

My walk along the river, through the neighborhood, or wherever I walked each morning was my time to have conversations with my Maker. I had much to thank Him for on my special birthday, and promised Him I would not request too many things for the days ahead. It was a time to clear my head, cry my tears, and plan what might be in store for me. I knew that no matter what my task was or where I traveled, my God was with me. I never was alone.

When people would ask if I had a lonely childhood as an only child, I never quite knew what they were referring to. I had a big imagination as a child, and I knew there was a God who was always with me. The security of loving parents was something a lot of people didn't have, so I knew I was lucky. I stopped for a moment to pick a fuzzy ball stem from a dandelion. All my life, I could never resist blowing them out with "He loves you, he loves you not." I would repeat the phrase until the fuzz was gone. Yup, he loves me, thank goodness!

The Missouri River was slowly rising, which always was a threat this time of year following the northern thaws. It roared so strongly and it was muddy as usual, but I loved it. There was nothing like nature's beauty to keep things in perspective. I saw more Queen Anne's Lace growing along the path, and thought of how beautiful they truly were. I then thought of the sweet young bride at the shop who had wanted them for her wedding. She loved the way they took to the color and it made me happy to be a part of such a momentous occasion.

It was also a lesson in life to watch the regular walkers here each day. I wondered what was on their minds, and if they were troubled or happy. One day I saw a young man bring his father, who was in a wheelchair, to see the river. I wondered if the father used to walk here every day as I did, but now he couldn't. I hoped someone would bring me here some day if I were not able. The river's edge was my church, and I would miss its presence in my life.

Oh, my gosh! Time had flown and I had to get home to shower for the big birthday lunch. "Thank you for my thirty years," I prayed, looking up to the sky.

There was quite a chatty bunch at a long table under the shade trees when I made my appearance. Birthday greetings came from family and friends, including Donna, who always made our family occasions so special. In the center of the table was a beautiful, white-iced chocolate cake decorated with very tiny red roses.

Jean and Sally had arranged lovely tussie mussies for everyone's place setting, and they presented me with a lovely red rose corsage to make me feel extra special. We all laughed, gossiped about our potting shed quilt, and passed around the silly and precious little gifts they all had brought despite my request that they not.

The color red was always on people's minds when it came to things I liked. Mother gave me the *Joy of Cooking* red-checked cookbook, which generated a huge laugh from my family who knew me so well. The lunch was as much fun for them as for me, no doubt.

"We need to send home cake with all of you," I suggested. "I'm going to be adding more calories tonight when Sam takes me to dinner, so please help me out here." Donna brought out take-home boxes for those who might take us up on the offer.

Many agreed to do so, especially Sarah, who already had enjoyed a couple of pieces. Mia had been left with a neighbor of Sue's so she could enjoy her lunch, but she was anxious to get back to her. I wanted to stop by 333 to see if Sam might be working, so

I said my good-byes as the last one left. Leaving to go to my future home would make my day complete.

When I drove up the hill, I could see some clearing had been done to install a gate of some kind. I had mixed feelings about keeping us so snug and cut off at the top of the hill. I didn't see Sam's car, so I had the place of love and beauty all to myself. I couldn't think of a better place to spend part of my day.

My arrival at 333 Lincoln was always focused on the yard itself as I approached the house and then the potting shed. The house was to the right of the road and the last to get my attention. I think part of it was because it was now the time of year when the gardens and yard were alive and well. It was now clear which of the plants and shrubs were not able to return and would need removing.

I first checked on how my herb bed was doing. I pulled a few weeds and admired the growth. I wanted to take some of the mint home to Mother to use in her iced tea.

Then I went to the area where I wanted the gazebo built for Sam's birthday. I wanted it to be custom made so that we could have dinners and lunches there. I wanted a round table in the center and the edges lined with benching, plus window boxes built around the railing for color. I knew it was a risk in Sam approving of it all, but I had decided to go ahead, knowing this house was half mine.

The potting shed was calling my name. I opened the door and knew at once there was something different about it. It was then I saw new gardening tools with dark green handles that were hung in place along a wooden strip above one of the counters. I had never had proper gardening tools of my own—just odds and ends from this and that, which worked fine for my needs. This must be my birthday present from Sam, I thought. He knew this place would be my haven, so how cool was this?

I picked one of them up and imagined what it might be used for. As I admired each tool, I wondered where the few old rusty ones had gone. Some of those were left here by the Taylors; I would have liked to have kept them. Surely Sam would not have thrown them away.

I watered the potted plants, told them I loved them, and then glanced at my watch to see that once again today, time had gotten away from me. Off I ran.

Sam was all dressed up in a wonderful suit and blue-striped tie when he picked me up for dinner. This man was so handsome, I reminded myself again. Mother was gone, so I suggested that we first have a drink and sit on the front porch and enjoy the nice weather.

I was wearing an off-white pantsuit with gold jewelry. I placed my hand close to Sam but he didn't pick up on my new ring. When I decided to show him, holding up my hand, his eyes opened wide as I explained its history. Sam was silent and then shared how much he admired such family traditions. So far, no word on how gorgeous it happened to be.

"Your mother is very special," Sam said with admiration. "I have a feeling she will make a wonderful mother-in-law. This ring is sure going to make my gift pretty insignificant. I hope you'll like this."

He took a small package from his coat pocket and presented me with a daintily wrapped box. I was a bit confused by the box and wasn't expecting another gift besides the tools. I removed the paper slowly, not saying anything other than telling him he shouldn't have gone to the expense. Lo and behold, it was a gold necklace with a small pearl that had the same gold rim as my engagement ring.

"Oh, Sam, this is precious! I will certainly be coordinated on our wedding day." I smiled and kissed him. "This is pretty over the top considering all the other gifts you've given me. I went to 333 today and found your surprise in the potting shed."

"Oh, and what would that be?" he asked with a puzzled look on his face.

"Well, I love them first of all," I said, smiling. "I will indeed use all of them!"

"I'm sorry, Annie." Sam really looked confused "Use all of what? I'm not following you."

I told him about walking into the potting shed and seeing all the new tools hanging there for me. He looked even more puzzled and his face mirrored more than mystery.

"You can see why I guessed it was you, don't you?" I was confused by his confusion. "Who else would know what I like? And who else would go into the shed? Who would take the time to hang everything so nicely for me? I really love it, honey, but the only thing that makes me wonder is—where did the Taylors' tools go? Some were quite old and part of the charm and history of the family and house. They were working pretty well for me, even though they were dull and quite dirty, of course."

"This is pretty serious." Sam got up and put his hands on his hips. "I did not give you new tools, my dear, but I appreciate your appreciation to that effect. I want to go by there and see for myself before we go to dinner. Are you sure none of your family would have had this done for you?"

"Hardly!" Now I didn't know what to think. "I got all my gifts from them today at lunch, and no one mentioned anything about gardening tools! Finish your wine first. The tools aren't going anywhere. Hey, maybe this Steve guy decided to make it up to me by doing something nice and helpful." I could joke about him now that he'd been arrested.

"This isn't funny, sweet Annie. We've got to check out the giver and hope they had a right to be on our property! That being said, I'm happy you like my real gift and I am all about you having a happy birthday!" He kissed me deeply. "Now," he said while I caught my breath, "Let's get some food. I'm starved!"

CHAPTER 34

It was hard to concentrate on our dinner at Q Seafood and Grill. I was quite amused by the anonymous gift of gardening tools, but Sam was not. I told myself to drop the subject and just enjoy the evening, but Sam couldn't seem to move on despite our drinks being delivered.

"Have you had any other mysterious experiences at 333 that you haven't told me about, Annie?" He looked straight into my eyes. "You don't suppose this has anything to do with the haunted stories that people tell us about, do you?"

"If it is the ghost of 333 Lincoln, she likes me," I smiled, trying to get him to lighten up. "I get good feelings there. I think the spirits like us. I've already talked to it—or them—a time or two when I've been alone. Who wouldn't like how we are making 333 come alive?" I sipped my merlot.

"After all," I continued, "Uncle Jim said he heard it was an unhappy mistress who kept the place haunted. The Taylors are

209

gone now. The mistress wouldn't have a bone to pick with us. I think we'll be able to find out who she was in time. It might be revealed in one of the letters of Mr. Taylor that we are trying to put together."

"Anne, if you do discover who she is, then what?" This told me he could believe in such activity, which surprised me.

"Knowledge is power, they say," I quoted Sir Francis Bacon. "Once we know the players, we have nothing to fear." I looked right at Sam. "I want 333 to be a happy place. I want our children to run around, play hide-and-seek, have picnics and parties with their friends. I want to grow old there working in my potting shed. I want to see Brown's Botanicals grow and perhaps pass it on to family. I want us to snuggle and cuddle on a wicker couch on that south porch. I want to write my famous novel there and have lemonade cocktails every evening at five thirty like the Taylors did. I want Colebridge to love and admire the Taylor house so that someday they will call it the Dickson Estate. Am I foolish and naïve, Sam?"

"My dear Annie, I think this is a marvelous dream and could quite possibly become a reality for us," he smiled as he put his arm around me. "I'm so glad you mentioned the children again, because I can actually see them running around catching butterflies. I think we share that dream, Annie, especially the idea of the 'Dickson estate.' I guess it's why I love you so very much. Happy birthday, my sweet!"

Later, Sam reluctantly took me home and we saw that the lights were still on in my house. Mother usually retired right after the ten o'clock news. I couldn't help but be concerned, so I asked Sam to come in the house with me. When we were inside I called her name and she responded from the basement. I felt at ease then and thought she was probably at work on the quilt.

"What are you doing up so late, Mother?" We joined her downstairs.

"I am so close to having this one letter completed that I just couldn't stop, if you know what I mean." She sounded frustrated. "Oh, hello Sam. Forgive me for not getting up. I don't know if I'm going to discover what I'm thinking, or perhaps this quilt is just getting to me."

"Well, it's getting late, Mother," I cautioned. "Maybe it would be better to call it a night and see what the morning perspective has on this."

"You kids leave me alone and enjoy a glass of wine or something," she said, not looking up from the quilt. "Did you have a nice birthday dinner?"

"Oh, yes! Look what Sam gave me. Won't this be perfect to wear with my wedding dress?"

"Ah, Sam," she admired my necklace. "This is so sweet and lovely. It's a match to the ring, isn't it?"

"Well, it was hard to compete with your generous gift, Sylvia," Sam joked. "That ring is amazing. I just hope she doesn't get robbed when she wears it."

"I told you I'd wear it only on special occasions," I laughed. "Tonight was certainly one of them. Mother, I told Sam we would like to celebrate his birthday on the 4th of July at 333 Lincoln, and by golly, I think I convinced him."

"Well that's great, you guys. It will keep you focused on getting some things done over there," she was still engaged with her seam ripper.

"You're right about that," Sam was emphatic. "If you're serious about that party, Anne, we've a lot to get done in the next two weeks to make 333 presentable. It'll be nice to have at least the bathrooms done. They have them walled out, so it probably won't take them too long. They may not have the finish work done, but they should be functioning."

"Sam, everyone will just love being there." Mother finally got up from her seat. "I think you should put us all to work that day and then let everyone enjoy your birthday food. Anne, did you say Kevin would barbecue for everyone?"

"Yes, and everyone will bring a dish to share." I was so happy, picturing it all. "It will be quite an old-fashioned picnic. Just leave it all to your fiancée, Mr. Dickson. You better get used to having a social director around."

"Okay, I'm becoming outnumbered here," Sam said as he headed towards the stairs. "I'll leave the two of you alone on your quest."

I followed him up the stairs to the door and kissed him with as much gratitude as I could. It was a grand birthday. Next year this time, we'd be having those lemonade cocktails on the porch and blowing out my birthday candles! I could hardly wait.

As I stood daydreaming by the door, Mother finally came up the stairs to call it a night.

"I hope to sleep on what I uncovered tonight and see if I can make some sense out of it all." She shook her head with frustration.

"We have lots of time to figure it all out, my dear Mother." I kissed her on the cheek. "You always said 'Tomorrow's another day,' and it will ring true for our potting shed quilt."

CHAPTER 35

Because I awoke extra early, I decided to drive over to my future neighborhood and take my walk on Lincoln Street. I might as well figure out a walking route, I told myself. I was also curious to get closer to the Brody house; it seemed to be our nearest neighbor. I wasn't sure if I would have to access it from the street or if I would have to cut across some trees and brush from behind our house.

I put on my walking clothes and shoes and went quietly down the stairs hoping not to disturb Mother. I would probably be back before she awoke. I stopped at Starbucks to get my usual coffee and proceeded to 333 to park my car. None of the workers had arrived yet. The early air and sunlight showing behind the clouds made my arrival seem special and quiet. As I got out of the car, I glanced at the porch where I knew I would be having my coffee each morning.

I walked to the back of the house and looked to see how I

could get from our house to the small cottage called the Brody house. The trees and bushes looked to be too challenging, plus I remember Sam warning me about poison ivy this time of year. I decided I would go down to the street and approach the Brody house from there. I walked a good block and then saw a gravel road that curved toward what had to be my destination.

It didn't sit as high as the Taylors' house, I observed, when I saw the cottage in full view. It reminded me more of a summer kitchen that would have been behind a mansion somewhere. It had a small front porch with two rusty 1950s-style metal lawn chairs on each side of the door. I wondered if knocking on the door at this early hour would scare the owner. I saw an older car parked in back of the house, which meant it was probably Miss Brody's and she was at home. I thought I'd better go and knock just in case she was already watching me out the window. I knocked on the door lightly and stood for a few seconds before it opened to a crack.

"Good morning, Miss Brody," I called out. "I'm your future neighbor, Anne Brown. I know I'm calling at an early hour, but I was out taking my walk and thought I would say hello."

She opened the door wide enough for me to see a small elderly lady with uncombed gray hair, but she was fully dressed for the day. She had an old-fashioned apron on; I remembered seeing one like it on my grandmother. I knew she was being cautious and I knew better than to expect to be invited in the house.

"I hear a lot of commotion over there," she said in a shaky voice. "I'm Evelyn Brody, but you probably already know that." I wasn't sure how to respond to the remark, so I ignored it.

"Do you have time to sit out here and visit a bit?"

"I do have some coffee made," she said as her face perked up. "I'm an early riser, too. Have a seat out there, if you don't mind those dirty chairs. I'll bring you a cup."

"You're so kind but I already had my cup for the day, which is my limit, I'm afraid. That's very nice of you though." I moved to one of the chairs and sat. "How long have you lived here, Mrs. Brody?"

"It's Miss Brody, ma'am," she clarified, as she sat down on one of the chairs. "It was just me and my brother living here until he died five years ago. The place has gotten away from me as I just can't do what I used to do. My nephew comes and mows the yard for me when he has time."

"Well, I think it's great that you can still live alone." I tried to sound encouraging. "May I ask you a few questions about the Taylor house next door?" I found my voice getting louder, in case she was hard of hearing like most older folks.

"I didn't know them like some people did in Colebridge," I continued. "My fiancé Sam and I will be getting married in September. He's the one who found the house and fell in love with it. I now love it also, especially since I found the potting shed. I love flowers and have a little flower shop on Main Street. I bet it was a very beautiful home at one time."

"Yes, that it was, but Mr. Taylor was not happy 'bout my brother and me living here." She made an unfriendly face. "He kept trying to buy our place, you see, but we kept sayin' no. I'm sure he thought we were a disgrace to his big house and all, but this is our home and all we had. Mrs. Taylor was never rude to us, but then I'm sure he told her not to talk to us."

"Did they just have one child?" I hoped to lighten the topic.

"Yes, just the one girl, but there were always rumors, of course."

How would she know about any rumors living way up here from civilization? This could be interesting! Hmmm.

"What do you mean by that?" I wanted her to continue.

"Well, Mr. Taylor was quite a ladies' man, and often they would

215

say things about him like he may have fathered others. You know how folks talk, especially about rich people. And they always said the place was haunted, which doesn't surprise me none."

"Well, yes, we've heard that." I was anxious to hear more. "We've not seen or heard from any ghosts yet, but we know older places like this can have such things. Do you believe in ghosts?"

"Well, my brother, who never told a tale in his life, said one man told him the ghost would repeat some woman's name; can't recall now what it was." Miss Brody was whispering like she was telling me a secret. "The house has been for sale a long time, but as soon as anyone gives it a look, ghost lady does her part and they don't come back. My brother and I would just laugh. We just figured the place would stay empty the rest of our lives, anyway."

What "part" does the ghost lady do, I wondered? A woman's name—how interesting. Now I knew we *had* to find out who she was if I was going to have complete peace at 333 Lincoln. Why hadn't this ghostly woman's voice spoken to Sam and me? Or why hadn't she tried to scare us in some other way?

To Miss Brody I said, smiling with confidence, "I'm not too worried. I feel she might like us. I had a mysterious good thing happen there recently. I don't know if she had anything to do with it or not, but I can't explain it any other way. Sam and I have good feelings about the house and want to make it beautiful again. Before I forget to ask, is there a path or road between our houses? I keep feeling there has to be."

"Yes, you're darn right about that feeling, but it's gotten pretty grown over since my brother died." She had started speaking normally but then went back into a secretive whisper. "Mr. Taylor didn't like us being able to use it. It's not a real road. It's just a path with the best blackberry patches you can imagine. They should be about ripe by now." Her voice got stronger. "I haven't had any of them since my brother passed. He used to love to surprise me with those berries when I least expected it. It's just too hard for me to get out and get 'em. I don't go anywhere much. My nephew doesn't like me driven by anyone but him."

"Miss Brody, you can come see us anytime." I hope I sounded neighborly. "I'll be happy to come get you anytime. You have a phone, don't you? I grew up with neighbors being an important part of our lives and we were always helping one another. Let me know if there is anything we can do for you. I'll put one of my cards in your mailbox on the street if you need to get hold of us."

"That's mighty kind of you, Miss Brown." She broke into a smile. "I don't have a phone anymore; no need. My nephew just comes by when he can to check on me and he's good about bringing groceries. He pretty much knows what I need. When you're home as much as me, you see a lot of things being on higher ground like our houses are. I look forward to seeing your progress over there. I used to love my flowers, too, but I can't tend them any longer. Some keep comin' up though!" She was still smiling when I said my good-bye.

I walked back down to the street. It felt and looked like a different part of Colebridge that I had never seen. It was as if time had stood still on this part of the hill and the rest of Colebridge kept on going. I could see why Mr. Taylor wanted to own their property, but I also felt like the Brodys had every right to their place called home. I went to my car and got out a business card from my purse to put in her mailbox. I couldn't even imagine not having a phone! I still felt she needed our contact information. Time was passing quickly and I needed to head home to shower.

"Well, you got an early start this morning!" Mother yelled from the kitchen when I came in the door.

"I went to walk on Lincoln Street and ended up checking out

the Brody house that's about a block away." I joined Mother for a half cup of coffee, testing my one-cup limit. "She was pretty pleasant and obviously quite lonely. We sat for awhile on her front porch and she gave me another hint about the ghost that might be at 333. She said that someone claimed they would hear a woman's name whispered in the house. Isn't that something? We have got to find out about her. Do you think you could finish at least one of those letters today?"

"Oh dear," Mother said with a sigh. "I'm sure you'll be hearing that name soon, if it's true. The name 'Martha' in those letters really bugs me, Anne. I guess it's because it was my mother's name. I'll do my best to get back to it, but I have to do a few errands this morning." She walked away, truly taken with the mystery.

As I showered, I knew what one of my missions was going to be when I went back to 333 again. I wanted to find those blackberries on the overgrown path and take Mrs. Brody a nice basketful!

CHAPTER 36

Mother stopped by the shop around two o'clock to make sure I was coming home for dinner. She was a good customer of the spice shop across the street, so she popped her head in to say hello to us at the same time. She was also anxious to tell us that she was about to complete one letter and had progressed on others. I was curious to know more, but I couldn't give her a time when I would be home. Sam had told me he was spending his afternoon at 333, so I didn't know if he was expecting me there or to meet up with him later.

Main Street was very busy and we were getting some of the walk-in traffic. Sally was working the front counter while Jean and I tried to finish up some arrangements that were going to be picked up by Trinity Church. Mother saw that we were busy and went on home.

When Jean heard that a letter was about to be completed, she chattered with excitement. "I'll probably be home at some point, if you want to stop by tonight," I said, knowing she was eager to be in on whatever was found.

"I surely would appreciate that, Miss Anne," she said as she stopped her work. "I collect we'll solve something soon enough. Sally told me about your visit to the Brody house. There's a connection here with that ghost, Miss Anne. I think it may be one of the names we found in the letters."

"Jean, I, for one, have not ruled out that 'Martha' may be my grandmother. Just because she didn't live around here doesn't mean she didn't know Albert Taylor at some moment in time. If they did know each other, my grandmother would have had to be pretty young. No sense in thinking about it further until we have proof. Anyway, seven o'clock should be a good time, if you want to stop by, but I'm sure Mother won't care when."

"Won't care about what?" Sally joined us in the work room.

"I told Jean she could come by tonight since we have a letter completed."

"You do?" Sally asked with excitement. "Can I stop by? We have a short class tonight and I'm dying to see what you've learned. I've been thinking about Martha all day. I wonder if the ghost whispers her name or yells it out loud. How spooky it must be to hear that! If it's true, that is."

"You guys are nuts!" I joked as they all laughed. "You're right: 'If it's true' is a big consideration here. Show up anytime. I have to pay some bills yet and don't know how long that will take, but they'll be turning my electricity off if I put them off any longer. I haven't heard from Sam about meeting tonight, but I'll be there sometime."

I called Mother to tell her I still didn't know my schedule but that by seven o'clock we could expect Sally and Jean to join us. She said we would have bacon, lettuce, and tomato sandwiches because of the great tomatoes she picked up at the farmer's market down by the river. That sounded good and would keep nicely till I got home. I called Sam on his cell and had to leave a message. I was hoping to have time to drive by 333 to see if he was there, but I was running late as it was. Just then my cell phone rang.

"Hey, are you still there working?" Sam sounded anxious.

"I'm about to leave here but Mother is expecting me. Jean and Sally are coming over," I explained. "I was hoping to stop by 333 but I'm running late. Are you still there?"

"Yes, but it's getting dark. I was going to call and see if you wanted to get a bite to eat."

"How about eating a big fat, juicy, bacon, lettuce, and tomato sandwich?"

"That sounds great!" I could hear Sam's mouth water. "Where do I find one of those?"

"Meet me at the Brown residence," I said with a big grin on my face. "Mother says that it would be our supper and I'm inviting you!"

"Count me in," he smiled through the phone. I did love his smile! "Meet you there shortly."

Mother was frying bacon as Sam and I arrived together, surprising her in the kitchen. That smell was like no other. Mother used to fix eggs and bacon for my father most mornings; now it was a wonderful memory smell that I missed. She was very pleased to see Sam and started bragging about the great tomatoes she purchased. I went and changed into jeans while they started layering the sandwiches. We had begun eating at the kitchen table when Jean arrived. She asked for a half a sandwich until she found out how delicious they were.

"You are spoiling your future son-in-law, Mrs. Brown," teased Sam.

"This is bloody good, Miss Sylvia," Jean said. "It's the best fry-up I've had in a long time! But I just can't wait to get downstairs and have a look at what's come together."

"Well, then we'll have dessert later," suggested Mother. "So you think Sally will be here soon?"

"Sure, Mother, but you don't have to wait for her." I hoped they would go on downstairs. "This is so cool having you here, Sam. Please don't leave yet. I want to fill you in on my visit to our neighbor, Miss Brody."

When we were alone, I filled him in on my early morning visit to the Brody house. He listened intently as we cleaned up the kitchen. I knew that he was calculating something in his mind, but I didn't know what exactly.

"Sam, I need to find those blackberries and take her some," picturing them in my mind.

"I think I know exactly where they are," he said, kissing my forehead. "They're probably ready to be picked about now. That would go a long way to being neighborly, my sweet Annie. It's mighty nice of you to think of doing that."

We joined the others in the basement. Mother and Jean were picking out more pieces from the quilt to match the other rescued pieces attached to the sticky boards. Their faces were so intent, as though they were preparing for major surgery. Sam seemed amused by the system we had designed to corral the messages attached to the potting shed quilt.

The doorbell rang, signaling Sally's arrival. Sam went to answer the door and brought her down the stairs in time for the evening's important highlight.

"It's time for me to read the blue letter," Mother announced, taking a deep breath.

None of us wanted to sit. Sally didn't even put down her purse.

We were all anxious to hear it read and urged Mother to go ahead.

"Some of these words were cut, but I think I have most of this figured out," she began.

"Dearest Marion, he says, "I arrived safely at the Prince Albert Hotel. How appropriate is that? How are my little tomatoes? I miss you both very much. My heart is breaking about the disturbing visit of Miss Abbott. Martha is a confused young woman. Please dismiss her story about bearing my child. I feel I am not able to defend myself from such a distance. Please console your tears and concern until my return. This small but elegant hotel is like no other I have seen in America. London has been dark and rainy since my arrival. The sun is probably shining in Colebridge and you are enjoying lemonade on the south porch. I will count the days to be there with you again soon. Love most heartedly, Albert."

"So Miss Abbott went to Marion and claimed she was carrying Albert's child," I said with uncertainty. "Do I understand this right? He has used 'Miss Abbott' and 'Martha' in the same reference. That's huge, Mother. How many 'Martha Abbotts' could there be in this world? He is pretty light-hearted about this news, don't you think? He right away starts talking about the hotel and the weather, for goodness sake." She made no comment.

"That poor soul," said Jean.

"Are you ready for most of the cream letter?" Mother had dread in her voice

"Are they dated?" Sally asked.

"It doesn't appear these two letters have one," she answered. "This also begins with Dearest Marion, Once again you need not be concerned about your visit from Miss Abbott. I assure you that this story is most disturbing and certainly not true. Please put aside your thoughts. She is probably seeking financial help by simply claiming our acquaintance. You must not worry, as we have our *own family for which we are concerned. I am sorry she was so blunt regarding me being the father of her child.*

She has always been fond of me. She even expressed so a time or two. If she is so determined to give up her little baby girl for adoption, she should do so, as we have our own little girl. I am told my mission here will be longer than I like. In my spare time I have been reading till the late hours of the night. Miss Milly has given me a couple of novels by F. Scott Fitzgerald. She is also a very good cook. This is all I have done on this letter, however there is a piece telling about her muffins and strawberry jam, remember?"

"He is disgusting," Sally immediately responded. "It sounds like she did or was about to put her little girl up for adoption because he wouldn't fess up to being the father. When he says, 'She has always been fond of me,' he is pretty much saying that he has known her and she has expressed her feelings to him. I think we can dismiss the idea that Miss Milly is the one having his child." Everyone murmured agreement except Mother.

"I guess it's just about their baby girl." Sam joined in with serious interest. "To heck with another baby girl that is probably his! What a man! It sounds like the topic of Martha Abbott is not going away, even though he tries to change the subject in each letter. That's how I read this anyway."

"Grandmother never put any baby girl up for adoption, so it can't be her," Mother said with certainty.

The room fell silent. We were all thinking. I was not as certain as Mother that we could rule out her mother. Who would be bragging about doing such a thing, especially in that day and time? There were many secrets back then. I could, however, understand that she didn't want to think of her mother as being a part of anything like this.

"Well, this gives us all something to think about as we finish up the other letters," Mother said as she started up the stairs. "I have a nice peach cobbler and coffee perking if anyone is interested."

Everyone *was* thinking, and it wasn't about peach cobbler. Most of our thoughts were not happy ones, by the look on everyone's face. We went up the stairs quietly.

Sam wasn't about to turn down the cobbler, so he ate my fair share. I was deep in thought, and decided it was going to have to be me, not Mother, who would find out if we were talking about my Grandmother Davis.

CHAPTER 37

I was starting to feel overwhelmed with all the responsibilities mounting up—seeing Sam, planning his birthday party and our wedding (oh, my gosh!), gardening, being an attentive daughter, and running my flower shop. Business was good, which meant more work but higher payroll. Jean and Sally were pretty much fulltime now so that I could devote time to my other responsibilities.

With Sam still dealing with a heavy travel schedule, I had become the contact person for many of the contractors at the house. I was starting to enjoy those demands, though, such as coordinating color combinations for the various rooms. The house was becoming more and more personal. My independent streak was useful now as I acted as "the woman of the house."

The bathrooms were the priority, by order of Sam, so they would be functioning for his birthday next week. He had thought of everything in making them bigger, adding another, and choosing gorgeous fixtures fit for a king and queen, as he put it.

Mother was actually helpful to me in picking out accessories that I had not thought of before. Sam had the kitchen remodeling under control because of his love for cooking; he was satisfying his "wish list" for the perfect kitchen.

As I saw the restoration evolve, I cringed at what it might mean financially for both of us. I couldn't tell if Sam had a budget or not. I would have to have a serious conversation about this with him before our marriage. He was counting on promotion as soon as a year from now, and had assured me the increase in salary would easily take care of 333 Lincoln. But could we take that to the bank?

As I opened the door of the shop to begin another day, the fluff from the cottonwood trees on the riverfront had taken over Main Street like the white snow of winter. I used to be allergic to it, but in recent years I seemed to handle their annoyance. Main Street would soon have the 4th of July festival and all the fireworks. Thousands of people would descend into our area.

There were always unhappy shop owners after this event, or, frankly, any other event. The preservationists didn't want to share this public property with anyone. Other shop owners wanted the business on the street regardless. Most were paying high rent, and for them, the income was necessary. Many landlords were caught in the middle, therefore this battle would most likely continue. We needed a balance of both, but few were willing to admit that.

I, too, was guilty of claiming this beautiful riverfront as my own. If my shop had included an apartment above, I would be living on Main Street for sure. My attic would not do; plus I needed it for storage. I did have an amazing view out the attic's front window, though. I had often thought I would clear a spot in front of that window and prop myself there to write when the winter months were dreary. I loved writing in different places. They all inspired me in various ways. My 333 journal was somewhat up to date, but that was all the writing I managed to do these days.

As I finished sweeping the fluff from the sidewalk, Sue pulled in front of the shop with her darling daughter peering out the window from her car seat. Mia grinned directly at me with a smile as if she really did remember me.

"Good morning, ladies," I greeted them. "Are you here to visit Brown's Botanicals today?"

"Yes, indeed Miss Brown," said Sue as she worked to get Mia out of her car seat. "I need to place an order for Mom and Dad's wedding anniversary. I thought a personal visit might be more fun than ordering on the phone or the web."

"Come here you precious thing." I took Mia from Sue's arms. "I have a pretty flower for you. Come inside and look for it with me."

"I heard you had quite a revelation at your house the other night with a couple of those letters," Sue said as she looked in the cooler for a centerpiece. "I can't wait to see them."

"Oh, indeed Sue." I put Mia down to explore the empty shop. "I was thinking of giving you a call. I need some advice since you are now the parent of an adopted child. Mother has strongly ruled out in her mind that the Martha Abbott in the letters could possibly be her mother. She may be right, but it isn't totally out of the question. If it is my grandmother, she gave her daughter up for adoption according to this letter. Back then, if this were to be the case, confidentiality would have been real important, so most folks would not know, right?"

"Right, but there is so much access to those records now that it could possibly be researched," she said, running after Mia, who had toddled behind the counter.

Jean and Sally now had arrived and our discussion was interrupted. All the attention was on Mia, and rightly so. She was precious, and no longer a stranger to any of us.

"Sue, I really don't have time to pursue this, but would you do me a favor and at least find out with whom and from where we could start? You met all the players when you went through your adoption with Mia. But please be discreet. Mother would kill me if she found out. She is in denial here and feels we should leave it alone. Last night I also remembered how our pieces to the letters were continually blown about everywhere. Why would that happen, I kept asking myself? Grandmother has always been active in our basement, right? If she is "the" Martha Abbott, it makes sense that she would be making it difficult for us to read about her in those letters, right? Am I crazy?"

"Oh Anne, you make a very good point," said Sue, now holding Mia. "It is pretty crazy, and I sure don't think Aunt Marie would be mischievous like that. I just thought it was Grandmother playing with us again, but you're right; this could have been for a reason. I'll do what I can, Anne, but I have my hands full, too, so I don't know when I can start checking it out." She shifted Mia to her other hip. "Hey, are you forgetting we have a wedding sneaking up in this family? We need to get our dresses made, don't you think?"

"Sure, you set it up and I'll make it happen," I joked, not really wanting to think about the wedding right now. "You mentioned having a shower for me, Sue, but please, please keep it simple and small. There's hardly anyone invited to the wedding, so I sure don't want to mislead anyone by inviting them to a shower."

"Well, I am going to call Mrs. Dickson and see when she and the sisters can make it," she said as Mia began to squirm in her arms.

"They may not come until the wedding, Sue. I'd love for them to come for Sam's birthday, but Helen was just here, and I doubt if his sisters will think it's that big a deal. I called Uncle Jim to get him thinking about who to ask from work."

"Oh, you don't think Uncle Jim will bring that Brenda girl, do you?" Sue asked cautiously. I put my finger up to my lips to indicate to Sue to not talk about this topic with Jean and Sally in hearing distance.

"Heavens no, Sue," I whispered. "She's married, and besides, Sam thinks that's about over anyway. I just hope Aunt Julia won't stay away because Uncle Jim will be there."

"I'll see to it she comes," offered Sue. "Mia and I will arrange to pick her up."

"Thanks so much, Sue. You're a real friend," I said giving her a little hug.

Jean joined us in the display room and asked if we had any news regarding our Miss Abbott. I no longer felt alone in my quest to find out who she really was. I told her I had researched the name in the computer; there was not a match. There was a Martha Abbott who won a spelling bee in New Hampshire. Who knows what last name she ended up with if she married anyone? We laughed and shook our heads in wonder.

Kevin had arrived and he approached me about the food details for Sam's picnic.

"Kevin, how is the gazebo coming along? It is so hard to think of a gift for someone who can buy themselves anything they want. I sure hope this was the right thing to do."

"We're in great shape," he assured me. "Well, if I could afford anything I wanted, I would have the latest technology tools available. He's a lucky guy. I think with him so engrossed in this house, he'll think this is cool. I think if you love it, he'll love it."

"You're right," I agreed as I cleared the work counter. "My case for this gazebo is that we'll have a place to have those spur-of-the-moment picnics. He's quite a romantic you know!"

"I guess giving him a quilt isn't possible," Sally chimed in jokingly. "Sorry, I just thought that would be kind of appropriate."

"I've been a little busy taking a quilt apart, not putting one together, haven't you noticed?" They all chuckled.

"You can't very well splash out on a chap like Sam, can you, Miss Anne?" Jean quipped. "It will be hard to strike his fancy."

"'Splash out,'" repeated Sally. "What on earth does that mean?"

"Well, like 'splurge,' I suppose you might say," explained Jean.

"You're so right, Jean," I nodded. "This gazebo will set me back a few bucks."

"Hey, Sam is a pretty cool dude, and he's not about how much you spend, I can tell," observed Kevin.

We got back to work. As I started creating a head table centerpiece for the Rotary Club banquet, my mind wondered again about my birthday gift. Was the gazebo more for me than what Sam would really like? He had begun to encourage me to spend more time writing, now that he knew how much it meant to me, so instead I could have written him a poem or love letter. I remember asking Ted to do that for me once and he thought I was crazy.

I think some people don't appreciate the power of words and how you can remember them forever. Writing is something to hold in your hand and reread all over again. Someone once said something like 'People may forget what you said or did but they would never forget how you made them feel.'

How true was that! This really was a special time in our relationship that we would never experience again. We were shaping our wedding and our new home at the same time. I was convinced that I could place a carnival in the yard and Sam would love it. Hmmm, maybe not!

CHAPTER 38

On the drive home after work I had to take care of a few errands, which took me near Walnut Grove Cemetery. I couldn't resist turning in the drive, knowing exactly where to go to find the Taylors' tombstones. It wasn't hard to identify Albert Taylor's stone, as it was the only one in sight to have fresh lilies placed in front of it, just as we had witnessed on our first visit. So much for thinking they were flowers left from someone else's funeral. Who would be doing this? Was it from family or a past lover? I thought about calling some of my florist competitors about the lilies, but felt rather silly about checking with them. I decided to stop by Walnut Grove Cemetery's office to ask a few questions. Maybe they knew who brought them every day.

Unfortunately the office was closed, just like my shop. I did see someone weed eating around some of the stones so I pulled over to see if he would stop and talk to me. I got out of the car and motioned that I wanted to speak with him.

"Sorry to bother you, but I wondered if you could help me out with something?"

"Sorry ma'am, if you want to know where someone is buried, I can't tell you," he answered like he had been asked this ten times a day. "I don't pay any attention when I'm working."

"Oh, no," I tried to get him to hear me out. "I'm just wondering if you know anything about the stone over there that has fresh lilies in front of it each and every day?"

"Pretty weird, isn't it?" He shook his head. "I guess he's pretty special to someone, huh? It must be mighty expensive to do that."

"So, you've never seen anyone put them there?"

"No siree," he laughed. "I figure someone may be doing it late at night when it's pretty dark out here. Who would want to be out here in the dark visiting the dead with flowers? Beats me, ma'am." He scratched his head in disbelief.

"If I could stay awake, I may just try to find out," I suggested as we both laughed. "Do you think anyone in the office would know anything?"

"Well, you can talk to them, but it's kind of a joke with everyone here," he chuckled. "We all talk about it now and then. Most folks that see them think they're artificial. We're kind of used it now and at a place like this, anything can happen, right? Sorry I can't be more help, Miss, but I have to keep going here." He turned on the weed eater and continued down the row of stones.

I got back into my car and couldn't believe such a thing would be so accepted. Did the press ever pick up on this? I wondered if I could convince my romantic boyfriend into sitting up all night in a graveyard to see who would show up. I drove away grinning to myself, knowing that whoever was up to this was probably having the last laugh.

As I reached the house, I wondered if Mother was expecting

me for dinner. When I walked in, she was reading in the den.

"Hey, mommy dearest," I greeted her warmly. "Did you eat?"

"Oh, I should have called you, I guess. I was impulsive at the mall this afternoon and had a barbecue sandwich. I was pretty hungry and I couldn't resist."

"Good for you." I put my purse on the kitchen counter. "Actually, I'm not very hungry. Maybe I'll just have a glass of wine and some cheese. Will you join me?"

"Sure, sounds good, but don't bring me any cheese." She sounded rather down. "I'm not very happy about what happened today in the basement. I decided I had to give it up, so I came up here to read." I joined her on the couch.

"What happened?"

"You need to go down and check it out for yourself."

"Did you learn something?" I poured the wine.

"Sure didn't and now we may not learn much more."

"What do you mean by that?"

"Well, I hope you don't blame me, but there are water stains on some of the letter boards like someone spilled something. I know it wasn't you, so go figure!"

"Oh, my word!" I jumped up to run down the stairs.

She described it pretty well. The pieces on two of the letter boards were now entirely blurred from something damp. I looked up at the ceiling, thinking maybe a water pipe or something leaked on them. The two completed letters were fine.

The good news was there were still many pieces in the quilt that needed to be assembled, so this mess would just be an unfortunate stumbling block. Poor Mother, I thought. This was turning out to be a stressful project and it shouldn't be. This was my quilt and my mystery. It was important to me, but now it had become a problem for everyone involved. The possibility of hurting my mother because of this nonsense was the final straw for me.

"No big deal," I said, coming back up the stairs. "There is still much to reveal in the quilt. It's just a weird thing, that's all."

"There is a lot of weirdness in that basement. I'm afraid I've had it with that quilt, Anne; it's all yours."

"I understand, and I am absolutely fine with that," I assured her. "I'm sorry I got you involved in all this. Besides, I also have enough other stuff to keep me busy! This darn quilt may just have to wait, or I'll let Jean, Sue, and Sally figure it all out."

"I started back working on your flower quilt today," Mother said, changing to a much better subject. "I need to move that along. It's so pretty. Wouldn't it be nice to have the quilt done by your wedding? Wouldn't you like to use it in your pretty new home instead of in the shop?"

"No, Mother, I want to have that on a wall where I can see it every day. This is for me, not Sam and me. Is that selfish?"

"I guess not, sweetie," she smiled at me. "It will be just for you!"

CHAPTER 39

I called Sarah to see if she wanted to go pick blackberries with me. She didn't like the early hour, but it was going to get hot later and I was afraid we had already missed the best crop. When I arrived in front to pick her up, her outfit was way too cute and impractical for our mission, but I decided it was her way to dress for the occasion. She'd find out soon enough about the thistles, brush, and blackberry stains.

"Aren't you two brave this morning?" Aunt Julia asked, coming to the car, wearing her morning robe.

"It'll be fun, and I never get to spend any time with my cousin!" I smiled with excitement. "I hope we see you tomorrow at Sam's birthday party."

"I'm not sure you will, so I told your mother to stop by and pick up Sarah," she said, looking down the street. "I really don't want any confrontation," she whispered, remembering Sarah was within hearing distance.

"Well, the food will be great," I wanted to sound positive if Sarah was listening. "Kevin is the best cook. Wait till you see what my birthday present is to Sam! He will love it or hate it, but he better get used to the extremes with me, right Aunt Julia?"

"This ought to be good, but I don't think you need or want any advice from me." She closed her robe tighter. "Your mother said she is done working on the potting shed quilt. I don't blame her. I can't believe the weirdness of the water spots. Our mother could be mean at times; I told you that, but this is pretty strange. Have you found out anything more about this name that is like our mother's?"

"No, but the pieces are coming together more and more. I just don't know where it's taking us. Jean is going to take the quilt from my house. She is really intrigued with it all. She was more than happy to come get it. I'm more absorbed with my own ghost at 333 Lincoln. Did Mother tell you about the fresh lilies I find daily at Albert Taylor's grave?"

"No." She looked puzzled. "Do you mean someone comes there every day to place them there, or are they artificial?"

"They are fresh and beautiful each day!" I said. Aunt Julia's face was full of wonder.

"Oh, how spooky," Sarah had come closer. "Why don't you try to catch them?"

"No one can seem to do that," I explained. "I talked to the folks there at the cemetery and they are as mystified as I am."

"Well, if the flowers were at Mother's grave, I could understand and tell you why, because she loved lilies," Aunt Julia revealed. "Remember all the lilies at her funeral? I know we kids made sure lilies were on top of her casket."

"Wait a minute!" A light bulb appeared in my head. "There may be a connection here. We kept trying to find out what the name 'Martha Abbott' was doing in Albert Taylor's letters. If my grandmother was his mistress, then she could be the one placing the lilies on his grave. It would be her never ending love for him!"

"Oh, please. Anne," Aunt Julia said with disgust. "You're going too far off the edge here, don't you think?"

"So you're saying that Grandmother's ghost is not only in the basement but in that graveyard?" Sarah asked in disbelief. "How creepy is that?"

"I've heard enough, you guys." Aunt Julia headed toward her front door. "Be on your way, and don't forget, Sarah—I wouldn't mind a few of those berries to put on my yogurt."

We found the berries buried by overgrown bushes as well as other sticky and protruding vines that made our adventure more challenging than we thought. Sarah picked the ones closest to the road, and then she was back in the car rather quickly, playing with her cell phone.

I knew I wouldn't have to take Mrs. Brody very many of the berries for her to be pleased. Aunt Julia would only have one serving from our harvest as I could see this picking would be slim. Since the berries were scarce, I thought maybe someone might have already found this patch. After a presentable basketful was picked, we had to be on our way. I was itching and pretty soiled from the challenge.

We drove up the drive to Mrs. Brody's house and I noticed that her car was gone. After no answer to my knock, I wrote her a note and left the precious berries by the front door and off we went. Sarah wanted me to drive by the Taylor tombstone to see the lilies. I accommodated her request but told her we had no time to get out of the car. She was not disappointed with the discovery of yet more fresh lilies and couldn't stop talking about it on the way home.

That evening Sam was arriving home, but when he called me from the airport, I told him he would have to wait to see me at his party the next day. I wasn't fibbing when I told him I had to help Mother prepare some food. He was none too happy about all the fuss, but he understood we had plenty to do.

"I checked to see if the lawn got mowed today, Sam, and it all looks great. My herbs are really growing, so we should have fresh mint for the lemonade tomorrow."

"Are the bathrooms in working order? Are you sure this is a good idea, Anne?"

"Everything is taken care of; I told you that," I reassured him. "I also put out some nice hand towels from home. Kevin will be there in the morning to start the barbeque and you, my love, do not have to do a thing. Did you tell any folks at work that they could come by?"

"I may have, but everyone seems to have traditional events that they attend on the fourth. You know I would have preferred everyone to see 333 when we were further along with our restoration."

"Yes, I'm sure, but I'm telling you right here and now, Sam Dickson. This is our first 4th of July tradition and it will be grand!" I was excited. "Your birthday is just an added plus!"

"I told you to wait until we're married before you get so bossy, Annie." It was good to get a laugh out of him.

It was hard for me to convince him not to come by and give me a kiss or two. I also stressed that he come to 333 around eleven o'clock, because that's when I'd be there. I didn't want him showing up when the gazebo was going up. I suggested he come and pick me up, but I didn't win that scenario.

I could hardly sleep the morning of the big day, so I got up very early to make coffee, dress, and pack the car with lawn chairs, paper plates, lemonade, utensils, and whatever else Mother had laid out the night before.

The sky looked cloudy, but the temperatures were already on their way to a very warm day. The weatherman said there was a chance of showers, but I wasn't worried. We had a gazebo and porches to turn into emergency shelters if we needed. I kissed Mother goodbye and went on my way to establish a future of the Dicksons' 4th of July and birthday celebration.

I had written a love note to include with a sweet birthday card for Sam. He would love that for sure, but the gazebo was a gamble. As predicted, Kevin and his two helpers were putting the finishing touches on it. The kit was painted and preassembled as much as possible before being brought to 333.

"Is it where you wanted it, Anne?" Kevin asked when I rushed up to him and the crew. "It went easier than we thought! I was thinking about it all night."

"Oh, Kevin, it's just like I pictured." I felt relieved and he smiled in relief, too.

"I think this will be where I'll write when it rains. We can use a table I have on the back porch. It should be perfect. Would you mind putting it right here when you're finished? The red-checked table cloth will be just the right touch. I have red geraniums in pots to go here and there. I really love it! I will settle up with all of you on Monday, is that okay? I hope you kept track of your time." I couldn't stop smiling or seeing a bright future for this place.

Kevin introduced me to the two guys who had helped him. They were polite and complimentary, unlike scary Steve. I invited them to stay for the meal, but they had their own family plans.

I placed more chairs on the porch and brought one of the potted geraniums to the food table. I decided to go into the house to see if there were any last minute touches to be done. I went upstairs and looked at the master bedroom and bath that Sam and I would occupy soon. I thought I could possibly live in this room right now, it was so beautiful. It was painted white and cream, and had the softness and innocence of the wedding itself, just like I pictured it to be. I had collected some white antique Marseilles bedspreads that would fit in nicely in this room. The hardwood floors begged for a large white area rug. Oh, there was just too much to think about and plan for.

"Anne, Anne," I heard someone yell.

I looked out the window and saw Sam driving up. He was early, but we were pretty much ready. Kevin was hanging the Happy Birthday sign on the gazebo. I ran down the stairs and got to the car door as Sam was getting out. He wasn't looking at me; he was looking at Kevin and my surprise birthday present. He wasn't smiling.

"What the heck, Anne? A gazebo, is that what I'm seeing? Where in the hell did that come from?"

"Happy Birthday, Sam!" I tried to act like all was well, but how could it be? No kiss hello after he'd been away, and this negative reaction?

"I had the gazebo made for your birthday. I thought it would be perfect on this big side yard and offer a place of shelter for picnics like today. Isn't it something?"

He didn't answer but walked towards the gazebo, not even responding to Kevin's birthday wish. I followed him, waiting for the response that I so dearly wanted. Most of the other folks who had arrived were silent. They wondered what all the attention to the gazebo was about. Some would think it had always been there. Sam walked all around it and then came towards me with the same serious expression. I prayed he would not yell at me in front of everyone. He was so invested in how this house looked. Oh, dear, what had I been thinking?

"I thought you would like it, Sam, but if you don't, I have someone who will take it off my hands." I hoped no one was listening. "It was a kit, so it can easily be taken apart, I'm sure. You told me the yard and garden would be my responsibility and I felt it would be a great addition. You know, this a very Victorian structure, just like the age of our house. If you look closely, you'll notice some of this same gingerbread trim is on the two porches." He kept staring at me. "This wood has a new kind of treatment that doesn't need painting, Sam, so the upkeep is nothing."

Kevin knew this was not going well and had walked away towards the house, leaving me alone to deal with Sam's big surprise birthday gift. He scratched his head, and again he walked around the gazebo, not saying a word. He walked over to me contemplating what he was going to say. I wanted to run away. How stupid I was to take such a big step on property that wasn't all mine! Without warning, Sam picked me up under my buttocks and whirled me around tightly with his arms.

"I think I love it, baby!" He gave me a big grin and a good kiss. I wanted to faint, right onto the grass.

"Are you sure?"

"This is really something," he said as he put me down. "How did you even think of this? My grandparents had a gazebo that I always played in as a kid. It wasn't as big as this one. This is really something! I've never seen one with window boxes on the side."

"Oh, my word, honey." I was so relieved. "I knew it was risky, but when I planned this party, it just seemed like we needed a place to picnic and have shelter. Most of the idea came from Kevin. Didn't he do a neat job? He had a couple of guys help him early this morning. He's over there cooking. I think he wanted to get out of your way. Maybe you better go tell him how much you like it."

"Sure, but first I've got to thank my sweet Annie." He gave me another big kiss and hug. "I love the gazebo and I love you!" Praise the Lord, I thought, as I said a silent prayer of thanks. Our guests, having seen his delayed positive reaction, clapped delightedly. The tension was gone, and the more I thought about it, I was so glad Sam had seen the gazebo before too many more folks arrived.

It seemed everyone was arriving up the hill at once. Kevin had also figured out where most of the cars could be parked. Mother took over organizing all the appetizing potluck dishes. Uncle Jim was in charge of drinks under the shade tree by the screened-in porch. There was no Aunt Julia, but Sarah came with Mother and hung around Uncle Jim most of the time.

It was probably a good thing Aunt Julia had decided not to come. The day was coming together with the chatter of birthday wishes and hugs. The table under the gazebo was now adorned with food. The smell of good barbeque from the charcoal grill was enough to make any stomach growl.

Ice cold lemonade in tall glasses was on offer on the south porch. I told Mother this was where the lemonade cocktails would be each evening. Until the snow came, I would do everything in my power to make the south porch our special time and place, just like the Taylors.

I smiled to myself, watching Sam enjoy each moment. I heard him bragging to others about the gazebo birthday gift. We laughed, chatted, and stuffed ourselves until, suddenly, we saw the sky turn black. A huge clap of thunder scared everyone and sent us all running to the gazebo, porches, or cars. Light rain began to fall, but the best of the day had taken place. The crowd broke up quickly, with fast happy birthday wishes and words of thanks for a great party. Mother was the last to leave, taking Sarah home with her. She said she'd pick up her things the next day, knowing we were anxious to bring the big day to a close. Sam and I huddled in the gazebo, waving our good-byes.

"What would we have done without this wonderful birthday gift, honey?" He tried to shelter me from the heavy rain that had begun blowing at us under the gazebo.

"It's a perfect initiation, don't you think?" We were getting wet as the rain blew in, so we grabbed a couple of beers and headed to the house. We were a sight to behold with soaked clothes clinging to our bodies.

"Come on, we need to get out of these clothes," he said, taking my hand and leading me up the stairs to our newly painted master bathroom.

"Oh, no, we're getting the floors all wet," I shouted over the thunder with in-between giggles.

"They need to be broken in for the many wet moments to come." He had a sexy grin as he unbuttoned my blouse.

It was there at the entrance to the master bath that we undressed in rapid fashion while dropping our wet clothes to the floor. We grabbed towels off the bars to dry our naked bodies and then made passionate love, knowing it was our first intimate connection in our new home.

I would never be able to forget this moment each and every time I entered this pretty, white, romantic room. It was no longer the innocent, sterile, and uninhabited suite I had observed hours before.

The thunder and lightning might have become worse, but we could only hear the closeness of our breathing as we stayed on the white bathroom floor rug, wrapped in each other's arms.

"Happy Birthday, Sam," I whispered in his ear.

CHAPTER 40

The girls were coming in later the next morning at the shop, since it would likely be a slow day after the holiday. I loved that private quiet time in my own shop—just me and my plants—when no one was around.

A favorite part of my job was one that others did now—watering plants. My flowers and plants were, to me, like people and their pets. I have a soft heart for them and they are my family. I sense when they need care and water, and, yes, I talked to them a great deal when no one was around. I couldn't stand the thought of them being thirsty and dependent upon others to keep them alive. I finished all the watering, making sure not one of them was neglected.

As I finished the ferns near the front door, I noticed how the Missouri River was once again rising. I was always more observant of this when I walked along the river, but this morning I had walked in my neighborhood. It was amazing how quickly the river could rise. The river was a natural beauty that I never took for granted, and I knew I would miss it terribly if I had to live in a different town. I had heard it was going to crest in the next day or two. The water would start seeping into the park, which would bring ducks and their ducklings to swim in the shallow puddles. I loved watching their activity, which never seemed to be interrupted by my visit. Fisherman would start appearing on the banks in hopes of landing some Missouri catfish. I was so lucky to arrive at this location each and every day.

"I thought I would pop in early today, Miss Anne," Jean announced as she came in the back door. "I ran an errand or two in the town so here I am."

"Good morning!" I jumped in surprise. "Thank you again, Jean, for taking the quilt from Mother. She was becoming disturbed by its contents, I think. Ever since we found the name 'Martha Abbott' she has been less than happy with the project."

"I don't blame her a bit, Miss Anne." Jean put her lunch in the refrigerator. "Are you sure your mother didn't have a bit of a spill on the two letters? After all, Miss Anne, she would have felt terrible about doing that. It's very hard to make out some of the snippets, but there still will be plenty to read, I'm sure."

"Mother would never lie about something like that," I defended her. "If you knew all the happenings in that basement of ours, you would not be surprised by any odd occurrence like this. Someone doesn't want us to find out what those letters are about. Remember how the pieces kept flying around? It's my theory, Jean, that the Miss Abbott we are hearing about *is* my grandmother. I think she could be the mistress, and that would be unacceptable to Mother." I stopped before deciding to go on. "I also haven't told you that Aunt Julia said her mother's favorite flower was a lily. There are fresh, and do I mean fresh, lilies on Albert's grave every day, and no one has ever seen anyone come and go to put them there. How about those apples?"

"Apples?" she asked in confusion. "There are apples, too?"

"Oh no, Jean." I had to laugh. "That's just a manner of speaking. It means 'What do you think about that?,' so just ignore that remark. Isn't that a coincidence about the lilies?"

"Bloody strange, if you ask me," she voiced from the front room. "So to strike his fancy, she shows her everlasting love with her favorite flower? If the goon dumped her as we think, she should give him a toss of coal each and every day, I say!" That sounded good to me!

When Sally and Kevin arrived we chatted about what a wonderful party we had had for Sam. I could tell I wasn't the only one who had fallen in love with this guy. Sally went out of her way to say how perfect Sam was for me versus my former love, Ted Collins.

"Guess what I brought us for lunch today?" Kevin asked, coming in the back door. "Does the smell give it away? I had lots of barbeque left over, so I brought us some. There's plenty to take to your mother, too, Anne."

"Was any of that cake left?" Sally wondered.

"There was, but we sent it home with Sarah since Aunt Julia didn't come," I answered, checking out his leftovers. "I think Aunt Julia did the right thing in staying home. Sarah had a really fun evening with her dad. Wasn't Mia cute? She sure is getting friendlier with everyone, isn't she? Sam just adores her."

"Yup," Sally said. "Next year this time we may be talking about Sam having his own little one, huh, Anne?"

"Stop it, you guys, and get to work," I instructed. "I have to go to the Chamber lunch today and I have lots to do before that. My riverfront committee has to make their report and I need to be there. Be sure to save Mother and me some of that barbecue!"

I did make it in time for the luncheon at the The Pillars. It was good to see some of the folks that were mostly known to me only in the civic world. I said hello to the Mayor, Sarah Felt, who was doing as fine a job as any female could do in this town. I was just about to find my seat when Ted approached me.

"Good to see you, Anne," he said, standing directly in front of me. "I hear that congratulations are in order. When is the big date?"

"Oh, thanks Ted." I felt somewhat uncomfortable. "It's September 12th, and thanks for the good wishes. How about you and Wendy, any wedding plans there? I guess you are still an item, right?" Oh, brother, why had I even extended the conversation? I told myself to just sit down and ignore him.

"Yes, I guess we are, but no wedding date or anything that serious," he stammered a bit. "I hear you and Sam have purchased the old Taylor house? The place up on the hill was always a big mystery to me growing up. I bet it needs a lot of work!"

"It's a fabulous place, Ted." Why was I talking to him, unless I was bragging a bit? "Sam is pretty handy and he loves historic buildings, as do I, but he's the one who will have to see through the restoration. I fell in love with the gardens and the wonderful potting shed on the property. It's heaven for me to play and grow things there. I'm happy to show you around some day when we get further along. How are your parents?" This was crazy; everyone else had taken their seat.

"Thanks for asking. Dad is going to retire soon, so it means more work and responsibility for me."

"Well that's a good thing." I decided to remain cheerful and end the conversation. "Tell them hello for me. It was good to see you, Ted. Take care." I turned immediately to greet the person next to me.

I didn't need or expect that encounter today. He did look great, as he always did. So it sounded like Wendy had not completely gotten her claws into him. He had to guess if they were still an item? That didn't sound logical. It was hard for me to concentrate on the lunch and program. There was no comparison between how I had felt about Ted and my love for Sam, but I did still feel somewhat bad that I had hurt Ted. I just couldn't keep dragging out that safe and lifeless relationship. I had needed more of a challenge and I needed my body and soul to rise to a higher level. With Sam, I had it all, and I had to pinch myself when I thought about how lucky I was.

Was I really, or had I convinced myself that this relationship was perfection? Hmmm.

CHAPTER 41

Mother never asked anything more about the progress of the potting shed quilt, although she was working diligently on my flower quilt. I was amazed at her appliqué skills and the details of her hand embroidery on some of the flowers. I began to check her progress every day. I told the girls I knew exactly where I was going to hang the quilt in the shop.

"This is really beautiful," I said at breakfast, watching her get an early start on the quilt. She worked on it upstairs, to avoid the other quilt, I think.

"I can see so much better in the morning, for some reason," she said. "I'm really getting hooked on the appliqué. Isabella gave me some good hints and it's going faster now."

"I'm naming this quilt 'Botanical Beauty,' Mother. How about that?" I was feeling the love she had put into it, so I said, "Or should it be 'Sylvia Brown's Botanical Beauty?' It should be named after you!"

"Don't be silly; I love 'Botanical Beauty.' I will put that on the label. I think we can start quilting on it after the wedding is over. No point in trying to make time for this, with all we have going on."

"How in the world are we going to have time to do it all, Mother? Did you decide on that green dress that you tried on at Miss Michelle's?"

"Yes, I think that's the one, if you approve. I feel good in it. At this age, that becomes more important than the looks. Good color for the outdoor affair, too!"

"Sure! So did you tell them to hold it for you?"

"Yes, they suggested I do so, but I didn't until you and I could talk about it." She took a break from her stitching. "I'll call them today. Now, tell me about the dresses for you and Sue. Does she have a dress in mind for Mia, in case we can get her to walk down the aisle?"

"Yes, but I'm not counting on her from what Sue has indicated. We should have fittings maybe as early as next week. The dresses are all simple, as you know, so they probably won't take long to be altered. I hope I can keep the extra weight off till then, Mother, so don't feed me so much! By the way, I'm going over to Aunt Julia's tonight to finish up the invitations. Don't look for me for dinner. Did you want to help? I can pick you up."

"No," she had started appliquéing again. "Remember, tonight I play cards and I'm the hostess. If you still need me after tonight, though, I certainly can help."

"Aunt Julia's handwriting is so magnificent; I'm letting her do most of the addressing. Sam will be working on the house this evening. So, these apples lying out on the counter must mean apple pie is going to be in the oven, am I right?"

"Yes, indeed. I'll make sure there is some left."

"Oh, better not!" I pointed to my waistline. "That wedding dress has to fit perfectly! I'm stopping by Jean's this morning. She's off today. She called and said she had some more information from the letters." Mother said nothing. I had to leave, so I said, "I'll see you tonight." She still didn't want to know about any of the progress on the letters. This worried my heart.

I pulled up in front of a charming, small brick house in Colebridge's Frenchtown area. It sat back from the street, and the stone siding made it really look like an English cottage. Roses on trellises were climbing along each side of the green front door. Jean loved flowers as much as I did, and I remembered she said she had a nice vegetable garden out back.

"A jolly good morning to you, Miss Anne," she said, as I entered her small entryway. "Will you have a cup 'a tea? I do not house coffee grinds, or a cup 'a Joe, as we say in England. Tea, however, I can offer."

"Oh, no thanks, Jean. I had two cups—more than my usual limit—with Mother this morning, so I'm good."

"Come in here a bit where the quilt lays about," she said, walking into the back porch off the kitchen. "I spent a sort of time on the matter, and here is the only legible part of the tan-papered letter."

"It reads as such: *your rose garden will survive* is the end of this last sentence, but then the next paragraph is all good. *Again, you must not worry your beautiful head about my loyalty to you. Miss Abbott is a very young, foolish girl. My best to all your family when you visit them on Sunday. Your loving husband, Albert.* The first part of this letter is gone drab with the water. I am now concentrating on the brown paper. A very fancy weight it is. This is the letter where we discovered a piece that read *have put aside your fears of any affair that.* It doesn't make a bowlful of sense to

252

read now, Miss Anne. I will write it down at an exceedingly good pace and have a final look for you as soon as possible."

"Oh, there's no hurry, Jean," I assured her. "So Miss Abbott was a very young, foolish girl, was she? I wonder how young and how foolish? Do you think she could have been lying about being pregnant to lure Albert, or was she trying to get financial support for her baby? Maybe she just wanted him to acknowledge that he was the father? She must have been very desperate to go to Mrs. Taylor."

"I give her credit to not put a sock in it about the baby," she said. "The mister's away in London and times a-wasting, she probably thought. Mrs. Taylor was probably a snob in nature and told Miss Abbott she was full of beans and to not show her face again."

"Well, she was upset enough to let Mr. Taylor know about it, and it sounds like he addresses this subject in each of these letters back to her," I reminded us both. "Good work, Jean. I sure hope you don't mind playing around with this. Your house is as adorable as I thought it would be, by the way."

"Nice of you to say, Miss Anne." She blushed a bit. "I am becoming exceedingly fond of it as time marches on. I guess I missed my calling in being a mum, but other than that, I am pleased to be here. Before you go, I have a swell garden out back. Come have a look. I have a tomato or two to send home to Sylvia."

CHAPTER 42

Aunt Julia and I had a pleasant visit that evening as we worked on my small list of invitees to the garden wedding of Anne Louise Brown to Sam William Dickson on September 12th. Seeing it in print was just as hard to believe as when I looked down at my engagement ring. We laughed and gossiped as we approached each name on the list. Sarah was out with a friend, so I felt comfortable in asking if she heard from Uncle Jim.

"Yes, I did, as a formality of course. In regard to the settlement," she said, as she neatly stacked the invitations. "I think he's actually going to be pretty generous. He wants me to stay in the house, which I appreciate. If all goes well, I will be a free woman in a month or so. Doesn't that seem wild?" It seemed more like weird instead of wild to me.

"I can't believe it'll happen that fast."

"My lawyer said that if we keep agreeing on matters, it will move along quickly." She smiled bigger than I would have thought she would. "Word has certainly gotten out there. I heard from an old schoolmate the other day who heard through the grapevine I was going to be divorced! How about that!"

"Oh, my word. Who was that?" If I was sad, why was she happy?

"You wouldn't know him," she suddenly sounded like a school-girl. "I dated him a time or two in high school, and then we lost track of each other when we went away to college. He was always considered a good catch, but don't worry, I'm not going there." She must have noticed my expression. "I hate and despise men right now and don't plan to expose Sarah to any such nonsense. I just want my freedom. I don't ever want to worry where a man is or who he is with ever again, so there!"

"I do understand, Aunt Julia." I put my hand on hers. "I'm sure in time you will feel differently after Sarah goes away to college. You'll want someone back in your life again." I straightened the stack of completed invitations.

"Oh, it's getting late. I told Sam I would stop by 333 after I left here. He's putting in some baseboards in one of the bedrooms. We have electricity now, so he can work at night, which is good." How could this conversation go from divorce to a high romance to someone who is thrilled about having electricity?

"I'm happy for you, Anne," Aunt Julia said, putting her arm around me. "You are old enough and wise enough to experience all this. I hope Sam will be a better husband than Jim was."

"I don't feel like I am getting into anything I can't handle." I felt like defending my decisions. "I'm getting married to someone I want to spend the rest of my life with. We didn't plan on 333 Lincoln, but I look at it as a bonus not a problem."

"I'm sorry, Anne. That didn't come out right. I guess the fact that Sam and Jim are friends colors things a bit, and I'm sorry."

"Accepted," I said as I kissed her on the cheek. "Thanks again for all the time you put in on these invitations."

Sam was indeed hard at work, down on his knees, pounding away with a hammer. His tight soiled jeans and rumpled hair were indeed an unexpected turn-on.

"Nice view," I said, walking into the room. "This looks really nice, Sam!"

"The work or me?" he joked.

"Both, so don't make me choose." He winked at me as he turned around to see I had brought him a cold beer.

"Now, this was nice," he grinned as he took the beer out of my hand. "Hey, before I forget, you missed a visitor tonight!"

"Oh, who was that?"

"Mrs. Brody." He took a big swallow. "She had her nephew drive her up here. They stayed in the car, so I went out and introduced myself. He is a quiet sort and a bit odd, if you ask me. Mrs. Brody was thrilled with the blackberries and wanted to come thank you. I think they were a little curious as to how things were going over here, too. She said they saw all the cars coming up the hill for some reason and thought maybe we had moved in. I offered a couple of times to show them around, but they refused."

"That was sweet of her," I smiled, picturing their visit. "I'm so glad she was pleased. We'll have to remember to do small things to be nice to her, Sam. She's pretty confined over there."

"She commented about the yard and garden. She couldn't believe how beautiful things were looking in such a short span of time. Then she asked if the gazebo was new, as she didn't remember it."

"Do you think her nephew comes around up here on his own? What is his name anyway, did he say?"

"Yeah, he did say his first name." Sam got back to his work. "I think he said Walter, but I'm not sure. Anyway, you did a good deed there, sweet Annie. How was your visit with Julia?"

"Well, the invitations are ready to mail. She was really a big help with that. She said the divorce is going quickly and that Uncle Jim is agreeing to most everything she wants. She seems to be looking forward to being free, as she put it. It's all so sad, honey. Why did he have to fool around?"

"Some guys fall into the pattern quite easily when they travel like that." He stopped working again to give me his full attention. He took another swallow of beer. "Some don't stay focused and want instant entertainment in their free time."

"I've never worried about you, Sam," I said carefully. "I know it's a different world than years ago, but I do hope you stay focused on our relationship."

"I haven't told you that my mother worried continuously about my father when he traveled." Sam stood up and stared off into the distance. "I didn't like even thinking about it back then. I always sensed he was probably cheating on her, but that she would never do anything to break up our family. I felt the deception and told myself that was no way to live."

He turned toward me. "I think it really aged my mother over the years, and now here she is, pretty much nursing him until he dies. The good news is that I think he finally appreciated her, and I think all and all, she is glad she didn't leave him."

"I'm so sorry, Sam." His revelation had me feeling sad. "It's strange how people live their lives when there are so many options to choose from. I hope we can work out the social situation with Uncle Jim and Aunt Julia. I want both of them in my life—in our life—and I hate the thought of trying to be careful around them."

"That's their problem, my sweet, isn't it?" He had come near to put his arms around me. "Our lives will be what they are, and they will have to be the ones to choose how they handle us." A comforting soft kiss went on my forehead, then on my mouth.

Sam always made things simple, which was one of the things I liked about him. We went downstairs together and then out to the south porch to enjoy the night air and the remaining half can of beer. We walked hand in hand to the gazebo and looked back to admire our house. Right at that moment, we noticed the lights were going on and off in the house.

"Oh, no! What's wrong with our lights?"

"Nothing's wrong." He was calm. "I had Ben the electrician double-check everything and they couldn't find any reason for the flickering problem. I guess it just happens now and then, if you know what I mean."

"What do you mean, 'it happens now and then!?'" I asked in fright. "This shouldn't happen at all!"

It was dark outside, so I couldn't see his expression. "Well, according to Ben, this was a problem with this house in the past, and there doesn't seem to be an explanation—other than a spiritual one. Everything checks out fine. It's not a big deal for me; is it for you, sweetie?" I guessed he was looking at me. "It rarely happens and, frankly, I take it as a sign of approval."

"Well, Sam, it's not normal." I hugged him around the waist. "Is it the ghost everyone talks about? Do you feel safe here?"

"Yes, I do." He hugged me back. "Do you?"

"I do, ironically. Isn't that weird?" We smiled our way into a laugh.

"I have a feeling that when we are all settled here, other things will settle as well," he said, comforting me. "A lot of things are going on here and lots of folks are wondering about it. How many people have an active welcoming party before they move in?"

We sat down in the gazebo and looked up at the moon, changing the subject to other matters. The spirit in our house had to be a good one, I decided that evening. We still had not figured out where my gardening tools had come from, but they were appreciated, and I would use them.

Whoever the spirit was, she—or he—had not frightened us or stifled our love for the house—or each other.

CHAPTER 43

Jean and I were working by ourselves on Saturday, so it was hard to get time to visit about how the potting shed quilt was coming. Although we didn't have any new orders for the morning, we had to make sure the deliveries went out before our early closing.

The walk-in traffic was slow, except for Gayle, who came over for some moral support, as she did often. She kept tossing back and forth whether to sell her business or not. It had become rather comical, because every time we encouraged her to do so, she would argue how much she loved it and had to keep it. If we said to hang on for awhile longer, she would complain how it was draining her physically as well as financially. This morning we teased her about it and then offered to share our large deli sandwich with her for lunch. This cheered her spirits, and we finished our lunch with Jean's delicious shortbread.

After Gayle left, I took the time to tell Jean how pleased I was with her designs and how I was depending on her more and more.

She was always in a good mood, the customers loved her, and she was very intent on pleasing me. She loved every word.

"Now that it's a bit slow, Miss Anne, I'd like you to take notice of the letter I finished just last night." She sat down at the counter. "Sometimes I think I missed my calling, as I love to solve a puzzle or two now and then. I have really taken a shine to this quilt."

"Yes, I'm really anxious to see it." I tried to listen as I straightened. "I'm afraid that since it's been out of our house, I've put it aside. The wedding is on my mind and then, of course, I want to be at 333 Lincoln any spare time I have. It's really coming along. They're doing a fair amount of painting now, and it has made such an improvement. I think Sam will be able to move in right before the wedding. I'll send some of my things over, but I won't officially make my presence known until I'm Mrs. Dickson. That should be pleasing to our resident spirit."

"Sally told me about the ghostly lights that flicker," she revealed. "It may very well be a lovely response from he or she, and I would take no notice if I were you."

"That's what I told Sam," I said, as I walked to the front room to see who had walked in.

"Hi Aunt Julia," I greeted. "What brings you to Main Street today?"

"I had to pick up something at the O'Connell's Gallery so I thought I'd stop by. How are you, Jean?"

"Fit as a fiddle, thank you." Jean grinned as she always did. "I was just sharing with Miss Anne that I've completed another letter to show her. I've had a swell time with it."

"Oh, I meant to ask how the progress was coming on that," Aunt Julia remembered. She turned to me. "Your mother said she will soon have your flower quilt ready for us to quilt after the wedding. That'll be such fun for all of us—to get back to the quilting frame. I bet it's turning out to be quite beautiful."

"It really is," I said with pride. "Mother is getting better and better with her appliqué. Isabella has been a big help to her. She goes into the quilt shop much more now since she doesn't work at Pointer's anymore. I really do love it, and it will go great on that wall right over there."

"I thought you'd fancy it there," giggled Jean. "I'm playing around with putting photographs on fabric and have dashing ideas afloat for a nice little quilt. Isabella is quite a good sort in helping and planning such a quilt, isn't she?"

"So what about the latest letter?" asked Aunt Julia.

"Well, if no one comes in, we can maybe read it," I suggested. But I hesitated. "We still have to put some bows on these two pieces before Kevin comes in, Jean. I want to close right at noon today."

"For sure, Miss Anne." Jean was so responsible. "If anyone pops in, I'll attend to them. Here is the board with the brown paper. Sit here a spell, Miss Julia; I'll keep an eye out!"

"Okay, here goes." I read: "*Dearest Marion, My train should arrive at noon. I do not relish the trip home, as my stomach is still ailing from the flu. My mission here has been accomplished for all concerned. I have gifts for you and the family. Nothing as pretty as the vase I brought you from Germany. The shops are few near here, but I hope you will be pleased with my selection. My hope is that you will be able to accommodate Edward when he comes to pick me up at the station. By now my hope is that you have put aside any fears of any affair that has plagued you since my absence. Soon to be in your arms, Albert.*"

"Who is Edward?" Aunt Julia asked.

"I think his brother," I said. "I can't remember where or when we decided, but I figure it must be family. The vase he is referring to is probably the one I found in the potting shed. How it ended up there is still a mystery. Poor Marion still has fear of his alleged affair in each letter. I think we can establish that now. We have the name Martha Abbott, Aunt Julia." I looked straight at her. "She could be your mother. Have you thought seriously about that?"

"Do you really think so, Anne?" She placed her fingers to her lips thoughtfully. "Age-wise, he would have been so much older, though." She looked away. "I can't really grasp this whole idea."

"Yes, he was older, but remember in the one letter he refers to Martha as 'a very young foolish girl,'" I said. "Mother refuses to go there, too, but Aunt Julia, think about it. How many Martha Abbotts could there be?"

I took a breath and went on. "I was told by Mrs. Brody that the ghost at 333 Lincoln used to say some woman's name over and over. Your mother—my grandmother—also loved lilies. There are fresh lilies on Albert's grave every day." Aunt Julia said nothing, so I went on.

"I think Grandmother Davis had an affair with him and was likely pregnant when she went to see Marion about it. Albert was in London, though, so when Marion wrote him, full of concern, he responded with these letters." We just looked at one another, but I had to finish my thoughts.

"These letters were saved by Marion, then cut up and used in a quilt. I come along as the new owner of 333 Lincoln and find the nearly-destroyed quilt in the potting shed wrapped around the vase Albert gave his wife. I remember now that Mother said that vase was German."

"Good heavens!" Aunt Julia was pacing in stress. "I forgot about the lilies. How could they possibly be fresh every day if you think Mother has something to do with it?"

"Hello! Aunt Julia! This has to be a supernatural occurrence," I stated as firmly as I dared. "Your mother has not moved on to wherever she was to be in the afterlife. She finished quilts in our basement, left open a book to show me a quilt design for my flower shop, and insisted on leaving a thimble for Sue to use. Do you want me to continue? You, of all people should know her dominance and determination."

"God only knows I do." Aunt Julia had a look of revelation on her face. "That woman was something else, and she and I were like oil and water. I didn't put anything past her then, and I certainly shouldn't now."

"Perhaps she 'ad a bit of aristocratic blood in her," Jean suggested from the front room. "We have a lot of those bloody spirits in England. We pay them no mind, but if they don't 'get on' as we say, they can make your life a bloody hell! She sounds angry like you describe, Miss Anne, but is she also crying out for someone to give her a notice? This Albert did her wrong and gave her a toss. I'd be angry, too!"

This was a pretty good observation, I thought. Martha Abbott, mother or grandmother or not, wants someone to hear her. Hmmm.

The door opened and a young man went right to the refrigerated display case to pick out a small basket of flowers. I remembered seeing him before—couldn't place his name—but Jean was right there to help him. As soon as he left, Aunt Julia continued our conversation about my grandmother.

"What happened to her baby, then? Did she have an abortion or give it up for adoption? She certainly didn't keep it!"

"The one letter referred to the fact that she told Marion she was going to give the baby up for adoption, remember?" I had the attention of both of them. "Albert replied that she should do so, as he had his own family to worry about." I could see I was getting through to Aunt Julia.

"What a jerk," she said curtly. "Men are inconsiderate. It's always just about them. This is what I tried to tell you, Anne. We are convenient distractions at certain points in their lives, but then when it's inconvenient, they move on, and we are trashed. It's always the woman's problem."

"Hey, ladies, keep a lip back there," Jean whispered, as she peered around the corner. "Someone just came in."

"I'm sorry, Anne," Aunt Julia said, softening. "I need to go and digest this." She hugged me.

"As much as I hate all of this, I think you are on to something. You are right; your mother will not want to believe this at all. She never had a bad thought about Mother. She always took her side in everything."

She went to the door. "I've got to go. Sarah will be home soon. I'm doing some redecorating and I'm anxious to see how this new paint will look. I'll be in touch." Off she went.

I felt as if I had just spilled from my guts a thousand puzzle pieces that I had barely put together. Even if all of this was correct, what now? What could I do to help Miss Abbott move on?

CHAPTER 44

When Sam left for another two-day trip, I told myself I would try to accomplish more at 333. Everyone was picking up the name "333" when referring to what used to be called the "Taylor house." I did so hope it would be called the Dickson house one day. With all the changes we were making, it would bear our influence, for sure. Still, I would certainly make a place for Marion's vase on our mantle. I wasn't sure what I would do with the Crazy quilt, however, once we had removed all the pieces. I knew enough not to discard it.

The Colebridge Historical Society was just two blocks from my shop on Main Street. The hours were so limited it was hard for me to get there when they were open, but I decided to try to stop by and see if anyone was there. I wasn't due in the shop till lunch time, so I decided to make it one of my stops, along with a short Beautification Committee meeting at City Hall. Fortunately, a nice, college-aged young man had just opened the doors to the handsome old building and let me in. It was hard to know where to start, but I told him I was looking for any information concerning the estate of Albert and Marion Taylor who had lived at 333 Lincoln.

"Well, that's interesting, because a lady was just here yesterday asking about them," he shared.

"Oh, well, that's interesting," I stammered. "Did she give her name?"

"No, she didn't, but I think Elsie knew her because they exchanged hellos. Elsie just works one day a week here. We're all part time. I'm going to school, but I love genealogy and I love Colebridge. I'm not sure I can leave here once I graduate."

"What's your name?" I had to ask out of curiosity.

"Carl Hogan." He answered as though no one had ever asked his name before. "And you are?"

"Anne Brown. I own Brown's Botanical down the street."

"Oh, sure, I've been in there," he said, grinning. "I like what you do with the boxes outside your window. You did a nice thing for my friend Jenny. She just got married. I think you dyed some flowers for her."

"Yes, yes, I did," I said, remembering her with pleasure. "I'm glad she enjoyed them."

"So, back to this Taylor family question," he said. "We didn't research very far yesterday, but we did find a picture of him as president of the Colebridge Chamber of Commerce Board."

"Oh, may I see it?"

"Their home was also mentioned in this book, *Colebridge Lives*, along with other residents. They especially mention the beautiful garden."

"Could you show me that as well, Carl? This is so great! My fiancé and I just purchased the Taylor home. The reason I fell in love with it was the garden and potting shed." Carl was as accommodating as a young man could be who heard such questions many times over.

I sat down at one of the large long antique tables and Carl shortly brought me the photo of the Colebridge Chamber of Commerce Board. Mr. Taylor stood prominently amongst his other officers. I carefully read the description of the installation dinner, held at the Hendrix Hotel, which had since been torn down.

Then I noticed that the name Edward Taylor was another one of the names mentioned. Maybe this was the "Edward" that Albert referred to in the letter. With that last name, he must have been a brother.

There was little description of the Taylor house from the locally published book of Colebridge houses. There was a distant view of the front, facing Lincoln Street. I had never given the front side of the porch much preference or notice because the south porch faced the drive when we approached the property from the driveway.

I barely made out some white rattan furniture that seemed to be placed on both porches. This was my plan for the porch as well, which seemed strange. I could see a potted fern on a side wicker table. I would remember the position of the table and fern and reproduce that as well, I thought. The book described the house as "grand" and referred to the magnificent gardens. It didn't say what year the photograph was taken.

"When I bring Mr. Taylor's name up in our computer, they also refer to him as an invested member of the First National Bank of Colebridge," Carl said, rejoining me. "I guess he was pretty rich, from what I can tell. He's buried at the Walnut Grove Cemetery, did you know that?"

"Yes, I did find him there. Well, I mean I found his stone." Carl laughed.

"So then you know about the lilies?" His grin did not go away.

"Yes, I do Carl," I answered with the same grin. "What do you make of that?"

"It's all pretty weird. I don't know who first told me about it, but rumor has it that they are put there by his mistress. That's pretty far out! I went with my girlfriend one day to see it for myself, and it's for real. The cemetery is closed-mouth about it. They don't want the publicity and refuse to elaborate on details. Someday, it will be written up in some ghost book, don't you expect?"

I don't know why, but I trusted this young man enough to say, "Well, you may as well know that I think she hangs around 333 Lincoln as well, but in a good way. She winks at us with blinking lights once in a while."

"No way!" He reacted. "That would freak me out! Do you know her name?"

"Yes, I believe it's someone with the name of Martha Abbott," I said, testing the waters.

"Martha Abbott? That's one of the names the lady asked me about the other day!"

"Well, it doesn't surprise me. Her name is getting about. What were you able to tell her?"

"Nothing, nothing at all." Carl shook his head. "She wasn't born in this county that I could find. I'll be happy to keep a lookout and research more when I have some extra time. But we are pretty short-handed here, so I can't guarantee anything. Leave your number with me. I have to tell you that the lilies are quite intriguing, and I would like to know more about their existence."

He wanted to continue the conversation, but time was getting away from us both.

"Would you mind making me a copy of this Chamber picture?"

"Oh, sure." He jumped out of his seat.

"Here's my business card, Carl." I shook his hand in gratitude. "Thanks so much for all your help."

CHAPTER 45

J ean had two customers waiting at the counter when I walked into the shop. It appeared Sally was out and she was working alone. I took over chatting with the customers so Jean could go outdoors to our patio to have a quick bite of lunch.

When the shop cleared out, I noticed on the tickets that we had had a nice run on the vintage vases that I had been displaying in the gift section of the shop. It didn't seem to matter if they were reproductions or the real thing. I made a point to display the variety of both as much as I could, and many customers liked their arrangements in one-of-a-kind vases. When I displayed them now and then in the window, it always encouraged walk-in traffic. Oh, I wished I had more time to get to garage sales and estate sales like I used to. I would always find the most unique vases and containers. Sometimes customers brought them in for me to purchase, knowing my buying habits.

"Miss Anne, do you fancy Jane Austen, or, should I say,

have you read her novels?" Jean asked as she spray-cleaned the glass countertop.

"Oh, my, yes! I haven't had the pleasure recently, however," I answered with a big smile. "*Pride and Prejudice* is my favorite, of course. It is the love story of all love stories! The idea of a single woman like Jane who focused on her writing excites me. I can only imagine how odd her independence must have been back then."

"I read quite a spell into the night," Jean said, "so I'm a bit out of sorts today, I'm afraid. I'm rereading *Emma*, her fourth novel. Boy, oh boy, if that story doesn't send a message to mind your own business, nothing will. This may be my favorite; I'm not sure."

"Is her work appreciated in England as much as it is here in America?" We both kept working.

"Indeed, Miss Anne! I was a member of a small Jane Austen book club there before I married my Al and came to America. Young school girls fancy her at an early age and sometimes have Jane Austen parties. Quite fun it is is!"

"It does sound fun and educational at the same time."

"We would have sinfully good teas as we discussed the characters like Miss Bennett and Mr. Darcy," Jean said thoughtfully. "Perhaps I will give the club a toss here in Colebridge and see what comes about."

"That would be awesome, Jean." My interest in her idea caught me by surprise. "I think I'd like to come to that. This is my problem; I want to do everything! How can I run this business, restore a house, plan a wedding, make a quilt, be a gardener, and become a wife, Jean? Sam doesn't know what he's getting into! That reminds me, I must go to 333 after hours and check on the work that's been done today. Every visit now I see some real improvement. It really makes it all seem livable."

"You are a lucky lady, Miss Anne." Did I hear envy in her voice?

But she went on to say cheerfully, "It would be swell if you would be an 'Austen Girl,' as we call them."

"Is that what they really call the members?" I chuckled.

"That's what we called our group, but Janeites is the official name for Austen fans." Jean smiled, thinking of happy times. "Having a Jane Austen book club here would remind me of home among the heather, as we say. Don't laugh, Miss Anne, but I have scraps and notes in a biscuit tin to make a Jane Austen quilt someday."

"I love that idea, Jean!" Now I was really enthusiastic. "By the way, Mother said my flower quilt will be ready to quilt soon. It may not happen till after the wedding, but would you help us? Maybe we can give you pointers on your Austen quilt!"

"Oh, indeed, Miss Anne," she said, getting back to her cleaning. "I most certainly will be a player. Oh! Excuse me—a quilter."

The shop hours went by quickly. I sent Kevin on his way to make a last-minute delivery and called Mother to tell her I was on my way to 333. I told her I'd eat a bite later when I got home. She had made chicken salad and said it would keep. She added that she was appliquéing a vine on my flower quilt and it was taking a long time to do. I reheard the words in my mind that Jean had said: "You are such a lucky lady." Hmmm, I was indeed. I was really lucky to have Mother still with me. Her whole life was about doing things for me, her only child. How all this would change after I became Mrs. Dickson, I didn't know.

I couldn't help but smile as I drove up the hill to 333 Lincoln. The painters were gone and the heat of the day was calming down. There was always shade somewhere in this spacious yard. I gazed at the weeping willow tree and didn't want to trim it back as had been suggested by the nursery. I had fond memories of playing under a willow as a child. It was easy for me to hide there and imagine all sorts of stories at play. When it died, Mother was as sad as I was, as she loved it, too. It was no wonder she was happy to see one growing in the yard at 333. I decided I was going to leave it alone for now and enjoy the memories.

I walked into a house that smelled of fresh new paint. The risk of choosing a deep green for the walls in the dining room was a good one. The contrast around the white marble fireplace in the room was striking.

The entryway was half painted in the dark red I wanted on one wall. The painters did a fine clean up each day, I noticed.

The next room to check out was the study. The dark oak woodwork and shelving were heavy accents for the room, so a light shade of terracotta was just enough color for the room. This would be where Sam would spend most of his time. I knew how much he worked out of his loft. I could just picture his desk in this large room. He wanted to bring the Oriental rug from his home office here and it would indeed be perfect on these hardwood floors with the terracotta.

Oh, why wasn't he here with me? I missed him. I couldn't wait to tell him that I had gotten a photo of Albert from the Historical Society. It was just a newspaper photo, but I was determined to find a real photo of him and Marion to display in our home.

I closed up the house, and while it was still dusk, I made my way to the potting shed. The humidity was pretty intense as I entered. I grabbed the hose and began watering. I would have to remember to water the herbs as well before I left. Out of the corner of my eye, I could see the single hanging light bulb on the ceiling sway back and forth. As soon as I turned around to gaze at it directly, it flashed off and on as I had seen lights do on one other occasion in the house.

"Oh," I said aloud, feeling a little silly. "Grandmother, if this is you, I know you're here and it's okay. I am not afraid. I thank you for the nice garden tools. I have used them just once so far, but please know they will be used for a very long time."

I was talking faster as I told myself it was okay to talk out loud to her. The light had stopped flickering, so I continued to finish watering. Then, for some reason, I felt compelled to be very brave.

"Grandmother, if it really is you, please flicker the lights again." Silence held the muggy air.

I stood very still for a good whole minute before the light began to flicker again. I took a deep breath and nodded to acknowledge her. Chills were going up and down my spine, but I was not going to show any fear.

"My heart goes out to you," I said, surprised, really, to hear only my voice. "I know from your visit to Marion Taylor that you were in love with Albert. I am so sorry he abandoned you and I respect who you are and hope to learn more about you. I am going to plant some white lilies in the garden, which I know you are fond of, in your honor. I will not forget you here at 333 Lincoln."

Just then my cell phone went off and I went out of the potting shed to answer. It had become dark! I saw the call was from Sam. I had to compose myself from just having had a conversation with my ghostly grandmother.

"Hey, love," I said, hoping he couldn't hear how shaken I felt. "I'm so glad you called. I'm at 333 checking out the newly painted walls and they are beautiful."

We chatted for a good half hour. I just couldn't bring myself to tell him about the communication that had taken place with our resident ghost. It would have to be another time. Right now I just wanted to hear about his day and how much he missed me. It was as if I could smell his cologne over the phone. His arrival back home the next day was indeed something to look forward to.

"Promise me we can have lemonade cocktails on the south porch tomorrow night," I said sweetly before hanging up.

CHAPTER 46

It was Friday night and the day was a mixed bag of problems ranging from the garbage man not picking up trash in the alley for some reason and a botched delivery that affected the Meyer anniversary order we had to do. I was edgy, knowing that I didn't want to be late to meet Sam at 333 for the cocktail we talked about the night before. The way things were going now, I would be late for sure.

I ran across the street to Nick's to get a container of lemonade to be mixed with vodka for our cocktails later. Nick always saw the glass as half empty despite his good business, so it was, as always, hard to rush in and out.

When I returned, Sally graciously said that if we could not close on time she would stay late so I could leave. Jean's husband was a stickler about her coming home on time, and especially tonight because they had dinner plans. I thought it interesting that she didn't talk much about Al, but it probably didn't mean much. She was coming over on the weekend to return the potting shed quilt, now that the pieces were all removed.

Sally never had a date, but she seemed to always be busy and yet helpful to me when it came to staying late at the shop. I sensed many times that she might be gay, but she never shared information. I never saw her with anyone that might be close to her.

We did manage to close on time. As soon as we locked the door, I went to the restroom to change into jeans and a sleeveless white knit top. I prepped my face and headed to my car with lemonade and a small bag of ice.

When I arrived, I unloaded my basket and then decided to water plants until Sam came. I got out two of the wine glasses we now kept on hand in the kitchen cabinet. I felt like I was playing house in a make-believe world with Sam. Where was he?

It was getting darker and darker. I looked at my watch and it was past the time that I thought we would meet. I decided to call his cell but that attempt got me nowhere. After I watered and walked around the grounds, pulling a weed or two, I sat down on the south porch feeling very sorry for myself. I started thinking of different scenarios about where he might be. The most likely one was that his plane was late and he couldn't call.

I didn't know how long to wait and it was starting to get chilly. I didn't have a sweater, so I draped a blanket from the car around me. When I started to doze off, I decided to go home.

Should I be worried? Did he forget? Why hadn't he at least called? Would he make a habit of this behavior when we were married?

When I got home, I iced up a glass of the lemonade and vodka and went quietly up to my room, not wanting to wake Mother. Much needed sleep was a blessing; I didn't stay awake long enough to drink half my cocktail.

It wasn't much longer before I rolled onto my pillow for a full night's sleep. I woke up in a panic to check the time and it was seven o'clock in the morning, which was past time to get up and dress for my walk. I had just finished brushing my teeth when the phone rang.

"Wake up, sleepy head," said Sam.

"Oh, Sam, I am so glad you called!" I tried to clear my head. "What happened to you last night? I waited for you until I nearly fell asleep on the porch. Why didn't you call?"

"I had my reasons not to call, Anne," he said slowly. "I was on my way to the airport to catch the plane when I had some pretty hard chest pains that seemed to be more than indigestion. I decided to make a stop at a medical center I had seen on the highway when I arrived in town. I had plenty of time so I thought I could still catch my plane."

I could hardly believe what he was saying. Chest pains?

He went on. "Well, as you can imagine, they made a big deal out of everything and I had to have an EKG and the works. Things were looking fine, but they insisted on keeping me overnight. I wasn't about to call and worry you. I knew I could catch the early flight and be back by the time you went to work."

"Holy cow, Sam," I finally said, horror in my voice. "What did they say it was? Are you okay now?"

"Yes, I'm fine," he reassured me. "They said it was probably stress. With what I have on my plate, that may be the case. They said stress has a way of affecting you in different ways sometimes. I just need to slow down a bit. This traveling is getting to be old; especially when I want to be with you and the house. We've got some issues here at work, too, where some folks may lose their jobs if we don't bring up the numbers in sales. I worry about them."

"Honey, I hope this was a wake-up call." I tried to be brave but

I wanted to cry with worry. "I need you. I don't want to be one of your stressors. When things get too big for me, I break them down in bite-size pieces and ask God to help me. Please promise me you will take it slower and let me help you where and when I can."

"Sure, Annie, that's just what you need," he teased. "A business, a wedding, and now moving to 333 aren't quite enough for you to worry about, right?"

"Sam, these are all choices that I have made; I want to do these things. If it starts to affect something in a negative way, I'll have to make changes, and so will you. Do you hear me?"

He paused. "Yes, I really do hear you. Now, when can I see you?"

"Where are you calling from?" I tried to picture him somewhere besides a hospital.

"I'm at 333, waiting for my lemonade cocktail!"

"Stay there! I'll grab a couple of coffees and join you in a few minutes."

I dressed quickly in my stand-by walking shorts and top and told Mother I had to run an early errand, and then I'd be back to shower. She was about to ask questions about the night before, but I cut her off with a goodbye kiss.

I could hardly take time to absorb what Sam had just told me. Even though his test results were fine, the stress factor was there. I was going to have to realize that my perfect man was going to have his limits just like anyone else. When I arrived at 333, he was sitting in the gazebo with his legs propped up on the side of the wall, his suit jacket and tie lying beside him. He looked like a traveling salesman taking a break without a care in the world.

"Hey, woman, get over here," he demanded. "I need to be waited on. I need some attention and some tender loving care."

He pulled me into his arms and kissed away a tear that had escaped down my cheek. Sam was a rock that I thought I'd never have. To think that my rock had any imperfections made it clear to me how much I appreciated him.

CHAPTER 47

When I drifted down to breakfast on Sunday morning, I saw Mother leisurely reading her Sunday paper. I thought it might be a good time to tell her about Sam's health scare and why I had rushed out of the house yesterday morning.

As I described the sequence of events, I could see her face intensify with concern. I knew that look, as I had caused it many times. To her credit, she waited until I finished. Then she asked if I were up to the mission of caring for him in case this did turn into something more serious. I got the whole lecture on how once you're married, then it's just not about "you" anymore.

I answered by trying to convince her that this marriage was what I wanted and I was ready. Avowing my commitment out loud made me love this imperfect man even more. A part of me sometimes felt like I could never measure up to such a fine specimen of a husband.

That afternoon, like clockwork, Aunt Julia and Sarah

arrived, chirping away in conversation like mothers and daughters do. They brought a heavenly, three-layer white coconut cake that could have served a whole wedding party. I said they might have to make my wedding cake!

Jean arrived with a bag containing the potting shed quilt. Following her were Sue, Mia, and the pet family member, Muffin. Mia was dragging her favorite quilt behind her. This was the quilt we all had started for her and miraculously finished, thanks to the spirit of her Great-Grandmother Davis. I was tickled to see her so fond of it, but wondered how her persnickety great-grandmother would have taken to seeing it drug on the ground. I wondered then if Mia could see her great-grandmother in spirit, as I have heard children do.

We went down the stairs together as always. Mother carried a platter of cheese and fruit and Aunt Julia followed with her impressive cake. I followed with my pitcher of leftover lemonade. We weren't drinking as much wine at our gatherings since Sarah was joining us more frequently.

"I have all the appliqué done on the quilt, thank goodness," Mother said. "I have been trying to remember how Marie said to layer this before it goes in the frame. Jean, you are better at this than we are. Although if we get stuck, I have a feeling there might be some unseen assistance ready to help us."

We acknowledged the thought, and when she laid out the beautiful quilt top on the table, everyone sang their praises for Mother's work.

"Well, Marie would have a much nicer way of lending us assistance than Mother," Aunt Julia said, unhappy. Jean looked puzzled, as if she again missed something important about our ghostly quilt meetings.

"Jean, don't mind them referring to Aunt Marie and my

grandmother, who have passed on," I explained. "We haven't told you very much about their spirits being present here when we quilt, but they do seem to let us know when they're here. And they have had different ways of being with us."

"Oh, indeed, Miss Anne," Jean nodded. "Remember, I saw some of their coming out when the paper pieces blew about the room for no reason. It doesn't frighten me none, as spirits roam fancy free in England. It's good you know a knock when you hear or see them rather than guess on the visitor at hand."

"Yes, we know their knock, so to speak," I laughed. "I'm beginning to learn that they sometimes knock at more than one place."

"What on earth do you mean by that?" Sue was busy getting out Mia's toys.

"I'll let you all know in due time," knowing I should wait first for Mother to question me further, privately.

"Oh, look at Mia giving an olive to Muffin." I changed the subject. We giggled and watched Sue, the new mother, run to Muffin's rescue.

"While we gather our refreshments, Jean has some exciting news to tell us about a book club she is going to start," I announced.

Jean was delighted with the opportunity to discuss her plan to have a small group of folks start a Jane Austen book club. After giving us a few details, Mother was the first to respond enthusiastically with her membership. Sarah said she wanted to join even though Aunt Julia said it was not something she would be interested in. Sue said it would be a good social thing for her to do although she had only read *Emma*. "I need to plan those little breaks for just me and get a sitter for Mia."

"I would be happy to watch Mia at the meetings if you want me to, Sue," chimed Sarah.

"I won't have any of that Sarah," Sue chided. "This is a good thing for you to participate in. Miss Austen is for all ages, and you will fall in love with her!"

"Sue, you drop off Mia at my house and pick up Sarah," suggested Aunt Julia. "I would love to spend time with her. I never get a chance when Sarah's around."

"That would be great, Aunt Julia. I can't wait. When is the first meeting?"

"Next Wednesday I think we'll give it a whirl." Jean sipped her lemonade.

As we continued eating, drinking, and talking, the planning of my quilt took a back seat. Many questions surfaced for Jean about what would happen in a "Jane Austen book club."

"I have always loved her," Mother said. "Her books are very popular at the bookstore, and we have other Jane Austen gift items that are so clever. Jane's mother and father were writers as well. She had a rather different childhood, didn't she Jean? She learned to read at a very young age and she had a very tenacious memory."

"I know she never married," added Sue. "I am one to pick up on such things. Does that surprise you?" We all laughed at her self-humor.

"My favorite book, of course, is *Pride and Prejudice*," I revealed to the others. "Miss Bennett and Mr. Darcy became quite a romantic pair. I have a DVD of that book, Jean, if you or anyone else wants to borrow it sometime."

"Jolly good, Miss Anne," she brought her hands together in satisfaction.

"Not to change the subject, Anne, but what are you going to do with the potting shed quilt now that the papers are out?" asked Sarah as she looked it over, trying not to touch it.

"I will air it out real good, for sure. Jean was nice enough to do a few repairs on it. She suggested we put a black backing on it. It will be easier to handle, plus protect the stitches. It's going to be at 333 someday. As Jean once told us, these Crazy quilts were to thrill the eye and not warm the body. I'll find just the right place for it, just as I will for the vase we found wrapped inside."

"I don't hear much chatter about the wedding these days." Aunt Julia changed the subject once again. "Is everything under control, Sylvia?"

"Yes, we think so," nodded Mother. "That's the beauty of having a small wedding. We do have to get Anne to settle on a bridal shower date. Nancy Barrister contacted me and said she wanted to be invited. She said she would try to attend the shower as well as the wedding; we just need to let her know when."

"Oh, you all, I don't need a shower," I said, humbled.

"Don't be telling your cousin such a thing, after what you all did for me," said Sue. "In fact, as the maid of honor, I insist that I be the one to host the shower. If the list is long, I'll have it at Miss Donna's. Wouldn't that be nice, Anne?" No one really waited for me to respond.

"Oh, that would be so special Sue," Mother said. "You know we will all help with that."

"Yes, my word, Miss Anne," Jean said. "The shop girls on the street have been asking about such an occasion, so I know they want to celebrate! They know you are planning just a half-pint wedding, so you may want to take a shine to the shower."

"Alright, Sue and I will look at the calendar," I said in agreement. "Just don't go inviting so many folks."

A half-pint wedding indeed, I said to myself. I don't think I could handle anything larger than a quart size. I guess this bridesmaid who was never a bride was going to be a bride indeed, according to all the talk. It made me smile.

Finally the quilt was secure in the frame. I looked around to see that most everyone had taken a seat where they had quilted before. Why do people have a tendency to do this? I guess it makes them feel they belong.

Mother was looking over the thimbles in order to make sure everyone would have one. We shared a story or two about how the thimbles had played a role in our basement quilting. Sue and Sarah had had their thimbles assigned to them by the basement spirits. We all agreed to place them in the silver dish as we had before so they would be ready each time we worked on my quilt. Jean, now our quilt leader, took time to refresh us on how to get started. Sarah reminded us of her newness to the craft, but we all assured her that our stitches were all unique despite the fine quality of Aunt Marie's and Grandmother Davis's.

"Before I make my first stitch, I now want to christen the name of this quilt 'Botanical Beauty,'" I announced. "Please lift your glasses for a special toast to Sylvia Brown, my mother, who created this masterpiece."

Yet another Kodak moment occurred in the Brown basement on Maple Street.

CHAPTER 48

I was pleased the next week to get a phone call from Carl at the Historical Society. He said he had found a newspaper wedding photo of Mr. and Mrs. Albert Taylor. He said there were some other articles that had to do with Mr. Taylor's accomplishments in the community. One mentioned that Mrs. Taylor had been elected President of the Colebridge Garden Club.

I couldn't wait to pick everything up around lunchtime, when I went to the post office. I was dying to read every word right then and there, but instead I went back to work and then to meet Sam for dinner at Charley's. We had planned a quick bite before going to check out what had been accomplished that day at 333 Lincoln.

Sam seemed to be back to his old self, doing many tasks that he enjoyed, not mentioning anything about his chest pains. I decided I was going to have to become a nagging wife early, to encourage him to slow down.

"I noticed you didn't have your usual cocktail at Charley's

tonight," I said as we were driving towards our future home.

"You're right about that. This business creates a lot of habits that you don't even think about. Sometimes I order a drink when I really would just as soon have iced tea. I think less alcohol will be better for me. I'm also not going to skip working out, which I have a tendency to do when I'm out of town. I usually have early morning meetings or have to catch a plane, so working out on the road doesn't always happen."

"I know what you mean. It's pretty easy for me to skip my walk when morning errands wait for me. I'm proud of you, Sam, in acknowledging some of the little things that can make a difference."

When we pulled up the drive, we noticed a nice car parked by the garage. We saw an attractive, middle-aged woman walking around the yard towards the house. There was also the painter's truck, which we were expecting to see.

Sam asked me who the lady was but I couldn't answer. As she saw us drive up, she waited until we got out of the car to walk forward. Surely we were not going to be approached by solicitors before we even moved in! We asked if we could help her.

"Yes, please," she said politely. "I am Amanda Anderson. I'm doing some family research for my mother, Mary Anderson. Are you by chance the new owners of this beautiful place?"

"Yes, we are. I'm Sam Dickson and this is Anne Brown. We're to be married in September and this'll be our home. We have a lot of work to do, but it's coming along."

"What brings you here?" I asked.

"I learned that this was the former home of Albert Taylor, is that correct?" she asked.

"Yes, Albert and his wife Marion lived here," I confirmed.

"My mother isn't able to get around much anymore, so I've taken an interest in trying to help her find someone. You see, she was adopted in 1921. Back then you were not told much about who your real parents were. She will never rest till she knows who her father was."

I interrupted her, knowing this was going to be more of a conversation. "Amanda, let's go on the porch where we can sit down and visit."

"You are most kind. I know this is of no concern to you, but perhaps you can shed a little more light on my quest. May I ask who you purchased the house from?"

"It was vacant for quite some time," Sam replied cautiously. "It was put in the hands of one of Albert's distant relatives, who lives out of town. They obviously had no interest in it and let it run down. Finally, they listed it with a Realtor and it's been for sale for quite some time. When I discovered the property, I couldn't believe such a beautiful house was untended and falling into disrepair up here on the hill."

"Well, the internet has been quite helpful to me, but it only will go so far," Amanda explained. "My mother has only bits and pieces of information left by her mother that lead to Albert Taylor. From what I understand, her mother didn't want to give her up for adoption, but she had no choice. She was very young and couldn't support a child. This is what the agency said on her record, anyway. My mother has always felt sorry for her mother and didn't blame her one bit for giving her away. She was very grateful for her adoptive parents. I have to agree that she was very lucky in that regard. My mother never came in contact with her birth mother before she died, but we have enough information now to know who she was. Since she wasn't married at the time of her pregnancy, the father is still unknown. I guess she has some negative thoughts about her father because he would not fess up and marry her mother. She talks about it more and more as she gets older, so I know it has bothered her. I really want to help her figure all this out to give her some peace, and for my own family record."

"I think I'm following you, but how and why does it bring you to 333 Lincoln where the Taylors lived?" Sam was as confused as I was.

"Well, we're not really sure," she said hesitantly. "We talked to a lot of people who knew of my grandmother, or I should say my mother's birth mother, and they said she had gone on to marry someone, but that she was heartbroken by a previous love affair. When I figured out the dates, this fits. One person mentioned it could have been an Albert Taylor. Some thought mention of his name could have been in reference to him being one of her bosses or something. It doesn't mean he was her lover or anything. I checked up on him and knew Albert had died, so it was kind of a moot issue. Then I became curious about his house, as I heard it was quite grand. I was heading this direction anyway today and I decided to check it out. I think I drove by this place more than once. It was hard to find."

"Where do you live?" Sam asked.

"In Illinois over in Collierville. My brother and I were raised there."

"Sure, it's a nice little town."

We were interrupted just then by the painter, who had to ask Sam a question about something he was working on. Sam excused himself and said he would be right back.

"Oh, I am taking too much of your time," Amanda said, getting up to leave. "I envy you moving into such a lovely place. How do you have time to plan a wedding and move at the same time?"

"Oh, that's not all," I laughed. "I also have a business to run. I own Brown's Botanical, the flower shop on Main Street here in Colebridge."

291

"Oh, so you love flowers a lot, which makes sense, seeing this lovely yard and all." Amanda looked around. "I, too, love flowers, as does my mother. She is now in assisted living. It just got to be too much for me to take care of her. Neither my brother nor I ever married. I'm trying to close up her home and all that goes with it and it's overwhelming. She has a weak heart and I know I'm not going to have her much longer. She has already had one attack."

"Bad hearts run in my family as well," I shared. "My Aunt Marie died last year and I worry about my mother. She has really slowed down lately, and since I will be leaving her when I marry, I worry how long she can stay in her house alone."

We started walking towards her car when she noticed the potting shed.

"See that potting shed?" I asked with a smile. "That's the reason I agreed to buy this house with Sam. Would you like to see it?"

"Oh, could I?"

When she walked in, you would have thought she entered a big castle. Amanda's eyes went everywhere with delight.

"You have everything you could possibly want from this place, don't you?" she said with admiration.

She went over to smell the red baby roses I was going to plant soon.

"Your garden tools look brand new and unused. They are beautiful. Do you really use them to work with?"

I laughed and told her they were a birthday gift and that I still preferred to use some of my older tools. I told her that I had found a beautiful vase wrapped in a Crazy quilt under one of the benches. I said the vase was pretty valuable and would have a place on our mantle one day. Then I described the back of the Crazy quilt and that it had pieces of letters written by Albert

Taylor himself used as the quilt's foundation. I told her I wanted to learn all I could about it. I started laughing when I told her how dedicated we were to putting all the pieces together.

"It's funny how you get into something like that and can't quite let go of it, isn't it?" I shared. Why was I telling her all this?

"Yes, I do know what you mean." She looked straight into my eyes. "That's the way I feel about trying to find out who my mother's father was."

"Well, we've learned Mr. Taylor was probably not such a good husband. There is reference to a Martha Abbott that has us interested because that is my grandmother's name. We can hardly believe it would be the same name so we're having fun with it."

"Excuse me," said Amanda, interrupting me. "Did you say 'Martha Abbott?'"

"Yes, and she doesn't let us forget it!" I smiled.

"This can't be." Amanda most definitely was not smiling. "'Martha Abbott' is the name of my mother's birth mother."

"No way, Amanda!" I exclaimed as we stepped outside the potting shed.

"Yes, indeed, and this is why I'm checking out Albert Taylor." She looked very concerned. "He may have been her boss, but I think she may have had an affair with him and he wouldn't do anything about her pregnancy because he was married. He may have been the father of my mother. Okay, I didn't want to be so blunt, but I suspect I'm not far from the real story. I can't believe we are talking about the same Martha Abbott!"

It was all starting to sink in. This made all the sense in the world, given the letters we had found. I told her we had letters claiming he was not the father of this young woman's child. I told her he had even mentioned that this "Martha" had threatened to put the child up for adoption. Amanda was turning white and I thought she was going to faint. Sam came along and asked how we were doing.

"We need to sit down again, Sam," I headed toward the porch. "I think we may have solved the puzzle of Albert's letters. Amanda just told me that her mother's birth mother's name was Martha Abbott. This has to be the Martha Abbott that Albert Taylor is referring to in his letters to his wife."

"So, how many Martha Abbotts can there be in this world?" Sam scratched his head. "How can you both realistically have grandmothers named Martha Abbott?"

"Oh, my word!" I said. "Did you say your birth grandmother went on to marry someone later?"

"Yes, that's what we were told when we were asking questions," Amanda said.

"Well, Amanda," I stated. "I think she went on to marry John Davis, who was my grandfather. He married a Martha Abbott. They had four children who were my Aunt Marie, who just passed on, then my mother Sylvia, my Uncle Ken, and then my Aunt Julia."

"This can't be real, can it?" Amanda was trying to follow my story. "So you never knew that your grandmother had a child named Mary? Are you thinking this through?" I had to slow down this information to digest it all before I spoke again.

"Amanda, let me ask you something," I said very slowly, to be clear. "Did your mother ever talk about having any kind of spirit around and any weird things happening that she couldn't explain?"

To Sam's credit, he remained silent in his confusion, ready to hear information that neither he nor I were prepared for. Amanda also remained silent for a while in order to think.

"I think there has been some of that, Miss Brown, but I don't think Mother would want me to reveal anything," she finally said.

294

"Please don't call me Miss Brown, Amanda." I put my hand on hers. "You can call me Anne because I think we just became cousins." Now the real stories would begin.

For the next forty-five minutes we went over all the timelines in the family. I even revealed how Grandmother Davis, née Martha Abbott, had played all kinds of tricks at the Brown house as well as here at 333 to remind us she was still around and not too happy with the way things turned out.

Her passion and love for Albert was real, and scary at the same time. Did she even love poor John, my grandfather? I guessed so, because they had four children together. As feisty as Grandmother Davis was, I bet his life was pretty challenging. I gave Amanda my business card and told her we both needed to confirm any doubts about what we had just discussed.

After we said goodbye to her, Sam and I agreed we would have to digest all of this. I certainly was not ready to announce this news to Mother just yet. We headed to the kitchen to get out one of our favorite bottles of merlot. It was dark now, and the day had revealed more than we bargained for. This family mystery had come full circle, right here at the Taylor estate.

We went back to the south porch where we sat on the new wicker couch that had been delivered earlier in the week. As soon as his arm went around me, I started crying as though someone had opened the floodgates. This was all so surreal. Sam held me closer as I cried on his shoulder. If he hadn't been present to see and hear what had just happened with Amanda Anderson, he wouldn't have believed it. Was Grandmother watching this all play out? Hmmm.

CHAPTER 49

It was difficult sleeping that night and I was glad Mother was asleep when I came home. I needed a way to soften the news so that Mother could believe that she had a half sister living across the river in Illinois. I thought perhaps I would share the news with Jean and Sally when I got to work. Maybe they would have some ideas on how to divulge everything to her. It all sounded simple, but yet so unbelievable. How many more mysteries would we uncover in the Taylor house?

When the girls arrived, they were discussing the first meeting of the Jane Austen Literary Club of Colebridge, the name we decided on. It was set to happen two days from now. I was deep in my thoughts and now wondered if I should even share the news with them since they weren't family. We all started on the orders and before I knew it, lunch was being ordered from the deli down the street. When the two decided to eat a bite and sit down, I kept an eye out at the front counter. It became quiet so I went back to tell them I had some important news to share.

"You're not closing the shop, are you?" Sally said in a half-joking way. "You haven't been yourself this morning, Anne. What's going on?"

"The quilt letter puzzles have all been solved," I said slowly, sitting down. "Martha Abbott is really my grandmother. She did give her child up for adoption and the father WAS Albert Taylor. The adopted girl's name is now Mary Anderson. She is in her eighties and living in Illinois. She had two children, Amanda and William. Amanda was doing research to help her mother find out who her father might be, and it brought her to 333 Lincoln, where she knew an Albert Taylor had lived. Albert's name had come up in conversation because her mother, Mary, worked for him many years ago. Amanda came to the Taylor house yesterday, because she heard it was so beautiful. Can you believe this? Mother and Aunt Julia have an older half sister, and I have two cousins that I didn't know about!"

I was talking faster and faster as I watched their eyes get bigger and bigger. They were truly stunned. I could hardly finish telling them how it all happened because they had so many questions.

"What did your mother say?" Sally asked.

"You're the first to know," I shared. "It's a lot to take in. I guess I didn't just want to blurt out everything to her because I saw how she was refusing to believe even for a second that we were talking about the same Martha Abbott. I need your help to figure out how I can tell her. I have to do this before she meets all of them or it would be too much of a shock, don't you think? I was so glad Sam was with me, or I'm not sure I could have handled it myself."

"So your grandmother is the bloody ghost in the basement and at 333 Lincoln?" Jean's eyes were wide with wonder.

"Jean!" Sally barked. "That is no way to talk about

her grandmother."

"That's okay, Jean," I said calmly. "She truly is the bloody ghost and she's caused a lot of problems. Do you think now that she has brought the family together she will 'give up the ghost?' No pun intended!"

We all laughed and then started putting the pieces all together from our quilting parties, as we finally got back to our work.

"Oh, I forgot to tell you that Carl from the Historical Society dropped off newspaper clippings about the Taylors," announced Sally.

I stopped working with the flowers in my hand and opened the folder he had left. Right on top was a picture and an article on Marion and Albert in their younger years. Albert was actually a pretty handsome man. He was more slender than in the Chamber picture I had seen before. As I read about others in attendance at their party, an Edward Taylor was mentioned again. I verified in my mind that it must have been him that picked up Albert at the train. I saw the signature of the photographer who took the picture; it was not a name I recognized. I would have liked to have had a real photo of the two, to frame for the house. As I looked at Marion, who was also quite attractive, I felt sorry for the pain she must have suffered as she suspected Albert of his many affairs. I wondered how the two had settled the matter between them, or if they ever did.

I told Sam that after work I would have dinner with Mother. Then I needed to be thinking of how to tell Aunt Julia, Uncle Ken, and Sue. I decided to tell Sue first and have her explain everything to her father. I called Aunt Julia and asked if she were free for the evening. I explained I had something important to discuss, but that nothing was wrong. She said she was curious enough and could join us for dinner. She wondered whether to bring

Sarah, and I suggested she not do so. I called Sue, who resisted the thought of coming over because she had had a stressful day. When I stressed the importance of the get-together, she finally agreed.

Then I called Mother and said I was bringing home Chinese food and that Aunt Julia, Sue, and Mia would be joining us. She was puzzled but thought it had something to do with the wedding. I prayed all the way home that everything would go well as the time approached.

"This is mighty nice, Anne," Mother said when I carried in all the cartons of Chinese food. "I haven't had Chinese for awhile. There's enough here for a family of five! Did you get the broccoli chicken that I love?"

"Of course," I said, opening up the cartons. "Can you arrange the dining room table? I want to put some of the Taylors' papers in the basement with the other quilt pieces. Carl dropped off some newspaper clippings of them for me that are quite interesting."

"Oh, that's nice." She pulled out the proper dishes. "You're getting quite a few things. Maybe you should start a scrapbook with all the Taylor memorabilia."

The doorbell rang and the first arrivals were Sue, Mia, and Muffin. Muffin smelled the aroma and immediately went running to Mother, who always gave her a treat. Aunt Julia arrived as we were pouring each other glasses of wine.

"I love Chinese." Sue eyed all the delicious choices. "It's also an invitation to a free dinner, which is even better! Mia has eaten, but she loves rice, so I hope it will keep her occupied."

"So, Anne and Sylvia, what's the occasion?" Aunt Julia spooned rice on her plate.

"It sounds like a serious matter to me," Sue said as she helped Mia into her booster chair.

"Is there something you've kept from me, Anne?" Mother had

a serious look on her face.

"Yes." I took a deep breath. "I've asked you all here because I have made a major discovery about our family. I had a visitor at 333 Lincoln when Sam and I were there working the other night. Well, actually we didn't get to do any work because we had a lady visit us who was looking for the Albert Taylor house."

I had to force myself to continue because there was dead silence. No one was eating except Mia, who was also making a big, happy mess with her rice. I began with what Amanda was asking me about the Taylors. Then I told them that when I showed her the potting shed and then told her about the quilt and cut up letters, all the pieces fell together.

I told them she came out and told me that her paternal grandmother was Martha Abbott. That statement brought several interruptions at the same time, so I quickly reminded them they needed to hear the whole story before they made comments. I was really watching how Mother was absorbing my story. I didn't want to upset her. When Amanda told me her mother Mary had a heart attack, I thought of how this family had a history of hypertension. When I finally got to the part where we decided we were cousins, I let the others join in. To my surprise, Mother was not the first to respond. She continued to look serious and calm.

"Good heavens!" said Aunt Julia. "Why did we not figure this out sooner? Sylvia, we have a half sister named Mary! Did you say she was not well?"

"No. Amanda just said she had had a heart attack some time ago and that now she is in assisted living in Collierville," I explained. "Does the family history sound familiar?"

"Oh, gracious." Sue put her hands behind her head. "Does my father know?"

"No, he doesn't," I plainly said. "I'm thinking you may want to be the one to tell him." She didn't look like she was ready for such a task.

Finally Mother spoke.

"I'm afraid I knew it all along, you all," she confessed, looking down, unable to meet our eyes. "I didn't want to really think too much about it, but when Mother started destroying her letters, I knew there had to be a reason. Maybe it was Marie, but I always sensed that it was really Mother acting up."

"Oh, no!" I yelled and jumped out of my seat to head to the basement.

I ran down the steps as fast as I could to the folder that I had brought home. When I opened it up, the articles were all in shreds and fluttered to the floor. I had realized when I was repeating the story that Grandmother was bitter about the marriage of Albert and Marion. Then it had dawned on me that she might not appreciate the articles about the Taylors. She was well aware of what I had just put in the basement. I cringed to think that now my plans for an album would not be carried out very easily.

"Darn, darn," I muttered as I went back up the stairs.

"What on earth is wrong, Anne?" Mother stood up from her chair.

Actually, they were all standing at the table waiting to hear about my unexpected visit to the basement.

"Here is what Carl brought me today from the Historical Society." I put the folder of paper sheds on the table. "This is what's left of the newspaper clippings about the Taylors, which I brought home less than an hour ago." I wanted to cry right there in front of them.

They remained silent, waiting for me to go on. Only Mia was making noise as she kept hitting her messy hands on the table.

"Hey, Miss Mia," Sue said sternly, as she held onto Mia's hands.

"I guess Grandmother didn't want me to own or read such material," I said with renewed anger. "Her hatred for Albert and Marion is beyond my comprehension. She is mean and unforgiving! I'm sorry you all, but this really makes me angry. What kind of person was she?"

"Hello!" Aunt Julia said, waving her hands. "Now can any of you understand the trouble I had through the years with her? Maybe she married our dad, but she never got over Albert! I know you and she did not have much difficulty, Sylvia, but for some reason, I did. She was never satisfied with anything I did and you and Ken know that, right?"

"She was difficult, Julia, I agree," said Mother, still very calm. "Oh, Anne, what a shame. I'm sorry you lost all that. I think, however, we have to cut her some slack here. She had to give up her baby. Think about it. How could anyone get over that? Then she had to see Albert live his rich life with Marion. It's no wonder she haunted 333." She looked at me closely. "Do you think you will be able to live there, Anne?"

"Well, I sensed it was her, or at least the unhappy mistress." I was still angry. "I've been talking to her at the house. Thus far she has only blinked the lights off and on, and one time she swung the light in the potting shed. One night I asked her if the ghost was my grandmother. I asked her to blink the lights, and she did!"

"Yikes, you all." Sue shivered. "This is kind of creepy and surreal, don't you think?"

I told them I had not heard back from Amanda but that we would be sure to get together once everyone got used to the idea. Now everyone was talking at once just like after I had told the girls at the shop. All the pieces were coming together. I was still pretty angered by my grandmother's spirit destroying the paper clippings. I was hoping Carl would be able to make me new copies.

After another hour of discussion and nibbling at our Chinese dinner, we raised our glasses to the new additions to our family. Then we made a toast to Grandmother in case she was listening. Of course, she had to know how unhappy I was. This was another Kodak moment in my home but this one brought very mixed reactions and emotions. Reluctantly, I would file this picture away with all the rest.

CHAPTER 50

There was no question that my bridal shower was the most important thing on most peoples' minds these days. I was trying to digest the revelation of having new cousins and an aunt that our family didn't know about. Had we not purchased the Taylor property, we may have never learned of Albert's mistress, who turned out to be my grandmother.

Jean, Sally, Sue, Aunt Julia, and Sarah were absorbed in the shower details. Donna Howard insisted on having it at her tea room so they could invite more folks, including some of my Main Street friends. Mother seemed distant and less excited these days about most everything. She was not as thrilled about the shower as I thought she would be and her interest in meeting her half sister was only so-so. I knew the reality of having me marry and leave the house would be a bit melancholy for her, but why was she not willing to embrace a close family member?

Staying focused at work with all the recent activity was

difficult. I wondered what I would have done without the great help I had to assist in each day's challenges. With wedding plans now spread to the public, customers wanted to visit much longer. I didn't know if they just wanted to be invited, wanted juicy details to tell their friends, or if they really cared about me.

"We'll have to have a splash of red at the shower, Miss Anne." Jean never stopped a minute in her assignments even when she chattered away. I tried to just listen and not respond.

"I went ahead and reserved some roses, Anne," Sally said. "You'll just have to turn the other way as we plan this. Donna said she would be showing off one her best sets of Haviland china. I wonder how many sets and pieces she owns."

"I would like to have asked that question when I toddled through her 'Haviland museum,'" agreed Jean. "I took a fancy to the many teapots that accompanied the patterns. My teapots are nothing of the sort. Haviland china is as sparse as hen's teeth in my family."

"By the way, should we invite your newly discovered family members to the shower?" Sally was being courteous.

"Heavens, no," I said quickly. "No one has met as yet, and I sure don't want them to be obligated to attend such an occasion."

"Some of the street folks have been asking if you and Sam have registered anywhere," Sally reported. "If you haven't, you may want to do so, or you'll have more crystal vases and picture frames than you can imagine!" We laughed in acknowledgment.

"No, and we probably won't. Sam and I have so much, and I think it's going to be a challenge to decide what we can and cannot use. Mother wants me to take china, crystal, my bedroom furniture, and goodness knows what all she has mentioned."

"Jean, is the Jane Austen Literary Club still scheduled for tomorrow night?" I changed the topic.

"Yes, by golly," Jean replied as she tied a bow on a basket of daisies. "I hope I can get Al off his duff to help me a bit."

"I told you I would bring something yummy," Sally chimed in. "Why do I always make things with tons of calories?"

"I can, too, Jean, so don't worry about making refreshments," I offered. "Mother has it all planned, most likely. I think I can actually cook, but I'm not totally sure. I know I can bake something!" This brought a big laugh. "I'm meeting Sam for a quick bite at Charley's, picking Mother up, and then I'll be there."

"It will be nice to get a start," Jean said. "The first meeting will be informational about Jane herself, and then I'll chat about the other Austen clubs. We can then decide our own fate and folly, so to speak."

The next night it was indeed a quick bite with Sam as he also had to go to a meeting; his was across the river. We hugged and kissed as we ate, and we talked about having a real date sometime soon. He was delighted to hear about the shower coming up, but he, too, had shelved the topic of Albert's mistress discovery. I guessed no one had really taken the time but me to try to solve the mystery, so when I did, they all moved on.

I told Sam to slow down as he shoved his hamburger and fries down so quickly. He gave me that look that said he was a big boy and could I please not treat him like a baby. I did try not to think about his former chest pains but when I observed his stressful nature after a workday, I couldn't help wonder if this behavior caused the chest pains. He dismissed the subject and off we went. Yup, I had no doubt this would be a more common practice in our future.

Mother and I arrived a few minutes late to the Austen party, thanks to me. They were already a lively bunch as we entered Jean's charming living room. Her English antiques were tasteful and very different than what most folks in Colebridge had. Mother was immediately impressed and had many questions about their history. Al came into the room to meet everyone and then he excused himself, announcing that he was going to the library. He seemed a nice enough person, just much more reserved than Jean.

After everyone was served tea from her very delicate English china tea set, we settled down to listen to our Jane Austen leader. Jean's English accent was perfect for this role. She said there were over sixty Jane Austen groups across the country. She said her former group discussed a different book of Jane's each month, but that tonight we were going to discuss Jane's birth and family.

Jean told us the timeline of Jane's life was 1775 to 1817. She was the seventh child for the Austen family, followed by her brother, Charles; she was very close to her sister Cassandra. Her father was a reverend; her mother ran the household and did a little writing herself. The most interesting part of what she told us about Jane was that after her christening, she was sent to be nursed by a nearby farmer's wife as were her siblings in their infancy. It seemed cruel to me, but Jean said it was the practice of those times. She returned home to the rest of the family after she had reached the age of two.

It was so interesting to hear about her life; it was a good way to start our group before we got into discussing each book. The time passed quickly and I noticed how we had also held Sarah's attention; she was usually checking her cell phone when she was with us. It was so good to be sharing conversation of another nature with family and friends. Jean was the perfect hostess, serving English brewed tea and some of her crumpets. She wore a crisp, white, ruffled half apron over the outfit she had worn to work that day. For a moment, we could imagine a charming teatime visit in a London home.

When two hours had passed, Jean suggested we start discussing Austen's first book, *Sense and Sensibility,* at the next meeting. Jean said she had a copy to lend if anyone wanted to borrow it. Mother jumped right in, saying the library usually had a couple of copies on hand. Of course, Mother had read it. I knew a little about it but had not read the entire book.

Mother and I left, feeling we had just experienced a very pleasant evening. "Just think, Mother, this little club will be a nice social event for the two of us to enjoy together after I'm married," I happily shared.

"Yes, I hope we can do these kinds of things, Anne," she said in a sad tone. "I'm going to miss you so much." Oh no, I shouldn't have brought this up, I thought to myself.

"Will you be okay, Mother?" I pulled into the garage. "I worry about that sometimes. You know I'll be just a phone call away. You can just come into the shop anytime you want or work your little self to death at the Taylor estate."

When she laughed, I gave her a peck on the cheek. I knew this wouldn't be easy on her, and had already thought of what might happen in the future if she became disabled in her old age. Our house and property at 333 Lincoln was certainly big enough for many family members. This was nothing I would share with Sam yet, but I had filed the notion in my mind along with all the Kodak moments.

CHAPTER 51

This is awesome, you all!" I exclaimed as Mother and I entered Donna's Tea Room. "Look at all this! Sam, you didn't tell me you were going to be here! Are you allowed?"

"The girls said I needed to see your face as you walked in and then I could leave!" He kissed me on the cheek. "Look who's here, Anne."

Elaine, Sam's sister whom I had met at Christmas, walked up to me with a big smile.

"Hi, Anne," she greeted me, giving me a little hug. "I was thrilled to be invited and decided I would make the drive. Mother wasn't quite up to it, so I'm here representing Sam's family. This place is so beautiful and everyone has been so nice." I felt her genuine love and acceptance, which meant a lot to me. I was, indeed, flattered that she took the pains to attend.

"I am so thrilled you came! This is so special!" I tried to take in the entire room. "Have you met everyone?"

309

"Yes, and I must say I have a favorite," she grinned and pointed to Mia. "I have fallen in love with this precious little girl."

When she picked up Mia to give her a kiss, I could understand what she was saying. I greeted Mia with a kiss as well.

Mother and Elaine started talking to each other as Sam took Mia in his arms. Why did this sight make me so happy? There is something so romantic about a grown hunk of a man caving into a little girl's world. She was all in ruffles, which was unusual. Sue always said her little girl would be dressed like a grown-up. Sue glowed with pride as she saw everyone's attention focused on her daughter.

After I greeted everyone, Donna and her two servers came out with dainty sandwiches, tea, and coffee. No doubt, the table settings were Donna's creations. Her selected china pattern had a touch of red, which coordinated perfectly with the red nosegay centerpieces. How in the world those were created at the shop without me knowing was a puzzle, but what a lovely surprise.

The cake was a work of art. I was told it was compliments of Nick across the street from my shop. He, too, had picked up a tasteful sprinkle of red in scattered rosebuds on the black forest cake, remembering my love of chocolate. The tiers were like a wedding cake, making the coming occasion all too real.

After we enjoyed the cake, I thanked everyone for coming and gave credit to Donna for the lovely food and place settings. I fussed over Elaine and told everyone what a lovely family I was about to inherit. I made sure to mention that Sue would be my maid of honor, escorted by my Uncle Jim. I gave special recognition to the shop girls in giving me such lovely flowers and filling in extra time for me at the shop.

Sue then started bringing me gifts to open. This was all so surreal to me. Where was my Sam, whom all this was about? He had slipped out the door during all the fuss and excitement. The first gift I opened was a precious red toile English tea set from Jean and Sally. Elaine brought me several gifts from the Dicksons, but the one I cherished most was a framed family photo taken when they were last together. I could see placing this on the mantle in the study.

"You'll be included in the next one taken," she assured me. "Everyone sends their love." How they could love me when they didn't even know me, I wondered.

I was nearly finished opening all the thoughtful gifts when Sue handed me a large, fancy wrapped box that had no card attached. I looked for one to no avail and then Sue started asking the guests who might have brought it.

"Oh, Anne, that was here when I arrived today, so it must have been dropped off yesterday," explained Donna. "Perhaps the card is inside. It's such a lovely wrapped present, isn't it?" Everyone sang their praises, as it was simply stunning.

Since it was the last package, Mother and the others were taking a photo of me slowly opening the big box; it obviously contained breakables. The tissue paper was abundant.

I was careful to make sure I didn't overlook a card. The center section of the box contained a beautiful crystal pitcher that no doubt was terribly expensive. Who would spend all this on my little shower? A similar remark came from my viewing audience. I then began unwrapping crystal glasses that matched the beautiful pitcher. There were eight of them. Together they were spectacular! Everyone in the room was impressed and visited among themselves about how gorgeous the set was. The person who made the purchase had excellent taste and a big pocketbook.

"That's for those lemonade cocktails you plan to have every night on the south porch," kidded Aunt Julia. "It's perfect for that.

For those of you who don't know, Anne has said she and Sam will have lemonade cocktails every night on the south porch just like the Taylors used to do." They all agreed this was a picturesque idea.

"Oh, that would be so Southern and so appropriate," Sue smiled. "I can just see the crystal arranged on that new wicker coffee table you have by the couch."

If no one in the room knew about the Taylors' habit, which we learned about from Albert's letters, who would have given me this personal gift? Everyone I was close to was at the shower. It wasn't from Mother, who did hear me tell of the cocktails. Was this from Sam, wanting to be romantic? I thought he would have included a love note for sure.

"Did you find a card?" Aunt Julia pulled aside some tissue paper.

"No, isn't that odd?" I shook my head in wonder. "I guess it was from Sam, but why didn't he include a note?" Hmmm.

"Anne, there are loved ones who are happy for you right now and cannot be seen," she whispered, putting her arm around my shoulder. "When Sue said this was a gift without a card, I knew it had to be your grandmother. Who knows, maybe Aunt Marie went in cahoots with her!" She giggled to herself, but I did not find it humorous.

"Oh, no, do you think it's possible?" I spoke softly so no one could hear but her.

"Didn't you get a nice birthday gift from her?" Aunt Julia reminded me.

"Yes, yes, I did," I said, turning away as tears trickled down my cheek. Aunt Julia gave me a hug to hide the emotion on my face. She then picked up the box off my lap and told me to go into the bar area.

I did just that with no one noticing my tears but my mother. She followed behind me, knowing what I might be thinking. She turned me around, saw my tears, and gave me a hug without saying a word. It was darker in the bar room but I couldn't hide. Sue, Sarah, Jean, and Sally all seemed to know what had taken place and no words had to be said. I could see other eyes tear up as we all embraced in the love of the missing, who always made themselves present. This Kodak moment needed no words.

CHAPTER 52

I was relieved to hear from Amanda the next week. I was beginning to think I had opened a can of worms that ended up going bad. No one in my family encouraged me to make the first contact.

She agreed that she would bring her mother to Colebridge; we agreed it was time. Her brother William said he would like to come and meet us also. She suggested a date, so I told her I would check it out with my mother. I offered our house for the privacy and convenience. After we settled on the timing, I had to finally ask the question I had been so curious about.

"What did your mother have to say when you told her that you verified who her father was?" I asked.

"She cried and cried," she said sadly. "She was almost sure of it in her own mind, but this sealed the notion and removed any doubts. She was delighted, though, to learn there were some half sisters and a half brother. When I told her that one of the sisters had passed on, she said somehow she knew that. She didn't explain. I was relieved it didn't upset her in a bad way, if you know what I mean. Her heart is so fragile. I didn't tell her that the deceased sister had died from a heart attack."

"That is so interesting, Amanda," I said, overwhelmed by the thought of it all. "There's so much to talk about. I'll call you back after I check with Mother, Aunt Julia, and their brother, Ken. I doubt if Ken will come to town to meet with us because of his busy schedule, but we'll certainly want to include him."

"Oh, yes, Anne," she said gratefully. "I really appreciate everything you have done to bring this all together. If I can help with anything, let me know." I was anxious for all this to happen next week, but how would the others feel?

On the way home from work, I went by Walnut Grove Cemetery. My inner self wanted to speak to my grandmother. Headed for her grave, I passed Albert Taylor's stone on the prominent hill. I could see from the car that live, fresh lilies were present, as always. That occurrence was one for the books, I thought, as I drove along the narrow winding graveyard road. When I arrived at Grandmother's gravesite, I got out of the car and didn't notice until coming closer that she, too, had lilies on her grave. As many times as I had visited, I had never seen that before. Why now?

"Grandmother," I said aloud, feeling a bit awkward. "Thank you so much for the pitcher and glasses. I love them and will use them, but please stop scaring me with your generous gifts. I don't know how to react. I'm glad you are happy for Sam and me. We'll always remember that living at 333 Lincoln will also include you."

I looked around to be sure I was alone. "I plan to plant a whole row of lilies along the side of the south porch in your honor. I miss you and Aunt Marie so much, as does everyone else. Your family will all be united now. As you probably know, your daughter Mary will become a part of our family. I have no idea if you are really hearing this, but I just had to get this off my chest." Thank goodness no one else saw me wipe away tears and talk to the dead.

I walked to my car feeling pounds lighter with a new sense of closure. I sat in the car for a moment to consider my behavior. When I arrived home, Mother was waiting for me on the porch swing with two glasses of merlot sitting next to her.

"Oh, I need one of those, Mother." I plopped down on the swing next to her. I didn't know what to share with her first.

"I thought you would, Anne," she said. Her voice was such comfort to my ears. "You have had quite a day, haven't you?" I nodded in silence. "I have some crab puffs about to come out of the oven. How about that? Would you share some with me?"

"I'd love that," I smiled, kicking off my shoes as I pushed back to swing.

When I filled her in on the phone call with Amanda, I saw her perk up with much better interest. It was likely she had had enough time to digest it all and was ready to face the rest of her family.

"Anne, we have to do a nice dinner for the occasion," she announced with excitement. "This is just too important to gather for coffee and tea! I'll call Ken tonight and the others. That date is fine with me. I'm glad Mary feels well enough to travel here."

"Well, she's not that far away. Are you sure you want to go to all the trouble? Of course we'll all help you."

"I've been hungry for that good brisket recipe," she went on. "I can make that ahead of time so all I'd have to do is heat it up. We'll make a fine table in the dining room. Let's see, how many would we have?"

"Well, Amanda wanted to bring her brother William along, so that's three," I started to count. "Then there would be Aunt Julia, Sarah, Sue and Mia, you, Sam, myself, and if you add Aunt

Joyce and Uncle Ken, that would be twelve!"

"Perfect for Mother's lily painted china," she said with no hesitation. "I haven't used that china in a long time. It is a setting for twelve. It'll be a good excuse to get it out."

"Grandmother had china with lilies on it?" I asked in amusement. "Good heavens, why didn't I notice? I never paid attention before. Is this the china you have stored in the hall closet?"

"Yes, I have four sets of china, my dear. It's time you took some of them off my hands. The way Mother has singled you out, I think she'd love for you to have the painted lily set. We never knew the proper name of the pattern, so we just always called it that."

"Grandmother always loved lilies, I guess. I would love to have it, Mother. It only seems fitting for 333 Lincoln."

"It's yours, my dear Anne." She gave me a big smile as she pushed back the swing.

The rest of the evening was full of planning and phone calls. Uncle Ken was not sure of their attendance but told us to keep the planned date. We stayed on the porch enjoying perfect weather for a Midwestern summer evening. We sipped merlot, ate crab puffs, and finished off the leftover apple pie from Mother's card club gathering.

I would remember this evening with her for a long time, and I knew she was thinking the same thing. She was taking advantage of every moment she had with her only child and loving every minute.

I knew Sam would check in with me at a late hour and he would be back in my arms tomorrow. I had my whole life ahead of me with Sam, but Mother was trying hard to realize that she did not have the rest of her life with me on Maple Street.

CHAPTER 53

Getting through the big reunion day at hand was tough. It was hard to contain my nerves because of the unknowns. Jean, Sally, and even Kevin were all excited for us and wanted me to leave the shop as soon as I could to help Mother with the dinner. They all expressed how anxious they were about the outcome. I was frightened to think of how it could all go wrong. Would Grandmother behave herself through the event?

"Can you believe all this started with that blessed potting shed quilt you found at the Taylor house?" Sally said, finishing up the table arrangement for me to take home. The white lilies and baby's breath with greenery was stunning, I told her. It would be a perfect complement to Grandmother's china.

Sam said he would arrive early to help be the bartender and host. When he called to offer his services, he related the fact that Uncle Jim would have liked to have been a part of this reunion, but Sam knew that would not happen. It was sad in one way, but divorce breaks up many a splendid thing. He arrived shortly after I did, looking like an ad out of *GQ* magazine. How had I managed to get such a handsome man, soon to be my husband?

Mother's table was set to perfection and she did indeed prepare much ahead, so it was not too hectic for serving time. Sue, Mia, Aunt Julia, and Sarah all arrived early and in one car. There was no question that we each had our share of nerves, anticipating this day.

Sue had fed Mia early so she could be put down for a nap while we all enjoyed our dinner, but that didn't go as planned. She sent her parents' regards since they could not attend; they asked us to take a lot of photos. Sue indicated it was not a significant shock to them to know that they now had a half sister.

We were starting to munch on stuffed mushrooms when the doorbell rang. I answered to see Amanda's face and then her younger, handsome brother William step into the entryway. I became breathless when Amanda introduced her mother, who followed behind them.

She was the exact image of Aunt Marie! Mary's dark hair only had streaks of gray, just like Marie's. She carried a cane and wore a big smile; tears welled in her eyes. Mother was the next to greet her and I knew the resemblance to my Aunt Marie would overwhelm her. They hugged with tears of joy, which spread to Aunt Julia who joined the two. Sarah was attached to Aunt Julia for assurance and wondered at it all. She knew this monumental occasion was important for her future as well. Sam stayed near me and embraced my waist in support.

After everyone shared hugs and shook hands in acknowledgement and greeting, Sam did as I had hoped. He tried to create a sense of order by offering everyone a drink, introducing himself as a future member of the family. The

Andersons embraced him, as they did little Mia, who ran up to him, trying to compete with all the excitement around her. William helped Sam pass the drinks as we made our way to the living room. In all the chatter, it did not take long for Mother to show Mary the photo of Aunt Marie. She, too, saw the resemblance between the two of them.

"Do you think our mother gave the similar name 'Marie' to her since she no longer had her Mary?" Aunt Julia bravely asked.

"I have a lot of unanswered questions," confessed my new aunt. "For now, I just know I'm grateful for Anne's due diligence on the quilt she found at the Taylor house. Of course, I'm also grateful for my daughter's many hours of searching on my behalf."

On Mother's signal, I joined Sam in bringing out the brisket and dishes; they all smelled so delicious. The familiar brisket brought back some of our best holiday dinner memories. Sue was explaining her father and mother's absence as we took our seats at the dinner table. Sue had been right; Mia's exhaustion finally had her asleep on Mother's bed.

Mother was the first to make one of many toasts to welcome our new family members. Watery eyes were glistening around the table. Throughout the meal, Sam would lift my hand and kiss it with his love and joy on this special occasion. He, too, felt he had played a role in this discovery. So many conversations were going on at once. Sue and I both concurred that it was all kind of scary and surreal in that it was like having Aunt Marie back with us again. The doorbell rang and Sam jumped up to answer the door so as not disturb the rest of us.

To our surprise it was Uncle Ken and Aunt Joyce! Sue was truly surprised. We cheered and stood to greet them. Mother immediately ran into Uncle Ken's arms and took him over to Mary.

"I want you to meet your sister," she said with uncontained joy.

He was the first to embrace her, followed by Aunt Joyce. I couldn't even imagine what a feeling it must be to meet a sibling that you had never met before.

Sue ran to hug her parents with such joy, their presence making her evening so much more special. Having them join us made the occasion complete. Uncle Ken was a large, masculine man, overcome with the emotion of it all. I don't think he had realized how meeting an unknown sibling would impact him.

"Did you know you have a floral delivery at your doorstep?" Uncle Ken looked at Mother. The hubbub had subsided and he and Aunt Joyce took their seats.

"Anne, do you know anything about that?" Mother asked.

"No, but let me check on it." I hurried toward the door.

Sure enough, sitting in a secured delivery box was a large bouquet of white lilies in what looked to be a crystal vase. I took them into the kitchen to unwrap completely.

It was a beautiful arrangement of fresh white lilies filled in with green ivy; it could only have been arranged in the last hour. This was something that only a flower shop owner would know.

Then I observed that the crystal vase pattern looked familiar. This might match my pitcher and glasses, I thought to myself. By now everyone was curious, and waited for an explanation as I carried the flowers into the dining room. The elaborate bouquet in my hands brought compliments and admiration in unison.

Sue was the first to ask where they were from. The look on Aunt Julia's solemn face was the same I had seen at my bridal shower. It didn't even dawn on me to look for a card. I guess I was getting used to unexpected finds.

But there was a card, I discovered. "What does it say, Anne?" Mother asked. "Who are they from?"

"It says, 'The lilies of the field have come into bloom, now that all are gathered into one.'" I had read as poetically as I could.

We looked at one another as if I had just read the giver's name aloud. How did we know? Did Uncle Ken and Aunt Joyce know as well? Mother was the first to raise her wine glass, followed by the others in unison.

"Welcome to our home and family!" Mother smiled happily. "May we toast all of those who brought us here to unite us as one."

"Here, here!" We spoke as one and joined our glasses.

We were creating the first of many Kodak moments as a new family; no further questions were asked. Those answers would reveal themselves as the Colebridge community continued.

What you can look forward to in *The Funeral Parlor Quilt:*

1. Will Sam's chest pains recur?

2. Will there really be a wedding for Sam and Anne?

3. What happens when Anne's longtime friend moves back to Colebridge?

4. What tragic event is learned over the TV news?

About the Author

Ann Hazelwood has written several books for the American Quilter's Society including *100 Things You Need to Know If You Own a Quilt*, *100 Tips from Award-winning Quilters*, and *100 Sweet Treats by and for Quilters*. A former quilt shop owner, Ann is an author of regional food and travel books about her home state of Missouri, and is an AQS-certified quilt appraiser and President of the National Quilt Museum's Board of Directors. *The Basement Quilt* was her first work of fiction. *The Potting Shed Quilt* will be followed by *The Funeral Parlor Quilt*.

Visit her at www.booksonthings.com to chat about the Colebridge community, share recipes, and more.

More Books from AQS

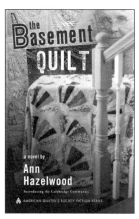

#8853 $14.00

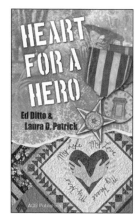

#7923 $14.00

#7558 $12.95

#8156 $12.95

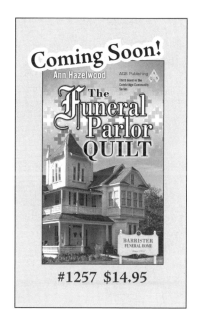

#1257 $14.95

Look for these books nationally.

1-800-626-5420
Call or Visit our website at
www.AmericanQuilter.com